# The Mao of

# Barkley
## Button Nose

Alexandra Claire

**A bit of pronunciation**


Miss Fi-Fi, a French feline, refers to Barkley as Monsieur Nez
– Mister Nose. Nose in French is nez, and is pronounced 'nay'.

# Contents


Chapter One .................................................... 1

Chapter Two .................................................... 8

Chapter Three.................................................. 15

Chapter Four.................................................... 19

Chapter Five ................................................... 25

Chapter Six .................................................... 40

Chapter Seven .................................................. 52

Chapter Eight................................................... 64

Chapter Nine ................................................... 70

Chapter Ten .................................................... 82

Chapter Eleven ................................................. 89

Chapter Twelve ................................................. 91

Chapter Thirteen ............................................... 98

Chapter Fourteen .............................................. 105

Chapter Fifteen................................................ 110

Chapter Sixteen ............................................... 120

Chapter Seventeen ............................................. 132

Chapter Eighteen.............................................. 146

Chapter Nineteen ............................................. 163

Chapter Twenty ............................................... 173

Chapter Twenty-One ........................................... 180

Chapter Twenty-Two ................................................... 191

Chapter Twenty-Three.................................................. 193

Chapter Twenty-Four.................................................. 203

Chapter Twenty-Five.................................................. 213

Chapter Twenty-Six................................................... 223

# Chapter One

The door opened, revealing a secretive room filled with hidden clues from past crimes – the skull of Patch, the parrot who had lived cooped in a cage at No. 3 Cherry Street for ten years; the foot of Bob the Bunnykin, who had dined on leftover carrots, lettuce leaves, grass and ghastly tasting pellets that made him leave extra deposits of poo in his cage. Then there was Simone's tail, which had been bitten off by the brute who lived at the top of the street. He had gotten out and knowingly raced down to her in an attacking frenzy. The case was solved when 'The Brute' attended a meeting with a silver car a few weeks later.

The matted sign at the door read 'Detective Inspector Barkley Button Nose'. Slowly and silently, a svelte figure moved along the narrow paths of stored antique furniture which led to an area of cat scratching poles adorned with piles of clawed paper. At the base of each pole were bones snatched from the dog next door during sessions of torment.

Eventually, her quest to find the detective led her to a desk decorated in opened packets of dried sardines. The odious smell permeated the small enclosure. On days when a south-westerly blew, the pungent odour of sardines would waft through the streets.

The overpowering smell made her feel nauseous. Trying not to adopt the vomit position, she swallowed hard and spoke with a delicate French accent, 'Monsieur Nez? I have come to seek your assistance.'

The figure sitting at the desk turned and gazed, his eyes widening in response to her beauty as he licked his lips to disperse the salt from the morsel of fish he had just devoured.

'D I Barkley, how may I be of assistance, Madam?'

Nervously, she cleared her throat and whispered, 'It is a matter most delicate. The family who give me my food are thinking of getting a puppy. I cannot have the puppy in the house with me.'

'Sorry Madam, a poo and pee? You mean the woman is having a baby?' Her pronunciation of puppy sounded like poo-pee to Barkley.

'No, I mean a puppy. A little woof-woof. I am a purebred and rare in this country. They have decided I am to breed to make them money. If they get the puppy, he will eat mes enfants when he is grown. What mother wants that? Monsieur Nez, please can you help me? I have brought the sardines.'

Barkley's eyes glistened as he took the bag of dried fish he so loved and stashed it behind his desk.

'My dear Madam, you must be extremely distressed. Please do sit down. May I offer you a drink?' asked Barkley, pointing to a bowl of water with dead bugs and fallen leaves floating in it.

'No, thank you. I am fine.' She gasped and sat, wiping her brow with a freshly licked paw. 'There is one other thing. Someone keeps stealing my collars. My family always give me pretty diamond collars and someone is stealing them. I go to sleep curled up and when I wake, no collar is adorning my pretty neck. Fifteen have gone missing so far. They think I am careless. My breed is very meticulous, Monsieur, vous comprenez? You understand?'

'Fifteen have gone missing already, you say? Hmmm, this is very grave, Madam. Very grave indeed. Please allow me to give you one of my cards. Tell me, to whom do I have the pleasure of this whisker?' queried Barkley as he handed her one of his fur balls.

'My name is Miss Fi-Fi. I have already commenced the breeding. My children will fetch a heavy price, provided they are not eaten by the woof-woof.'

Barkley took note of Miss Fi-Fi's address, then sent her home and commenced work on her case. Suspicious of the missing collars, he needed an action plan and he needed to work fast. Sorting out the problem of her family getting a puppy was easy. He would do as he had done many a time before – shred letters from paper he had collected and send a ransom note:

```
No dog or Fi-Fi gets it. We know what you are doing
```

The letter would be dropped at the back door every day for a week, along with one of Regie's bones that Barkley had stolen. The bone was to stop the note from being blown away in the wind and to notify the owner this was not rubbish but meant to be picked up and read. It was Barkley's way of saying, 'I am serious!'

As dusk approached the following night, Barkley made sure he was in position, hidden in the garden at Miss Fi-Fi's place. It was going to be an all-nighter, so provisions were brought. He scouted the garden and made sure all was safe and secure. Trees and shrubs were slowly being decorated with the fine silken thread from spiders as they wove their dinner plate for the evening. Barkley swished his tail, bringing some of the invisible filament down to shrub height. If the web was broken in the morning, he would know someone had passed this way.

The night-time music began as crickets chirped, bats clicked, possums growled, birds roosted in the trees and those darn cicadas deafened Barkley's thinking. Getting himself comfortable, he fixed his gaze on the cat flap.

*No one is going in or out of there tonight,* he thought.

A beautiful dawn greeted the weary detective as he waited for Miss Fi-Fi to emerge from her slumber.

'Bonjour, Monsieur. Thank you for guarding me throughout the night. However, as you see, my pretty neck has no lovely collar and I found this,' she handed him a small piece of paper she had found next to the cat flap.

Barkley unravelled it and read:

*At the ultimate outcome to all dilemmas, I will still be loved, heard and accepted.*

*Confucius of Mao*

'Where did you find this?' he asked.

'Right here, next to my door,' replied Miss Fi-Fi, pointing to a spot on the floor inside the house.

'This was placed here intentionally, Miss Fi-Fi, for us to see. When I find the culprit, he will be dealt with! You didn't see or hear anything last night?'

'No, Monsieur.'

'Is it possible one of your family members has been taking your collars? One of the nutrition people?'

'Non, Monsieur. Pardon, Monsieur, but have you not been here all night? Did you not see or hear anything? I thought you were guarding my door.'

'I have been here awake all night, Miss Fi-Fi. I too saw and heard nothing. I did a surveillance of your garden, every vibration of my whiskers. There was one disturbance of a pot plant falling from a ledge, which I went to investigate. Perhaps they entered then, although how they got out again, I am not sure. Miss Fi-Fi, is it possible this Mao is hiding inside your house this very minute?' asked Barkley as he shot through the cat flap into the laundry, with Miss Fi-Fi following.

'Quick, where do you eat and sleep?'

'My food is given to me here,' replied Miss Fi-Fi, pointing to a small corner in the laundry. Barkley checked behind the door, then ran into the kitchen, quickly surveying the place.

'This way!' cried the pedigree as she ran into a room and showed him her sleeping area. There was a lovely, soft, pink cat bed, a few scratching poles and some toys on the floor. They searched in every room possible for the mysterious Mao and found nothing. On the way out through the kitchen, Barkley suddenly thought about Fi-Fi's family.

'Have your family seen the note I left them about the puppy?'

'Yes, Monsieur,' replied Miss Fi-Fi, panting. 'Although they did not seem to understand. They were laughing and repeating your note. "No bog or I get it. We know what you are booing."'

*Ugh! Not again!*

Barkley shook his head and squeezed through the cat flap. He always had trouble with the letters 'b' and 'd'. One went one way and the other faced the other way. He was fine if he practised a lot, but he had fashioned the note quickly and stuck it down onto the paper with his special glue. In the beginning, he would get his 'bs and 'ps mixed up, so some of his notes read 'No bog or dus gets it. We know what you are pooing.' The readers would be in hysterics over his note wrapped around a bone.

'It will be alright, Miss Fi-Fi. They can't read my writing. I will be sending another note tomorrow,' sighed Barkley in frustration over his spelling errors.

Barkley made his way home to get some rest. Sleep did not come easy to him as his mind pondered repeatedly – who is Confucius of Mao? He pretty much knew all the pets in his area. Confu... Confushus of Miaows mmust... be a new kid on the... blo...

Dreams... slumber had arrived.

*'Ah-ha! Now I have you, Confoozed Us of Miaows! You will not be stealing any more collars!' shouted Barkley as he took out his sword and began to duel. He found it difficult to parry in his oversized boots and his hat kept falling over his eyes so he could not see his opponent.*

*'But I am not the Confused Us of Miaows, Barkley! It is you who are confused. You really should learn your alphabet better. You have been practising for years and still you get it wrong. Bog, pog, dog, booing and pooing. How many letters in the alphabet are there, Barkley?'*

*Barkley parried and counter-attacked, performed a feint and lunged forward. 'There are twenty-three letters, forty-six letters, twenty-nine letters. Miss Fi-Fi lives at number ten. Fifteen collars are missing. Miss Fi-Fi is having thirty-four poo-pees.' He was swimming underwater now, no longer wearing his Puss in Boots outfit. 'What happened to my sword?' he thought. He was talking to Miss Fi-Fi about the fifteen dogs coming and why would she not wear her collar. The darkened figure was chasing him and catching up. Barkley swam faster, faster. He could not make out his face in the dark. Who are you? Mao of Miaows. Mao of Miaows. Mao of Miaows...*

'Miaow, miaow, miaow.' Barkley woke with a start. His eyes quickly focussed on his surroundings and met Budge and Florry staring at him.

'You alright there, Berk? Only you were talking in your sleep. I didn't want to wake you, but he made me do it!' Budge pointed to his brother. 'It's just that we wanted to speak to you about something, didn't we, Florry?'

'Yeah, that's right. We think something funny is going on. Someone keeps stealing our collars. Budge here had a new one last week. He only had it a day and then whoosh, it's gone. What do you reckon then, Detective Berk, have we or have we not got a case?'

Dumbfounded, Barkley stared at the two brothers. He could not believe his ears. More stealing of collars? He was not dreaming anymore now, was he? This was real.

Waiting for a reply, Budge gave Florry a nudge.

'Oh, yeah. We found this next to our breakfast bowls,' Florry handed him a piece of paper.

Barkley read:

*The only cure to being lost is to teach your heart to sing.*
*Confucius of Mao*

Barkley began to test the paper and writing for clues. He sniffed it excessively, taking in its smell to see if he could decipher anything. He looked at the ink and the style of writing. Whoever this Confucius of Mao was, he knew how to write and hold a pen, something Barkley could not do. Barkley only knew how to scratch out letters from magazines and newspapers and stick them down with glue. If Mao knew how to hold a pen and write, perhaps he should not be looking for a fellow feline, but something else that had a dexterous hand, like a possum, koala, wallaby or even... or even a snake! Snakes were prophesied to carry wisdom and Mao was certainly not dumb if he could hold a pen.

*No, it must be someone from a family. They are the only ones who can do this with such precise ease of paw.*

The agonising grumblings of hunger gnawed at Barkley's ability to think. Not wanting to appear rude, he began to usher the brothers out so he could get a proper feed from his people/family and have a cuddle and play with the children. He needed to get out and have some fun for a bit, clear his mind and remind himself that, at least to them, he was an ordinary cat.

'Please take one of my cards,' said Barkley, handing them a half-decomposed fur ball.

'No thanks. We've got enough of our own,' replied Budge.

When Barkley spent time with his family he did normal pussycat things, like clawing the carpet, jumping on the furniture and miaowing as loudly as he could till food was placed in his bowl. As a kitten, he enjoyed trying out his climbing abilities on the curtains, till the frequent smacks were too much to bear.

A quick game of chasey with the young people, a nap and then outside for the night to commence searching, gathering clues to outsmart this Mao character. Barkley wanted to come face-to-face, whisker-to-whisker and if need be, claw-to-claw with Confucius of Mao.

Gradually, the house became quiet as bedtime for his family approached. Barkley got up and made his way to the back door.

*Must take a few little snacks with me.*

He went to push the door open – it was locked!

*Right, I shall sit here and miaow till someone lets me out.*

Slowly, the laundry door closed and the words, 'Night Barkley, sleep well,' were uttered through a stifled yawn.

*Darn! Trapped inside for the night! How on earth am I going to do any detective work now?*

Barkley hurled his body against the laundry door to gain attention, then waited, listening for sounds of movement, of someone coming to rescue him, but the only noise he could hear was the creaking of the house as it, too, settled for the night.

*Ok, if I am to spend the night here, I shall examine the clues I have so far. Miss Fi-Fi, Budge and Florry have had their collars stolen on numerous occasions. Why? Why these three cats again and again?*

Barkley pondered as he scratched an imaginary flea.

*Someone who calls himself Confucius of Mao is leaving notes, which are written by paw and don't make much sense in relation to stolen collars. Why steal a collar and leave a note in riddles? Perhaps this is a second case entirely that I have not distinguished? Yes, perhaps it is. The first note said, if I can remember correctly, seeing as I am in the current situation of being locked inside all night long, something about accepting dilemmas. Well, I am in the current dilemma of not being able to perform my duties as an inspector and solve this case for the cats who have paid me my sardine fee. So, I shall go to sleep.*

Barkley dozed off, wondering how he was going to find Mao.

# Chapter Two

Barkley did not sleep well. He could not get comfortable and was sure someone was walking around outside. There were too many noises he could not explain. Perhaps it was just the stillness of the night and the full moon that made him jumpy. Eventually, daylight began and there sat bleary-eyed Barkley, patiently waiting for someone to get up so the bursting feeling in his bladder could be relieved.

Movement.

'Ugh! Finally, someone has risen. Miaow? Miaow?' he pleaded.

'Morning, Barkley. Off you go out then.'

*Freedom!*

Barkley dashed outside to underneath the trees. Steam slowly rose from the puddle now being left on the cold, fog-filled morning. He then made his way directly to his office so he could continue solving the case. As he rounded the corner, Barkley saw a figure through the fog and froze.

*Storm! Storm is here? What can he possibly want with me?*

Thoughts raced through Barkley's mind.

*What if Storm is Mao and he has been stealing the collars? There is no way I can take him on.*

Storm was the biggest ginger cat there was. Lean, with muscles bulging out of his muscles, he never spoke; he just stared at you and would not move till you had figured out what he wanted. His real name was Albie, but everyone called him Storm as they were terrified of him. His riveting gaze could unnerve the toughest of cats, rendering them a quivering mess, just like thunder does. Nobody messed with Storm. Just about to turn and slink off the other way, Storm looked around and locked his silent gaze onto Barkley. As cold, emerald eyes like the swell of the ocean penetrated his core, Barkley took a deep breath, plucked up his courage and tried to stroll along to his secret enclosure in as nonchalant a manner as he could summon.

'Morning Storm, lovely day for a fog, dog, pog… jog. What pings you rother this day on wuch a—' Barkley gulped as Storm got up slowly and moved toward him, his gaze never faltering once. The muscle now standing before him like an impenetrable barrier, Barkley stood and stared. *Where is Puss in Boots when you need him,* he quivered silently.

In one swift move, Storm handed him a note. Cautiously, Barkley took it and read:

*All that matters is held together with belonging glue.*
*Confucius of Mao*

Barkley stared at Storm, 'Oh, my Felidae, not you as well! How many of your collars have been stolen?' he asked, before remembering that Storm never spoke.

*This conversation is going to be difficult.*

Then it happened, a deep rumbling occurred that Barkley had never experienced before in his life – Storm spoke! A voice resonated out of the giant and seemed to reverberate and echo off the walls in stereo sound.

'I found that note next to my water bowl. I found three more notes on my way here,' Storm said, handing folded pieces of paper to the detective of the moment.

*So, this is why they call you Storm. Your voice is so deep my bones are vibrating.*

Storm continued, 'I saw someone prowling around my yard last night and gave chase. I found those notes along the way and figured they must have dropped them. Their muddy footprints came this way and have gone under your house. It was me you heard out here last night moving around, Detective Inspector Barkley Button Nose.'

Barkley sat down with a plop. Storm had such a deep voice that if you just sat and listened, it was actually quite soothing and melodious once you got used to it. Then he realised what Storm had just told him – this Confucius of Mao character was LIVING under his house!!

*Oh my enormous Felidae, Puss in Boots where are you,* prayed Barkley silently.

'Look, Storm. I may be a detective but brave I am not. You are a formidable looking chap, how about you go under the house and have a look for this Mao character and bring him out alive so I can box his ears? Hmmm? What do you say?' asked Barkley, trying not to show Storm he was terrified.

'That would be all well and good, but I am too big to squeeze through the gap,' said Storm, pointing to the small opening that led into darkness. 'You're going to have to go in there yourself. I'll wait here and catch him when he comes out. Come on Barkley, you can do it. You're the greatest detective around these parts. What about being the hero of the hour as well?' Storm puffed up his chest to show Barkley what heroes looked like.

Barkley was close to tears.

*Face my enemy? Can't I just write them a letter with bad spelling? Make them laugh? Attach one of Regie's bones with string and pull it along or something? Why do I have to be the one to go under the house? Isn't that where the children said the boogey man lived?*

'I can't possibly go in there, Storm. The children's monster lives under the house! What if I am attacked by both of them? I won't get out alive,' he whimpered.

'Now see here, Detective, get a whisker! When have you ever seen the children's monster? Have you ever heard anything living under your house? C'mon Barkley, make Puss in Boots proud. Don't you want to be able to tell the great King Cat when you get to Kitty Cavern that you managed to foil Mao and the children's monster in one fell swoop? Just think of the accolades. They'll still be talking about it when Miss Fi-Fi's children are granddads,' reasoned Storm with the hero-in-training.

'Have you found Mao, have you?' asked Miss Fi-Fi as she approached. 'Bonjour, Monsieur Nez et Monsieur Storm. I hope it will not be long before you catch him.'

'It appears he has been living under the detective's house, Miss Fi-Fi. Barkley is just going in there now to have a look,' Storm informed her, tipping the detective a wink of confidence.

'Mon Dieu! Your voice is very deep. It is very soothing to my being. How come you never speak?' Miss Fi-Fi asked the giant.

Not wanting to reveal his fear of the boogey monster to the beautiful mademoiselle, Barkley put on a brave face and prepared to climb through the gap that led into unknown danger.

'Stand aside, Miss Fi-Fi. It appears this Confucius of Mao has been closer to home than I had originally anticipated. I am off under the house to catch him.' Barkley wriggled through the gap, giving Storm a nod of confirmation to remain and keep a lookout.

Barkley's heart was pounding.

*What if there really is a secret monster under the house who only eats children and anyone who comes into its lair, like inquisitive cats? Well, if there were, Mao would have been eaten by now, wouldn't he? Wait a minute, what if he already has been eaten? Storm gave chase and Mao ran this way – what if he inadvertently ran into the boogey man's dungeon?*

Then he remembered from playing hide and seek with the children that the monster of the night only came out when it was dark.

*But it is dark here – permanently dark. When do monsters sleep? Must be during the day, as they only come out when it's bedtime! That's it! The boogey man must be asleep now as it's not bedtime. Phew!*

Calming down somewhat, his eyes adjusting to the darkness, Barkley began sniffing the air and taking in odours that normally did not see the light of day. Slowly, he began to explore. He saw skeletons of small birds who had gotten trapped looking for a worm and could not work out where the exit was, spider webs galore and an untold amount of dust that made him sneeze. Possum poo seemed to be littered everywhere – or was it monster poo he was looking at? There was even the skin from a few lizards. Slowly manoeuvring his way around the house posts, he sighed with relief when he found no evidence of eaten children or pussycats.

*No boogey man down here.*

BANG!

Barkley jumped with fright and ran. 'Gotta get out! Gotta get out!' He bolted to the other side of the house as the whirling noise became louder and louder. 'There's a hole, I can climb through there.' Just as he approached the opening, he tripped and fell. Something had gotten caught around his hind leg.

'Oh no! The boogey man has got me! Miaow! Miaow! The boogey man has got me!'

Barkley turned to face the monster and saw… nothing! Wrapped around his leg was a bright red collar with pretty diamond studs. Barkley sat and giggled over his belief of the children's monster. 'Storm was right. For all the years I have lived here, not once have I ever seen anything that ate children at bedtime. This must be one of Miss Fi-Fi's collars that Mao has dropped in his haste to get away. Running under the house was a trick to get away from Storm as he knew he wouldn't be able to follow.'

Near the opening he was going to escape through, he found another piece of paper neatly folded into a note. Unravelling it, he read:

*Through acceptance we become one.*

*Confucius of Mao*

'Well, I accept my paws are in the right place as they are here under my house. Where are your paws right now, Mao? Paws. Storm said his muddy paws came this way, which means there could be paw prints!'

Barkley looked around and noticed the whirling noise was still going.

*What is that? Some sort of trick to scare me off?*

Using his sharp hearing, Barkley worked out that the noise was coming from above.

'That noise is inside the house! Oh, my Felidae! I think I have woken the monster and he is inside eating everyone right now!' screamed Barkley.

Standing up on his hind legs, Barkley managed to get half his body out from under the house. With a few strong wriggles, the rest of him came too as he plopped onto the concrete face first.

'No time to be afraid now, Barkles! The boogey man is eating everyone!' he said as he dashed inside to avenge the child-eating monster. Lunging into the laundry stood the detective of the moment, face-to-face with the whirling and banging noise. Gradually, the shaking came to a halt.

'Have you eaten everyone already?' he demanded of the large object.

'Barkley, what have you been doing? You're coated in dirt and cobwebs. Have you been exploring under the house again?' asked the children's mother as she put the clothes the monster had eaten into a basket. Barkley stuck his nose in to smell the fiend's dastardly deed.

'Miaow?' asked Barkley, wondering what had happened to his night-time playmates.

Storm and Miss Fi-Fi waited for Barkley to emerge from his detective activities. They sat in silence for a while, watching the fog dissipate when Storm spoke.

'What is this May-Seer-Nay you keep on calling Barkley?'

Miss Fi-Fi puzzled him a look. 'What do you mean? It is his name – Monsieur Nez.'

'Is that his name in French, is it? Barkley is pronounced May-Seer Nay? Odd.'

'Please allow me to correct you. It is Monsieur, which means Mister. Nez is his last name,' replied Miss Fi-Fi, pointing to her nose.

Storm pondered for a bit, then realised, 'Oh, Nay is nose in French, but his name is Barkley. Why don't you call him by his proper name?'

'Because his name on the door says Detective Nose. He knows everything through his nose, does he not?'

Storm smiled, then a deep, rumbling, infectious giggle gurgled up from within his belly and he laughed and laughed. Miss Fi-Fi joined in, although she did not fully understand what she was giggling about.

'Did… you… hear… the bang?' puffed Barkley, having bolted around the house to his two friends, who were having a good giggle over what Miss Fi-Fi had said. 'The bang and whirling noise. I was… (gasp) under the house. It was very loud. I went to investigate and met it just inside the door. I found this under the house too,' he said, handing Miss Fi-Fi the red collar.

'Ooh! How brave you are, Monsieur, to go searching in the dark for Mao. However, this collar is not mine. It is very lovely, but alas, it does not belong to my pretty neck,' declared the French Fi-Fi, then smooched the inspector as her way of saying thanks.

Storm sat, staring at Barkley. *Bang? Whirling noise? Monster? In the house by the back door? I will let him figure it out for himself.*

'I found another note too,' Barkley said, handing it to Storm to read. 'Oh, I almost forgot. Where were the muddy paw prints you saw?'

'They were here, along the path, which has now been covered by the morning dew,' the ginger giant responded, pointing to where Barkley now sat.

Barkley rolled his eyes over the fact that he had just covered up potential evidence; then grabbed the other notes he had not read yet and took them to his office for further analysis, salivating for a sardine and some quiet time.

Back at the bureau of hidden clues, Miss Fi-Fi and Storm sat on top of the scratching posts and gave each other a bath, their gentle purring sending an air of calmness throughout. Fortunately for Miss Fi-Fi, Barkley was down to his last packet of sardines, so the overpowering smell that normally permeated his office did not nauseate her.

# Chapter Three

Barkley got all the notes he had so far and spread them out on his desk.

One from Miss Fi-Fi:

*At the ultimate outcome to all dilemmas, I will still be loved, heard and accepted.*

*Confucius of Mao*

One from Budge and Florry:

*The only cure to being lost is to teach your heart to sing.*

*Confucius of Mao*

Four from Storm:

*All that matters is held together with belonging glue.*

*Confucius of Mao*

*Too much reflection stifles.*

*Confucius of Mao*

*He who lives through the ideal lives in sorrow.*

*He who lives with gratitude lives with peace.*

*Confucius of Mao*

Plus the one he found under the house:



Barkley sat and stared at them. What did all these notes have to do with stealing collars? His nerves were frazzled from confronting the boogey man and there was only one sardine left. He needed a break, and that meant Reg was in for another session of torment. Marching out, he left Miss Fi-Fi and Storm curled up asleep on top of the scratching posts as he stuffed the last salty fish into his mouth and wiped his whiskers.

Barkley jumped up onto the fence and surveyed the landscape.

Wagging his backside, Barkley called, 'Oh Regie-weggie. Where are you little Regie? The nice inspector has come to play with you! Podgie Reg.' Barkley jumped down and started roaming around Reg's yard, sniffing here and there. He wandered over to Regie's bowl that sat on the back patio and had a sniff of his food.

'Yuk! Ghastly stuff! Oh look, there's a bone – just what I need and oh, would you look at that, Wittle Wegie has a new toy.' Squeak, squeak it went as Barkley pressed on it with his paw. 'Ah, here he comes. Oops! That would be the table, Regie boy,' teased the inspector as Reg, the Red Pointer, came bounding along, slipping and sliding over the polished floor and crashing into the furniture.

'Woof, woof!'

Barkley stood squeaking the toy, watching Reg head for the patio door. Suddenly, the door slid open all by itself and out came Reg, ready to attack.

Barkley did not know which way to escape. He had to get away from Reg quick or it would be his own hind leg being buried in the vegie patch. With lightning speed, he grabbed the bone and fled to the nearest secure place he could find, with Reg snapping at his tail.

'Woof! Woof! Woof! Come out of there!' barked Reg at the top of his voice.

*Is he mad,* Barkley the antagonist wondered from the safest place to hand, tucked under the bushes at the back of Reg's kennel. Peering at him through the narrow gap between the fence and his outdoor home, Reg yelled, 'Almost had you then, Captain Berk! Next time, watch out!'

'The name is Detective Inspector to you, Regie boy,' replied Barkley, trembling from the close encounter.

'Well detective, I've got plenty of fleas that need inspection. Why don't you come have a peek?!'

'Nah, I'll let you inspect your own fleas. I wouldn't want to take the pleasure of your favourite past-time of scratching all day away from you,' responded the detective inspector as sarcastically as he could.

'Grrr! You give me back my bone, berk-brain! One of these days I will be having YOU for supper!'

'Fat chance, noodle-paws. You'll never catch me. One wittle teensy-weensy scratch on your ginormous nose and it's goodnight with a Band-Aid.'

'All the better to smell you coming, button head! What sort of name is Barkley Button Nose anyway? What do you do, smell through buttons? Or is it because your brain is so small you could thread it through buttonholes?'

'Actually, it's because I have the cutest nose, that's why! Haven't you ever heard of Button Nose before? With ears like that, I would think you could hear a moth cough from ten families away!'

Barkley stayed put. He was not going anywhere with Regie breathing so close down his neck.

*How did that door manage to open all by itself?*

After what seemed like an eternity, Barkley settled and sat quietly on top of his latest acquisition. Reg sat en garde, waiting for his tormentor to exit. Finally, the dog was dragged away by his collar to go 'walkies', much to the inspector's relief. Slowly, Barkley got up and stretched, then gingerly stuck the bone out first, knowing if Reg was still around he would be snatching his bone, which would give Barkley time to make a run for it. Nothing happened.

*Just a little peek to see if the coast is clear – great! I'm off and I'll take the bone as well as payment for the torment!*

With the bone in his mouth, he stopped and looked at the glass door, then went to see how it worked.

*I am an inspector, after all. It is my duty to know what is going on.*

As he approached the door, it opened all by itself.

'What is this? Magic?' Barkley wondered aloud. He moved away and the door closed, approached and it opened.

*Must be some sort of device to assist the family. Dare I be bold enough to go inside? I think not. If the door shuts while I'm in there and doesn't open, I could end up in a terrible predicament. Maybe later, when I know tweedle brain is permanently out.*

Barkley jumped back over the fence and…

'Barkley! What have you been doing? What have you got there? A bone?? Since when do you eat bones?'

'Ay don't. It's just vat ay need vis for my fup-wy,' he said, giving his cutest look.

'Right, I'll have that, thank you! You have enough food at home and are well fed already!' demanded Jean (the mother of his family) as she prized his trophy out of his mouth and threw it back over the fence.

'Miaow! Great! Miaow! Miaow! Now I'll have to go get it!!' he cried, stamping his feet. 'Dear woman, that could have been potential evidence you just threw away! Don't you realise I am in the middle of a serious case?'

Barkley was angry and did not care if he showed it, so he took a swipe and scratched her legs, then ran off to cool down.

# Chapter Four

The following day, Barkley wandered over to Storm's place. Something had been bothering him all night long. He had to ask someone, and Storm was the only chap he felt he could trust; why, he did not know. He had never been able to trust anyone before. Maybe he felt comfortable with Storm because of his deep voice and the fact that he gave an air of enormous strength.

*Storm will give it to me straight.*

Barkley found Storm sitting in the sun, warming himself on the cool morning.

'Good day to you, Storm. I see you are partaking of some beautiful sunshine.'

'Good morning to you, detective. What brings you my way so early? Have you lost a sardine or found another note?' enquired Storm.

'I am wondering if you could set me straight on a matter. I was talking to Reg yesterday...'

'You mean you were toying with him so you could get a bone and be the hero after losing to the washing machine?'

*Is that what you call that thing?*

'Well, actually, Reg made mention to my name, and I was wondering if you could tell me – what is a buttonhole?' he blurted.

Storm turned and looked away from the inquisitor, trying ever so hard not to roll around in laughter. *No, this is a time for seriousness,* he said to himself.

Barkley waited patiently.

'Come with me,' replied Storm and walked his new mate to the back of his home.

Storm was so serious, Barkley thought he was in for a hiding.

He took him into a shed in the garden and pointed to a coat hanging on the back of the door.

'See those round things attached to the garment? They are buttons. They hold it together when it's being worn. On the other side are what they call buttonholes. The button is pushed through the hole and that holds it in place,' explained Storm, looking at his student for confirmation of comprehension. 'Buttons also have holes of their own so they can be sewn, stitched onto the garment,' Storm explained, gesturing the action of a needle and thread sewing as he was confident Barkley did not know what sewing was. Barkley was dumbfounded.

'Do you mean to tell me my nose has been named after a button? What am I? A coat in the making?' Barkley was depressed. 'How could they do this to me? I, the greatest detective known in these parts! Tell me truthfully, does my nose look like a button to you?'

'Well, now that you mention it!' smirked the ginger muscle with a large twinkle in his eye. 'You seem to have forgotten that "Button Nose" is a term of endearment for people. Your nose is exceptionally, how shall I put it? CUTE! Miss Fi-Fi seems to think you are able to decipher all your cases through your nose.'

'Yeah, okay. I guess I am just being silly.' Barkley turned and did a little dance, wiggled his tail, jumped around and looked at Storm with the cutest look he could summon, then asked, 'Hey Storm, does my nose look cute in this?'

'Who knows?' giggled Storm, ushering his friend outside.

'I can only know what my nose knows, and my nose tells me that "At the ultimate outcome to all dilemmas, I will still be loved"! My Felidae Storm, do you realise what this means? It means I can misbehave as much as I like and still get fed and pampered! It means I can go back to climbing the curtains! Ha ha!'

'I used to get HUGE wallops when I was halfway up. My back was sore for days. Every time I went to try out my climbing skills with my newly sharpened claws, I was yelled at, grabbed from the neck and put on the floor with my bottom smacked. Eventually, it was not any fun and having my toenails cut made scratching those things they get us to play on boring,' reminisced Storm.

'Yeah, I too got lots of smacks for that and for climbing over the places where they sit and eat, especially along the catwalk thing where they prepare their own food. In fact, I remember being knocked to the floor several times. What am I supposed to do when what they eat smells better than my food?' pondered Barkley as he kept swinging his tail and jumping up and down. Suddenly, he felt like a kitten again. The burden of detective work escaped his thinking for a while.

'You should try being fed the same food they eat and it tasting awful! After several nights, I knew I had to do something drastic, so I left deposits. Finally, they took me to the doctor and he said I was malnourished. I have been fed lovely dinners ever since,' Storm smiled.

'Which is probably how you grew so big, hey Storm?'

'All my family are big. Some of them are bigger than me.'

Barkley's eyes were wide in surprise, ''There are cats bigger than you? Amazing!'

At that point, a black rabbit appeared in the yard and handed Barkley a note. He uttered not a single word; just ran back in the direction he had come.

'I see you've managed to get out of your cage again, Blackberry!' yelled Storm to the hopping shadow.

Barkley looked at Storm inquisitively.

'Blackberry lives over in what was Armstrong's place. A new family have moved in with a feline. I have not had the pleasure of a whisker yet,' explained Barkley's teacher.

'This could be Mao. I think I ought to go and investigate,' said Barkley, setting his detective mind on the case.

'Don't you think you should read the note first?' queried Storm, pointing to the small piece of paper that was neatly folded like all the others.

Barkley carefully unravelled the paper and read:


*G.E.N.T.L.E.*

*Confucius of Mao*


Barkley re-read it and handed it to Storm. 'What do you make of this?'

'I don't know. What is a Mao, anyway? Is it some sort of code?' Storm replied in his wonderfully deep voice.

'A code? Perhaps you're right! Well, I must be off now to visit Blackberry's feline friend, where I hope to find Mao. Thank you for your assistance today, my friend,' replied the serious detective.

'Wait, I'll come with you.'

Next to the house that always had lots of cars parked in the driveway, was a laneway that took Barkley and Storm into the next road. Cautiously ran across the road and into the place diagonally opposite to Ponchoo and Coco, the yapping Pomeranians. They sauntered up the driveway and went into the backyard to see Blackberry in the hope of obtaining information about Mao. What they saw was a small child underneath the clothesline, playing with a fluffy brown and white kitten that had been submitted to being dressed in dolls' clothes. Blackberry was sitting outside his cage.

Storm called out, 'Hey Blackberry, where did you get the note from?'

Blackberry looked up from his lettuce and pointed his ears in the direction of the detective and his muscular bodyguard. Behind them stood ferociousness. Fear instantaneously took over their questing curiosity as they raised their backs in defence mode. Barkley and Storm puffed themselves up to look twice as big to scare off the massive dog standing in front of them. Most dogs would know to back away but this one was advancing towards them, growling. Barkley told Storm to scratch the dog's back leg while he scratched his nose, then it would be goodnight with two Band-Aids. Storm hissed and moved around the dog to the tail end, ready to slash when Barkley gave him the signal.

The dog did not know which cat to attack first.

'Okay! Storm! Scratch his leg, scratch his leg!' yelled Barkley, then stood up and swiped. The dog was too tall – Barkley's claws missed his nose completely.

'Barkley, quick! Up onto the fence!' directed Storm.

In a split second, Barkley escaped harm's way, safe from the life-sized monster. Slipping and twisting as he grappled for grip on the fence, Barkley had no time to worry about any injury he might do himself in his efforts to reach safety. The dog yelped from Storm's scratch and inadvertently kicked the huge ginger cat away, then whizzed around to face the cause of his pain, just as the little kitten appeared and got under the dog's massive feet. As the dog tried not to step on his minute ward with his oversized paws, Storm took the opportunity to jump to safety. With great speed, he hurled himself up onto the fence.

Visibly shaken, Barkley and Storm cautiously took to safety in the overhanging branches of next door's tree with the monstrous dog jumping up at them, barking. Hearts were pounding and bruises were forming as they sat perched in their rescue tree, whispering whiskers of gratitude that they were safe. After a while, his heart still thumping in his chest so loudly he was sure the whole tree was vibrating, Barkley asked Storm, 'Was that Mao or the boogey monster?'

'Did you see the size of his legs and feet? Not even my brother Harley could take on a canine that big! Come on. We need to plan a safe journey home. You must be gnawing for a sardine to calm your nerves and I need to rest and lick my wounds,' said Barkley's new buddy.

Cautiously they climbed down from their security net, making sure the life-sized boogey monster did not have a counterpart next door. Scampering across the road, Barkley knew Storm was covered in bruises and noticed he now walked with a limp.

'Storm, I owe you huge gratitude for saving my life today. If I'd gone over there alone as I planned, I doubt I would be standing here now. Thank you! I will say a blessing to the great Felidae that your wounds heal fast,' said Barkley with such appreciation, silently promising himself the next packet of sardines he got were for his hero.

Barkley returned home with Blackberry's note that he had left in a garden pot to collect on the way back, quickly dumped it in his den, then snuck inside for some dinner and hid under the couch so he would not be locked into a cold laundry; he needed some peace, quiet and warmth to clean himself up and nurse his nerves. *It has been an eventful day,* he thought as he curled up and went to sleep, making a mental note that there was no way the monster was getting one of Regie's bones and a badly spelled note.

Barkley remained inside for the next few days. He wanted to feel cosy and spend what he called ordinary time with his family, listening to the children laugh and play games. He even had a go at climbing the curtains and marching up and down the kitchen benches while miaowing profusely for his dinner just to see if creating a dilemma would get him more love and acceptance, but all he got was a smacked bottom and being fed in a locked laundry. He needed to clear his mind and replenish his nerves. Waking only to lick his imagined wounds from the nightmares he was having of the monster attacking him and to eat a couple of mouthfuls of whatever was placed before him, Barkley tried not to flinch when someone stroked him.

When he was ready to venture out into the cold, Barkley got up, paid the garden bed a visit and went to his office. He sat there for quite a while staring at the notes, not knowing what to make of any of them. Letters and words jumped up from the paper and floated around the air.

*'Belonging is a reflection of silent glue; dilemmas talk in peace; mastering strength is waiting in the sky; stifling ideals reside in sorrow.' What does it all mean? Where are my sardines? Sardines....*

Barkley sat watching an ant march over the pieces of paper, holding a crumb high in its claws. He wished he had that crumb but it was too small to satisfy his craving. He stretched out a paw and tapped the paper the ant was crossing; the insect jumped into the air, still holding its prize. This gave him the giggles, so he tossed the notes into the air like he was playing with string, then ran around in total glee, up and down scratching posts, across the furniture, into open drawers and out again, imagining the letters had risen up off the paper and disappeared – case closed. Only they were still there, staring at him like they wanted him to step through their meaning into a world he had never seen before.

Barkley sat down and sighed.

*Perhaps if I lay down on them, the clues will somehow sink in and all the answers will be revealed?*

Still too mentally exhausted to contemplate anything, he curled up on the notes and fell asleep, hoping that when he woke the insights would be revealed and his head would be clear.

# Chapter Five

Peering at him from atop the scratching poles were three pairs of eyes. 'Good afternoon to you, sunshine! Did you have a nice sleep? We tried ever so hard not to wake you!' said Budge.

'Yes, it is true. The boys wanted to wake you, but I said no, let him sleep. Monsieur Storm has told us of your ordeal. You, too, look like you have been in the war,' said Miss Fi-Fi, looking worried.

Yawning, Barkley greeted the trio.

'Miss Fi-Fi, Budge, Florry. Yes, I thought I had found Mao and went to investigate. Storm came with me; we had a meeting with a massive hound instead. Storm was almost killed by the ferocious monster living with a young'un. He saved my life. Have you found more notes, have you?' he asked, cleaning sleep from his eyes.

'No, we have found something better than a note. We have found three collars, two that belonged to Budge and one what belonged to Zenya, but most of all, we found this – writing with pictures of us!' said Miss Fi-Fi, pushing a book in front of Barkley.

Barkley gazed at his friends in utter astonishment. This was real evidence, something tangible that was bound to be full of clues, paw prints, smells and the odd discarded strand of fur, perhaps even saliva.

His mind was racing. He had remembered his dream when Mao was chasing him, asking him how many letters there were. He had no idea. So many of them looked the same – b, d, p, q, not to mention how they changed when they became big. It had taken Barkley ages to figure out that lower case 'g' and upper case 'G' were the same letter. The stress he went through to work out that big 'I' was not the same as little 'i' left him unable to eat for a few days and had him scratching for a week.

In his dream, Barkley felt humiliated as he could not answer Mao's question. Looking at his three mates, Barkley asked, 'How many letters are there? How many letters are there to write with? Words are made up of letters. In all my newspapers that I have collected,' desperately, he pointed to the shredded papers that lay strewn atop the scratching poles, 'are written words. These words are made up of letters. How many are there?'

'We don't know. Neither of us can read, can we?' replied Budge, looking at his brother.

'What do you mean, neither of you can read? You brought me the notes you found. Those notes were given specifically to you as they have meaning, I think,' Barkley muttered, as he was not too sure. He could not figure out what the notes meant, thus he concluded they must have meaning to the recipient. Barkley looked to Budge and Florry, wanting an answer, but the brothers just looked at each other to see if either of them knew.

'So, you mean to tell me you have been given a note with specific meaning that pertains to you, and you have no idea what it says? How come you didn't ask what it said?'

'Don't know. We've had our collars stolen, haven't we? You've been talking about this Mao character. We just figured you'd let us know in the end what it all meant. Didn't we?' said Budge, with Florry nodding approval.

'Could you count them?' suggested Florry.

'Great idea! Let's all take some newspaper and count how many different letters we can see,' said Budge.

'I can only count to seven, what about you?' asked Florry of his brother.

'I'm only just learning how to tell the time.'

Barkley did not know what telling the time meant but he was not going to admit it.

Gobsmacked, Barkley responded, 'Do you mean to tell me that none of you can read, count or tell the time? How on Felidae do you manage?'

'Mais, Je peux lire et compter. I can read and count,' interrupted Miss Fi-Fi.

'Look Barkles, we're cats. What is there to know? We eat, we sleep. End of story,' replied Budge.

'But, but… how did you know to bring me the notes you found if you can't read?'

'The great King Cat from Kitty Cavern told us, didn't she?' said Budge, with Florry nodding.

'Wait on a minute – the great King Cat from Kitty Cavern told you? You mean THE great King Cat from Kitty Cavern, where all cats go when their nine lives have passed?'

'Yeah, that's right.'

'Well, what does he look like? When did you meet him? How did he tell you? Why hasn't he come to see me? If he were here right now, I could ask him to help me with my alphabet.' Thinking about spelling made Barkley despondent. He enjoyed scratching out letters and glueing them down. Finding out he could not spell was just horrible.

'I can count and read,' purred Miss Fi-Fi again, to deaf ears.

The brothers responded in unison, 'The King Cat is a girl.'

Barkley did a double take.

'What?! Kitty Cavern is run by a GIRL?!! And I suppose Hound Haven is run by a puppy, is it?'

'We don't know stuff like that, now, do we? All I know is I had a dream to bring you the note,' said Budge.

'Yeah, me too. He had his dream just after falling asleep and I had mine just before waking,' collaborated Florry.

'What about you, Miss Fi-Fi. When did you have a dream from the King Cat?' asked Barkley, unable to fathom that what he was hearing was true.

'I did not have a dream, as you say,' replied the French mademoiselle. 'I found the note in the morning, remember. You were there at the time,' reminded Miss Fi-Fi.

'Yes, that is true. I had spent the night in your garden waiting for Mao to appear. So, if you can't read, how did you know the book was for me?'

'I have been trying to tell you for the last five minutes,' said Miss Fi-Fi, holding up her paw, 'that I can read and count in French and English. There are twenty-six letters in French, and as most of English contains French words, you have the same, do you not?'

Barkley sighed with relief. 'Twenty-six letters in the alphabet. Now I can tell Mao when I see him. He will be so pleased with me.'

'How do you know that is what he wants to know?' asked the French linguist.

Barkley deflected answering by responding with a question, 'Um, so where did you say you got the book from?' as he stared at the evidence in front of him.

Full of anticipation, they watched as Barkley passed his paw over the plain cover, then extended a claw and opened the book.

'Where did you say you got this from?' asked Barkley again, wishing he had a dried sardine to chew on. How could such a lovely book with such incredible detail be before his eyes? Mao must have worked on this for years!

*So how did he know I am here? Why only come forward now? Miss Fi-Fi is new to the neighbourhood, yet here she is on the first two pages.*

Miss Fi-Fi continued, 'Storm found the book; no, he didn't really find it. Missus Andrews was reading it to her grandchildren. Storm has borrowed it.'

Barkley asked after Storm.

'Storm has been staying with Missus Andrews to recuperate after the ordeal. He heard her reading it to her grandchildren. Storm has borrowed it without her knowing,' Miss Fi-Fi continued. 'He has terrible bruises and walks with a limp. Storm is incredibly strong, Monsieur Nez. For him to sustain such injuries, the attack must have been great.'

'I must go to Mrs Andrews and ask her some questions and see Storm,' declared the sardine muncher. 'Deciphering the book and analysing it for catification will have to wait.' Barkley was off to gather clues. There was no time to lose. 'Miss Fi-Fi, would you do me the honour of taking me to Mrs Andrews' place?' asked the detective, wiping an imaginary crumb from his mouth.

Barkley Button Nose followed Miss Fi-Fi's pregnant, swaying body out of his office, through the labyrinth of scratching poles, decorations of torn newspapers and discarded Regie bones. He did wonder if he should take a bone to give her as a thank you, so she knew he meant business. No, maybe he'll give her a fresh one later.

'Budge, Florry. You coming?' quizzed Barkley on the way out.

'Barkley! Dinner time! BARKLEEE!' was heard as they jumped over the back fence and tip-toed around the fishpond (a favourite pastime of many a cat, reminisced Captain B as he remembered the hours he had spent there dappling his paws into the water, playing with the fish). It was there that he got the idea of his detective services. Barkley did not realise Mrs Andrews lived nine doors away, at the back of Storm's place. How on a whisker did he manage to find her? All four of them ran across yards, climbed up and down fences and balanced along branches to get there. Barkley sniffed the air continuously to pick up clues and make note of the way home.

Simmo threw his slippers at them when they were squeezing along on the top of the fence to avoid the dog; one of them bounced off a branch and hit Barkley in the face. 'Keep going!' he yelled. 'Keep going!'

Upon entering Mrs Andrews' backyard, Barkley noticed how neat and tidy the garden was. The lawn was immaculate, the trees provided good shade and large pots with flowering plants decorated the edges of the patio. The entire back of Mrs Andrews' house was glass, so Barkley could see into the kitchen, dining and lounge room from where he stood. As ordered by Barkley, Miss Fi-Fi, Budge and Florry waited amongst the shrubbery at the corner of the house to keep watch in case something happened.

Barkley let out an almighty Miaow. 'Hello? Hello?'

'Oh, now Mister Ginge. What's the matter? Are you hungry again? Are you?' came a voice from inside a room down the corridor. Barkley sat patiently and waited for Mrs Andrews to approach the door.

'Goodness me! Who are you?' Gently, the back door opened and Barkley met Mrs Andrews, a kind-looking lady with grey hair tied up on top of her head. She wore a very nice plaid skirt and white blouse, a pearl necklace with matching earrings and a pair of good, practical walking shoes. Here was someone who was sensible, caring and took pride in her appearance (well dressed and coiffed) and kept a neat garden and immaculate house, noted the detective the moment she opened the back door.

In a clear voice, Barkley spoke, 'Good day to you, Madam.' Pointing to his name tag, Barkley continued, 'I am Detective Inspector Barkley Button Nose, at your service. I have discovered you are in possession of a book, a book that your grandchildren are now aware of that is vital to my current case. Can you tell me where you got the book from? How do you know Mao? How do you know me? Are you in any way affiliated with the monster at

Blackberry's place, the monster that hurt Storm? How come you are in possession of such a vital clue in my current case of the missing collars? Did... did YOU write the book, Mrs Andrews? Because whoever did has a very dexterous paw!'

Barkley sat, glaring into Mrs Andrews' eyes as he waited for a response.

Mrs Andrews stared at the cute cat before her and listened to the constant miaowing, then said, 'Goodness, what a racket! What is it you want? Are you hungry? Alright then,' she said and turned to go back inside.

'Not so fast!' cried Barkley, running up to her, trying to block her attempt to return inside. He did not want her out of his sight until he had some answers.

'Just a minute, for heaven's sake. I've got to go and get it!' said Mrs Andrews.

Barkley stood by the back door, ready to pounce when she re-emerged.

*At last! Someone who can answer my questions!*

Barkley pranced up and down with excited anticipation for the answers to all his questions to be placed before him, miaowing as much as he could.

Mrs Andrews bent down and placed a small dish in front of Barkley.

'I don't want to be fed! I want answers! Do you know how long this case is taking me to solve? I'm out of sardines! That's how long! Now tell me, how do you know Mao and where did the book come from?' yelled Barkley, stamping his feet.

Kind Mrs Andrews opened the tin and emptied the contents into the bowl. Immediately, Barkley's nostrils were filled with the most fragrant smell. 'Sardines? You brought me sardines dressed in oil? Oh, my dear woman! You are too kind! I couldn't, I just couldn't...' Barkley was salivating. Unable to help himself, he sat down and slowly began to devour his favourite delicacy. 'Sardines!'

Mrs Andrews stroked his back and Barkley purred the loudest he had ever purred. Lost in his moment of delight, he did not even notice a second bowl appear with special cat milk. When he had devoured and drank all he was in heaven. His eyes glazed over as he flopped down onto his back, his belly in the air with a gentle hand scratching it.

'Oh, Mrs Andrews, you do the most wonderfullest things! You've got the best tucker and you know how to give a detective a good scratch!' Barkley was rolling around in sardine and milk delight, when a huge ginger face appeared above him.

'Hello, Storm.'

'Hello, Barkley,' said Storm. 'I see you got my message. How's it going?'

'Just dandy, matey! Just dandy! Have you met Mrs Andrews?' asked Barkley with a hundred twinkles in his eyes, stretching out a paw to where the kind lady stood watching the two chums chat. 'She's got the best tucker!'

'Yes, Mrs Andrews and I have known each other for years.'

Barkley continued to roll around on his back, moving his paws around in tai chi 'waving clouds' while Mrs Andrews watched her new visitor paw Ginge's face.

'This is the life, heh Storm?' daydreamed the detective.

Storm stood looking down at the Button Nose, when the sardine whiskers started buzzing.

'Where did the book come from, Storm?'

Suddenly, Barkley was up on his paws. Suspicious, eyes narrowed, he stared at his pal, then turned and stared at the elderly lady who had sat down in her favourite chair. Quick as a flash and without warning, Barkley was standing on her lap, miaowing profusely. Then he stood up and placed his front paws on her shoulders so he could gaze into her eyes more closely.

'Oh my!' she exclaimed, startled, not knowing what to think. 'A few sardines and some milk – don't they feed you enough where you're from? Well, you are welcome to come over any time. Ginge is here quite a bit, aren't you, Ginge?' stated Mrs Andrews, looking over at Storm. Barkley put his paw on her chin so as not to avert from gazing into her big blue eyes (this was one technique of catification). You could tell a lot from staring into people's eyes and smelling their breath.

'MIAOW! MIAOW! MIAOW! MIAOW! MIAOW!'

'It's no use,' thought the sardine deli-cat. 'I'll have to send a note. She doesn't understand a word I'm saying.'

Mrs Andrews stroked Barkley down his back and with her other hand, looked for the tag on his collar. 'Barkley Button Nose. Huh!

Well, I'll be! Barkley Button Nose from "The Shambolic Decision" by… hmmm, what's-her-name? Goodness me! I didn't think anyone knew about that!' With all the attention he was getting, Barkley was purring loudly.

'Yes,' purred Barkley, smooching Mrs Andrews' face, 'tell me about the book. Tell me everything you know. Miaow?' quizzed Barkley.

'Ooh! You are such a smooch, aren't you Mr Barkley! Or are you a Miss Barkley?' And with that, Barkley was held up and turned around to face the other way while a gentle hand poked around his nether regions.

'Ooh, so you're a boy Barkley, not a girl Barkley. Well hello MISTER Barkley Button Nose!' giggled Mrs Andrews.

Barkley jumped down, turned and glared at her. With indignation he declared, 'Well really! We have only just met! This is most indelicate! A detective must uphold decorum at all times, Mrs Andrews! AT ALL TIMES, PLEASE!'

Mrs Andrews picked up Barkley's dinner plates and took them inside.

Trying to regain his composure, Barkley sat in front of Storm and cleaned his nether regions and face. Sardines were just the best, most delicious repast for a detective such as himself. For a split second, he considered moving in. It would make deducing a lot easier, after all, she was the primary holder of all the clues thus far but then he would miss play time with the children. Barkley liked the game 'Tag' best. When the children were climbing into bed, he would dart underneath and whip a paw out and try to touch them. The giggles were enormous! Barkley liked making the children laugh; it was how he let off steam after a day's detecting.

Barkley's whiskers were twitching.

'Storm, will you stay here and try to get as many clues as you can? I'm going back to my den to catify the book you found. Well done, Storm! Well done to you! My paws would be missing a beat if it weren't for you!'

Storm nodded to Barkley. He knew what he meant, as every cat has a link to the Great Cat Star in the sky and their paws automatically feel the rhythm of the ground they walk upon. Storm told Barkley he was not going anywhere till his leg was better and the bruises were gone. He had already been there for eight days, listening to his family calling for him morning and night.

Barkley knew Storm was the strong and silent type. What he did not know was his mate had endured years of the twins' patting, pulling and poking; no sooner had they grown out of that phase did another one arrived. That one did not cry – it screamed the house into deafness. Then another one turned up and Storm hoped things would be better.

Barkley was deep in thought, muttering, 'Gotta get back to the den, catify the book, look at the clues and think, think, think!' This was his greatest case yet and he did not want to disappoint the Giant Felidae in the sky when he got to Kitty Cavern. Deep in thought, he did not even spot his fellow companions, Miss Fi-Fi, Budge and Florry, waiting under the shrubs like silent spies who had witnessed a crime.

With a big sigh, Barkley marched down the driveway and onto the footpath with his head held high and his chest out proudly – he liked the feeling he got when he knew he was on the right track and the case was progressing – then he realised he had gone the wrong way.

'This way, Monsieur Nez!' declared Miss Fi-Fi, scooting off. In silence, they hugged front fences and letterboxes, ran past the yapping dog that somehow seemed to smell them coming, up the driveway to the fishpond and back to Barkley's thinking post.

Barkley's Secret Service was located at 52a Oakdale Drive, at what he called Gumnut Alley, although there was only one eucalypt in the yard, it was too big for him to climb. It grew straight up into the sky and went higher than the house, only then did the branches appear. The 'a' of 52 was Barkley's address. His office was in the wooden shed down the side of the house. Years ago, one of the gumnut branches broke off and left a hole in the roof that let in extra spiders, bugs, rain and, of course, leaves during autumn and winter. Adjacent to the door sat a scattering of small plants that delicately hid the matted sign of Barkley's detective services from his family. The labyrinth of antique furniture was from Grandma's place and the cat scratching posts came from the days when 'Captain Dark' and his assistant 'Thunder Ada' fought the invading destroyers, Simeon and Anastasia, from the starship next door.

As a kitten, Barkley would run up and down the curtains, so a construct of scratching poles was assembled to keep his boisterous energy entertained. These made their way into the secret 'spaceship' to form passageways to the central control room. The rest of them were begged from neighbouring homes, while some that had been placed on the curb for council pick-up were whisked home on the billy cart, tied to the back of bicycles. The desk was an old door that sat on top of a chest of drawers. In the top right corner was a pot of pens, coloured pencils, crayons, a ruler and scissors.

Memories of fun and laughter had long since fallen down the back of the chest of drawers, where walkie-talkies and maps of star systems drawn on butchers' paper lay. Surrounding the disused toys were numerous strewn packets that once contained dried fish. The rest of the shed stored furniture – a walnut dining table with matching chairs, two walnut chests of drawers, a silky oak wardrobe and writing bureau and boxes of Grandma's fine china and crockery.

Barkley had learnt how to read with the children. He, too, loved listening to bedtime stories and singing the alphabet song 'Ay Bee Cee Dee Eee eF Gee…' He was most excited one day when he got up from sleeping on Sarah's bed, stretched, yawned and with bleary eyes, strolled to his eating area to see that the newspaper that got thrown into the garden each morning had fallen onto the floor. He read the headlines 'Golden Goals in Soccer Frenzy'. Barkley knew what soccer was; sometimes he played soccer with the children. He was the goalie. He would hide under the furniture and when the ping pong ball came his way, he would flick it back with a quick swish of his paw, then listen to delightful giggles.

Back at the Detective's den, Miss Fi-Fi said, 'I am thirsty, Monsieur. I think I will go home now.' Barkley looked at his water bowl and thought perhaps the numerous dead bugs and rotting leaves that made their way into the container did not seem appealing to sensitive stomachs. He looked directly at her, yet uttered nothing. His eyes told her he was absorbing all that had occurred – the odours, the way there and back, what was said and especially gazing into Mrs Andrews' eyes (this clue was vital to the whiskered detective).

Barkley got into his reading position in front of the book that had been lying open on the table all this time. From the outside, there was no indication as to what the black portfolio was about. Larger than most books, with a coil binding down the spine, it was not till you opened it did you find it was heavily illuminated with beautiful script that had historiated initials for each section.

'Go on, Barkley. Tell us what it says,' said Florry.

'Yeah, go on. I'm starving, but this is too good to pass up,' agreed Budge, with Florry nodding.

Starting at the beginning, Barkley ran his paw over the page that showed various pictures of Miss Fi-Fi amongst the writing. There she was playing with a ball of wool, licking her paw, and walking across the bottom of the page with kittens in tow. Then he noticed it was not printed like the newspaper but was a painting, and so was the writing. He began to read:

To Be Cared For
To feel wanted.
To stop being disloyal to myself.
To allow all aspects of myself to be heard by me and
others in a safe place.
To know at the ultimate outcome to all dilemmas, I will
still be loved, heard and accepted.
To understand if I make a mistake in life, it is not a crime.
To know that mistakes are to be laughed at, a lesson
seen for what it is and the creation of Plan B
implemented with honour, integrity and joy for the
existence of the experience.
To know at the end of each day, as I climb into bed,
that all is well; I am safe, loved and wanted and
tomorrow's excitements are a restful sleep away.
To be gentle.
To be kind and patient with myself.
To see in my heart a flickering flame that shines.

Barkley was dumbfounded.

*Doesn't Miss Fi-Fi feel loved by her family? Why would she feel that making a mistake was so terrible? And when did a cat ever make a mistake? Cats know already that everything works out for the best. The Great Cat Star in the sky says Paws Walk on Sacred Ground and that chance is there for luck to flourish; this is why cats are given nine lives. A cat's paw is linked to the breath of the ground that it walks on. It beats to the same drum. This is called instinct. Why does Miss Fi-Fi feel that she is being disloyal?*

He could understand feeling insecure. Who wanted to raise kittens knowing there was a brute of a dog around? Barkley had had his fair share of brutish dogs. He read on:

*The meaning of To Care is:*

*T – Total*
*O – Observance with*

*C – Compassion*
*A – Awareness*
*R – Respect for their*
*E – Existence*

This was amazing! Barkley was in awe of the words. He could not believe that to be cared for simply meant to pay respect. Barkley stopped and thought about being nice to Regie. He felt rather disappointed with not being able to take out his frustrations on him and steal his bones to use as blackmail. Barkley yawned, turned around and looked at Budge and Florry, who stared wide-eyed at him. Swallowing hard, Barkley knew this would be the most demanding case he had ever tackled; it would take all his strength to solve.

Budge broke his stare and said to Barkley, 'That's great, isn't it, Flor?' Florry nodded. 'We had better leave you to it, Barkles. The gnawing in our stomachs is too much for us to bear. We'd love to hear more, it's just that we can hear our dinner calling us.'

Budge and Florry were already making their way towards the labyrinth to wind their crying hunger past the paraphernalia along the alleyway to the door. 'Come on Budge, if I don't eat soon, I'll die right here, I will!' drooled Florry as he kept nudging Budge towards the exit. A few seconds later, Barkley heard the fence bang as the two cats jumped over and made their way up the street.

'A few more fences and they'll be inside having their dinner,' thought Barkley, listening to his own hunger pangs. It was getting dark now, too dark to read. Soon the back door would be shut and his miaows would take forever to be heard above the evening din. Standing up and stretching his back, Barkley made his way through the dusky light to go inside and be fed. He might even see if he could sleep on the couch this time!

*'Not so fast, Detective Barkles!'*

*Barkley looked up, startled. 'Puss in Boots! What are you d—?'*

*'I have come to show you the way!' said Puss, prodding at Barkley's chest with his sword. 'You think you can escape my almightiness and solve this all by yourself, do you? Huh? Well?'*

*'Captain Boots!' Barkley gasped. 'I wasn't going to solve this without your help. I can't solve this! I don't know where to start!' he cried. 'I've got so many clues; so much running through my head it hurts!' Barkley put a paw up to his head but it was not there. Where had it gone? It had disappeared! How come he could still talk? Barkley put his paw up to give it a lick in the hope that his tongue would appear but nothing seemed to happen.*

*Meantime, Puss in Boots kept prodding Barkley with his sword, demanding to know how many letters there were in the alphabet.*

*'I don't know, Puss! I can't find my head!' whimpered Captain B. Nonsensical words ran through Barkley's mind. 'Nog, pog, dog, Doing, pooing. Watch it or the gog det's it! What gog, where?'*

*Barkley heard laughter and watched Puss turn and fly up and out through the top of the wall.*

*'Just listen to the clues, Captain Beeeee, the clues. What's the purpose? What is the purpose of the clue? Why is Mrs Andrews' garden so neat? What is Miss Fi-Fi doing with all those words? Baaaahhhh-kleeee!'*

Barkley startled himself awake. Quickly, his eyes came into focus as he realised it was all just a dream. He was curled up asleep on Jean's lap, being gently stroked as the discussion being held over the kitchen table led to more laughter. The children were in bed and all was well. Barkley stood up and arched his back into a good stretch.

'It is really quite extraordinary, you know! If Barkley can write a note, then he can read as well! I could give him a cookbook to read that will teach him how to make broth with the bone!' giggled Jean.

Barkley gulped!

*They know of my expeditions with the notes and Regie's bones? How did they find out?*

Sitting quietly on a warm lap, Barkley noticed the evidence sitting on the kitchen table. Mrs Longford had angrily knocked at the front door and emphatically claimed that their cat had dropped it off at her back door.

Jean looked at Barkley, 'I didn't know you knew how to write, Barkley! You been writing notes to the neighbours have you, about what they've been pooing?'

'Just don't make any poo soup!' said the husband. Hysterical laughter filled the kitchen, whereupon Barkley jumped down, had another bite of his dinner, then went and hid under the couch so he did not have to spend the night in a locked laundry; his head hurt too much to reply to any comment.

In the middle of the night, Barkley's nose twitched. There was someone outside! Crawling out from under the lounge, he nudged his way behind the closed drapes and looked out the window to see the local fox stalking up the street. He could sense something going on. Something he had never sensed before. Someone was up. He heard a door open, then a light came on, the toilet flushed, footsteps, a door closed and the house went back to its slumber and snoring. Barkley sat quietly behind the curtain and continued to look out the window.

Something… something was not…

*Just a minute! What was that?*

Across the road, in the dark, Barkley's whiskers told him someone was…

'There!'

From behind the telegraph pole, two eyes glistened in the moonlight. Barkley thought they were looking directly at him. Then they disappeared and he saw a shadow move away and jump over Mr Rowan's front fence.

'Who was that?!' quizzed Barkley aloud.

He thought of waking someone up to get them to open the door so he could go out but that never worked.

Barkley sighed.

*I will have to wait till daybreak.*

# Chapter Six

'**U**gh! Good grief, woman! I don't want this for breakfast! You gave me this yesterday and I'm bored with it! If you can't come up with anything imaginative, give me the salmon one! Salmon!' miaowed Barkley, nudging the can of salmon with this nose. Profuse miaowing made no difference, so Barkley put his paw on the one he wanted to pull it out of the cupboard. It fell on the floor and more nudging and miaowing ensued.

'Hey, Mum! Did you see that? Barkley pulled the can he wants out of the cupboard!' declared Sarah with excitement, handing her mum the desired flavour; however, the can was quickly whizzed back into the cupboard and the door firmly shut.

'Did you know, according to Shirley Longford, he's been writing notes to the neighbours and dropping them off at their back door with a bone? God knows where he got the bone from, or the ability to write!' declared Jean, having forgotten the scratch on her leg. She nodded to the kitchen table where the note was as she emerged from the fridge, only it was no longer there. With astonished looks, they both searched everywhere for the note and eventually saw it in shreds underneath the chairs.

'Mrs Longford? Really? She's got a cat already.'

'Has she?' quizzed Jean.

'Yes, it's a purebred. It's pregnant and about to give birth. She's breeding to help with the bills. Mum, can we get—?'

'NO!'

'You know Nicholas, in my class? His cat, Albie, has gone missing. He's been gone for over a week now. They're really worried.'

'Oh, how dreadful! I hope he's alright and nothing terrible has happened. Are they sure he isn't shut in someone's garage?' asked Jean, tossing breakfast crumbs into the bin.

'I don't know. They've asked all the neighbours and they've been calling every morning and night. Apparently, he goes off for a few days on a regular basis but never this long.'

One more glance at the clock, then, 'Right, well, I'm off to work. See you when I get home.' Jean kissed her daughter goodbye, gathered her things and whizzed out the back door to the garage with shouts of 'Goodbye!' to anyone listening.

Sarah flung her school bag over her shoulder, stroked Barkley, who was still munching on his breakfast, and went to school. The small Burmese cat tried not to flinch from the caring touch.

Barkley's brain hurt, but he was still determined.

*Right! To work! Keep gathering clues and try to solve this case. What if I don't solve it? What if it can't be solved?*

Barkley shook his head. This was not worth thinking about. It was his duty to be a detective and prove to the Great Kitty Cat in the sky that he was worthy of the position he had nominated himself to be in.

The house was now quiet and felt empty, but the back door was still open. Barkley dawdled out the door towards his den, muttering, 'Miss Fi-Fi is about to become a mother. That means she has to care for her kittens, that's only natural and a mother's instinct, yet it spoke of being gentle, well that would be her request to the 'poopee', I mean puppy. The dilemma is the dog, which surprisingly has not turned up yet. Perhaps my bone and note worked. Could there be another dilemma? What is the mistake though? What mistake could Miss Fi-Fi, who is extremely meticulous, possibly make? Why have all her collars gone missing? How come this house is so quiet? Where did everyone go?'

He did think of snuggling up on a bed for another day and staying nice and warm, but he had already spent enough time inside on top of the heating vents recovering from sore nerves and counting his blessings. Besides, sleeping was not going to piece this case together and he had long since run out of his favourite delicacy. Barkley was so engrossed in his thoughts he did not notice a black and white cat watching him from the roof.

As soon as Barkley squeezed through the crack in the door, he heard cat shrills and barking.

'That monster is in my den!' pounded his heart in fear.

Barkley ran back inside the house and hid behind the back door, shivering in terror, his mind racing.

*Do I defend my territory or run away? Do I rush in and attack or do I wait till he's left?*

Underneath his fear he was concerned his nose would be scratched and ruined – no more Mr Cute Button Nose!

Titch with his loud voice was picking a fight with anyone and everyone who was prepared to take to him on. Titch was king of his street and made sure everyone knew it. He had fur missing, scratches on top of scratches and his ears were notched from top to bottom from all the fighting he had engaged in.

Everyone knew about Titch and tried to stay clear as much as they could. Last winter, they all got together and came to Barkley with numerous treats to plead and bribe him to 'go and have a word'. After eating half a packet of dried fish to pluck up his courage, Barkley went to see the street fighter, who at the time was fast asleep in the front yard (he was also covered in fleas and frequently woke to have a scratch). Hearing someone in his territory, Titch woke and it was game on. Up he stood on bulldog-like front legs and started to march around and hiss.

'D-De-Detective Inspector B-B-Barkley Button Nose at your s-s-service,' Barkley said in a hurried voice, throwing one of his business cards down on the grass. 'The G-Great King Cat in the sky sent me. Your… your b-boxing days are over!' and with that he ran off, with Titch chasing him. A week later, the street fighter came into Barkley's garden, dropped a small bone at his feet and through gritted scratches said, 'Fleas!'

Barkley took the small bone that looked like the letter 'Y' and wrote his first note:


                No Fleez or bus gets it


He dropped it at Titch's front door early one morning, figuring Titch would be inside going to sleep after a night of strengthening his claws. The following week, he wrote another note:


                Fix fleez or you get it

On the third week, he saw an ad for fleas and ticks in the newspaper, scratched it out and left it on their doorstep with a business card he had from last summer. Titch bringing him a bone was how he had gotten the idea to attach a bribe to his notes. He did not know how he was going to find a bone but then Regie next door started barking and Barkley's problem was solved.

Back to the present, the commotion continued as Matilda scratched Peppu's nose while trying to defend herself against Titch, who was trying to pick a fight with anyone game enough.

'OI, YOU! WE DON'T WANT ANY TROUBLE! THAT IS ENOUGH OF YOUR BULLYING!' demanded Budge and Florry in unison, but Titch continued to stomp around, hissing and shrilling like his territory was being invaded.

'Come on, let's go,' said Budge to his brother. 'We can't be bothered with that sort of behaviour,' and the pair walked out.

'PACK IT IN!' screeched Matilda at Titch, puffing herself up to look twice her size. Leia, a retired greyhound, was barking at Blackberry, who in trying to escape had taken refuge inside one of the drawers that housed empty sardine packets. Peppu was jumping up and down, barking in excitement from copying Leia. He wanted to know what she was after, only he was not tall enough to see.

'Oi! You two! Be quiet and go and sit over there!' yelled Matilda at Leia and Peppu, pointing to the other side of the investigation zone. Leia retreated to sit underneath a workbench, young Peppu copying her every move.

'Old habits die hard. I have not smelt rabbit in ages. It's all the training,' she explained.

When Leia arrived at the den, her heart had been all a flutter. All she could smell was rabbit, which made Peppu, her newly acquired Italian whippet house mate, excited, wondering what game they were playing now. Blackberry thumped from inside the drawer, asking for help, while a long snout sniffed him. Titch lost his patience and flicked his paws around Leia's legs, which made her yelp.

'Blackberry! Stay out of sight! It's crowded enough as it is,' snapped Matilda, trying to direct the chaos into order.

Zenya hid in the corner, waiting for the ruckus to end. Being an Abyssinian, she was not used to confrontation.

Having left the zone of beautiful words waiting to be read after the ruckus had aired its anger, Budge and Florry were making their way into the detective's backyard when they suddenly noticed Barkley hiding in the doorway.

'Barkley! What are you doing there? We've all been waiting for you,' said Budge.

'Budge! Florry! What's that monster doing in my office?'

'What monster?'

'I heard shrilling and barking,' gasped Barkley in terror.

'That's just Titch showing off his muscles to everyone. The barking is from one of those dogs that can run fast. She seems to be after Blackberry.'

'Yeah, and there's a miniature one there too,' said Florry. 'Not seen him before.'

'Nah, we haven't, have we, Flor,' said Budge, with Florry nodding in agreement.

'What do they want with me?'

'Don't know. We figured they've come to listen to you read the book, just like us. You want us to go and find out? Only, we can't be bothered with Titch, so we left, didn't we Flor.'

Just then, a large ginger shadow silently appeared by the back door.

'Storm!' cried Barkley. 'I'm so pleased to see you! How are you?' he asked, jumping in excitement to see his giant pal.

Budge and Florry gulped and quickly shirked away from the ginger giant. They were disappointed now that they would not get to hear the rest of the book being read by 'the greatest detective that ever there was'.

'Hey! What are you cats doing here? Go on, shoo! Scat!' said Tom, the father of the house, pushing Barkley out the back door with his foot. The two brothers ran to the opposite corner of the backyard and jumped up onto the fence, where they stayed in watchful silence. Storm sat and stared at Tom, who had never seen a cat that big but said 'Scat!' again and locked the back door.

Barkley and Storm sat in the cold air listening to Titch demonstrate his boxing skills, while Leia and Peppu yelped and barked. Storm stood up and made his way to Barkley's office with quiet determination. He had long since learnt that silence also has a voice. Before long, Titch was being ushered out of Barkley's den with his loud protests following him.

Barkley, still sitting near the back door, heard Tom on the phone, talking to someone about fixing a hole in a roof.

Barkley watched angry Titch stomp into the backyard and grumble his way homeward. Titch was a male tortoiseshell cat with a white mark down his back. His family, Felicity and Marcus, found their kitten at the pound and took him home with excited giggles, with Marcus declaring their kitten's name was Titchous the Fearless, because the white stripe looked like an exclamation mark. The kitten, not happy with his name, stomped around miaowing loudly in protest, which made his family love him all the more. The thing was, no cat ever wanted to meet him because there were too many stories of him scratching anyone who stopped for a pat and attacking all the dogs that walked past.

Considering the commotion he had just heard, Barkley sighed with relief that his ears were still intact and finally went to empty his bladder. He walked to his favourite corner and made two deposits, not knowing Budge and Florry were sitting on the fence watching his personal moment till he heard the brothers whispering.

'Budge! Florry! What… what are you doing watching me from up there?' he called, feeling embarrassed. 'Titch has gone, you can come down now.'

'Nah, it's alright Barkley. You go on without us,' said Florry, sounding nervous.

Barkley walked up to the boys and looked up.

'What's the matter? What's got you spooked?'

'It's nothing,' said Florry.

'We can't go in there because of the giant,' explained Budge, nodding towards the shed.

'Because of Storm? Why not? He's alright, his voice is rather deep but you get used to it,' Barkley said.

'Go on Budge, you explain. I've not got the stomach for it,' said Florry, looking ashamed.

'Well, you see. Florry here had a sore tummy, didn't you?'

Florry nodded.

'Terrible experience having a sore tum tum. You ever had the trots, Inspector? Nasty stuff. I almost gave it to my brother!' said Florry.

'He did too, you know! I said to Florry, if you don't hurry up and get better. Anyway, what with all the pooing, he filled up our corner of discretion. Then to make matters worse, he goes back to visit his girlfriend, Lilly, and pigs out on her tucker again. Then on the way back, he feels sick again, doesn't he? So, to avoid being dragged to the doctor, he stopped in someone's yard and there is this huge cat, sitting there staring at him.'

Barkley's eyes widened and his open mouth began drooling in utter disbelief.

'You we-ent putting your… your what's-it in someone else's C-Corner of Discretion? And you still have all your fur? What is going on?' Barkley could not believe what he was hearing. Fair enough Florry had been gorging himself again at his girlfriend's place but using another cat's corner? That was just not on. After all, there is the Kitty Cat Code that all cats instinctively live by.

'I know. It's not good. Storm was not happy but…' Florry had lowered his head in disgrace, 'I'd gone over to see Lilly and had a snack. On the way back over the fence I'd gotten past Pickles' place when I was desperate again. I didn't think there was a cat that lived there. Then I heard this grumbling noise like thunder. I looked up, and just as I'm covering my, y'know, I hear "SHUN!" and there is Storm, in his bed on the porch, glaring at me with those piercing big eyes that make you feel like you're going to be swallowed any minute, whiskers vibrating full bore. I was trembling, so I started bowing and apologising to him. Then he says in the deep, rumbling voice of his, "Evidence. Mao Book." I ran as fast as I could over the fence, leaving a mess behind me. I told my brother what happened. He went and got Miss Fi-Fi to talk to him, as I am petrified. He looked like he was hurt or something. Now that Storm is here, I'm shaking all over.'

'Miss Fi-Fi had been looking for him anyway, so she went to see him at his other home. How was I supposed to know he had two homes? That was when he told her about the book. It was left on the table out the back. Storm grabbed it and hid it. Then when you said you were going to see Mrs Andrews, I didn't know it was the very same place, so I said nothing because I'm too scared of what might happen to me. I don't want to get squashed by a giant or swallowed up into those big eyes!' said Florry, panicking.

'What a Felidae! Well, look at it this way Florry, if you hadn't deposited your whatsit into Mrs Andrews' garden, the book would still be there and I'd be none the wiser. Why do you only see Lilly when you're hungry?' asked Barkley, his ears exhausted with what he had just heard.

'Nah, that's no good. It's her tucker that makes him sick, isn't it? He gorges himself here, then goes over for a second helping. He tried to talk me into going and I said no. I would've been sick myself otherwise!' said Budge.

'Well, I don't know what to say. Let the King Cat in the sky sort it out. I heard Storm jump up onto the fence earlier. I do wish someone would tell me what is going on!' sighed Barkley, his whiskers twitching.

The brothers looked at each other and decided they would jump down and come and listen to the reading. As the trio crossed the garden to the shed, Tom opened the back door and yelled at them to get away. Budge and Florry escaped down the side of the house, into the detective zone that held all of Barkley's clues of past crimes and the current pandemonium. The detective inspector's paws followed them through the doorway and along the narrow path to a small beam of sunlight that shone down through the hole in the roof and lit up a hundred-thousand particles of dust looking for a new place to settle. Barkley gazed at a new bug swimming in his drinking bowl of debris, then turned to face the bedlam that was slowly beginning to settle. Excited faces waited for him to speak. Budge and Florry were ears and eyes sharp, ready to listen and grateful the enormous deep voice was not there to thrash them to a pulp.

'Good morning, Barkley,' they chorused, trying to look like good students.

'Why are you all here? Have your collars been stolen too? Do you have a note from Mao?' quizzed the nervous D.I.

'I'm only here because I saw a rabbit and followed it,' said Leia. Peppu wondered what was going on.

'I came because, well, I don't know why I came. I think I had a funny dream, although I can't remember it,' said Matilda.

Zenya, who was still hiding in the corner, said nothing.

'How did you get in here?'

'I came up the drive,' said Blackberry, sticking his head out from the drawer far enough to hand Barkley another note before diving back under the empty packets to hide from Leia's long nose.

'I too came up the drive. The gate was left open,' said Leia to Barkley's question. This was odd, as the gate was normally shut. Barkley wondered if the moon had been playing tricks on everyone again, including his family, who had gone out and left the gate open. Barkley's thoughts were interrupted by chewing noises coming from under the scratching posts where he saw Ponchoo and Coco, the Pomeranians who lived opposite Blackberry.

'What are you doing here Ponchoo? Coco?' asked the detective, trying to get their attention, but they were too engrossed in their bones to respond to the discussion being thrown around the investigating room. Barkley looked at the Pomeranians, disappointed — he had gone to a lot of effort to steal those bones and now they were being devoured without so much as a thank you.

Barkley turned and read Blackberry's new note.

*L.O.Y.A.L.T.Y.*

*Confucius of Mao*

Slowly, the room hushed. Barkley looked at the innocent faces staring at him in anticipation and wondered where Storm had gone. Like a conductor about to display his first piece of work, Captain B sat down before the opened book and gave a small miaow to make sure his voice was clear. Peppu sneezed from the dust that was searching for a place to rest. The audience of ears was ready.

Barkley looked at the book, extended a claw and turned the page, shuddering when he saw a picture of the monster at Blackberry's place. Sitting there looking at you with buckets of innocence was the kitten. In the background was the giant dog, lying down on his side, gazing at the kitten. He was so big his nose and eyes seemed to jut out of the page. Underneath the scene was the word G.E.N.T.L.E. The second page was framed in giant feet and legs punctuated from above with a huge snout looking down at cuteness. This bundle of fluff was standing on its back legs, trying to reach up, its small paws too tiny to grab its prize. Above the kitten's head was the word L.O.Y.A.L.T.Y. Barkley was not sure if the kitten or the words were going to be sniffed up the dog's nose or eaten for dinner.

'Blackberry, this is for the m-m-monster and the k-k-kitten,' Barkley faltered.

'George.'

'What?'

'The monster, as you call him, is George. The kitten is Sebastian,' explained Blackberry from under a blanket of empty sardine packets.

'The monster is called George?' Barkley was too afraid to pass his paw over the monster's presence in the room.

Trying to remain focussed, Barkley began.

### G.E.N.T.L.E.

Growing Enormous Nurturing Thoughts Lovingly Experienced

### L.O.Y.A.L.T.Y.

Love Owning Your Attitude Listen Trust Yourself

*Do not take loyalty as a gig of expectation.*
*It keeps you stuck in a world going nowhere.*
*Loyalty is best sponsored through nurturing,*
*To grow beyond the best of intentions and perceived*
*    expectations,*
*To hit the mark of potential and keep expanding,*
*Strengths exploring.*

'Any ideas what this means?' asked Barkley, trying not to break out in a sweat over George's enormousness on the page and how minute the kitten was.

'Yes,' said Blackberry, trying not to be seen. 'George thinks he has to be strong and brave to protect his family. This comes across as aloof bullying. When he first arrived, his understanding of protection extended to grabbing the wet washing out of the laundry basket and running around the garden with it in a frothing frenzy, then burying it in his kennel. It kept me amused over a bowl of pellets while I watched the woman run around after him. She tried enticing him back to her with the lead, crying, "Walkies!" in a shrill voice, yelling, screaming, squirting him with a high-pressure hose, throwing meat at him, opening a tin of food and trying to get his attention by shaking his dried food bag.'

'Eventually exhausted,' Blackberry continued, 'she sat and cried. George went over to her with his newly acquired wet toy in his mouth. When she tried to yank the shirt from his jaws, he ran off, thinking the game was back on. After the tears stopped, she dried her eyes, sat quietly and George went back and sat loyally by her side. George would even pull the washing from the line and run around with it when she had gone out. He didn't understand her anger and frustration. He thought he was keeping a watchful eye on all of us. Both Sebastian and I have been for a ride in his mouth in his attempt to herd us together.'

This brought laughter to the group, as they all knew what it was like to play games and have such frivolous fun, only to have the adults squash them into quiet behaviour. Zenya commented that the only time she saw her family in fits of giggles was when they spent time looking after the grandchildren, as playing with children brought spontaneous giggles. They all agreed making children squeal with laughter was glorious.

Barkley reminisced over how long it had been. It was so therapeutic for him to chase the young people to bed and then listen to their parents read them a story; Barkley could never decide which one he liked best. As each child arrived, the same stories were read. Barkley would sit, watching the adult fingers pass over each word as they taught Sarah, Beth and Corey how to read and pronounce the words. 'Cee and aitch makes tche, es and aitch makes shhh. Tee and aitch makes thth,' he remembered from his lessons on their bed.

Barkley wondered why the letter aitch had to change itself to suit the other letters. Why didn't they just create another letter for the sound they required?

'Does anyone know what Love Owning Your Attitude means?'

Barkley waited for more explanations, for someone to speak up, but silence was the ensuing response.

'Just a minute — where's Miss Fi-Fi?' he asked, suddenly remembering the French feline was absent.

'She's at home, getting ready to give birth,' said Budge and Florry in unison.

Barkley nodded, noticing how absence made the heart grow fonder.

*I do hope all goes well and that she and all her kittens are happy and healthy.*

# Chapter Seven

Just as he went to turn the page, Barkley suddenly noticed that George was not standing on grass but on tiny print dressed in green that said 'Magnanimous Affection Overdone'. Grateful that he now had the monster out of his eyes, Barkley said, 'Zenya, this is for you.'

Zenya came out from the back of the shed and sat next to Barkley to listen attentively. There she was amongst the words on the page, looking calm, regal, serene and glowing beautifully. One image showed her lying on a mat, gazing into the reader's eyes, only the mat was made up of words that read 'Maximising Authentic Options'. On the top right of the page she was chasing a ball of string. Other parts of the page were just of her paw prints, like she had wandered through the words knowing what they meant. The historiated initial showed her standing on her hind legs with her front paws on the top, like she was ready to jump up and sit on the gold letter.

*On quietude there is silence*
*Yet much talking is done.*
*Talk of greatness, of magnificence,*
*and storming of barriers.*
*In quietude, there is such talk.*

Barkley turned to look at Zenya, wanting some clues as to what it all meant.

He continued:

*Meditation*
*To discover what is underneath incessant chatter,*
*To greet self and meet glory,*

*To realise I am more than my original perception.*
*To breathe,*
*To discover the force in the Breath of Life.*

*To realise...*
*Magic in life is created by me,*
*Lessons in life are created by me.*

*To allow new energies in and release what is no longer needed.*
*Meditation...*
*Where peace resides.*
*Where acceptance is.*
*Where inner knowing is.*
*Where I am.*

Barkley looked at Zenya, awaiting her response.

'What's meditation?' asked Budge.

'Yeah, and how come if you are sitting quiet like, you are still talking? I don't get it. Are we supposed to sit quiet? How long can you be quiet for, Budge?' asked Florry.

'I don't know. I've never thought about it. We are quiet when we sleep, aren't we? Although you sometimes snore.'

'Yeah! Do you remember the time when...' started Florry with a giggle.

'Okay, boys!' said Barkley, trying to keep the group focussed. 'Does any of this mean anything to anyone?'

'Do you mean like when the Great King Cat from Kitty Cavern came and told us to give you the note? That was in quietude; we were asleep,' said Budge.

'What?' stirred everyone. 'You've had a visit from the Great King Cat as well?' they all asked in astonishment.

Barkley could not believe his whiskers.

*Am I the only one who has not seen nor heard from the Great King Cat? How could the Great King Cat forget about me? Am I not known far and wide?*

'The Great King Cat has come to visit ALL of you? When was this?'

'When I fell asleep in the flowerpot.'

'Last moon visit.'

'When we came to you Barkles, with the note.'

'Were you all asleep when the visit occurred?' Barkley asked.

Nods replied yes.

'What happens?' asked Barkley, so he knew what to look out for.

'There is this purring that is ever so comforting and nurturing. Then it gets louder and louder, only you can't wake up because the purring makes you drift off even more. Then someone you know licks your head; it feels like your mamma from when you were little. The purring continues and she says stuff to you, only you can't quite make it out. In the morning, you find the note and then you come here,' explained Budge.

'We don't know if the notes appear during the purring, licking or whispering,' added Florry.

'Ponchoo, Coco, Leia, Peppu, have you all had a visit from the Great King Cat?' asked Barkley, not believing what they were saying. 'What about you, Blackberry. Have you seen George with the Great King Cat?'

'There's been a black and white cat sitting on my cage sometimes when I get to visit the grass,' said Blackberry.

'When did you first see him?' asked the Collector of Clues.

'I saw *her* just before the last full moon,' said Blackberry, pondering the timeframe. 'The first time I saw her, she was sitting in the tree next door. That was about three visits to the grass ago.'

*Ahh, a full moon.* Barkley drooled. *The time when all cats like to be outside paying respects to their inquisitive nature.*

'Did you ever speak to her?'

'I did. I never got a reply though.'

'I saw a black and white cat walking across the roof over the road one morning,' said Leia, while Peppu got a bone and started munching on it. Barkley looked sadly at his disappearing bribes.

'Had you seen the feline before?'

'Yes, just before Peppu arrived I saw her sitting on a fence when I was taken to get my toenails cut. At least, I think it was her.'

'How long ago was that?' asked a furrow-browed detective.

'That was just after the last full moon,' said Leia, scratching an imaginary flea.

'The next time you see this elusive feline, come and let me know immediately. This is vital to my catification. I will need to speak with her,' directed Barkley to his newfound classmates.

Nods in agreement confirmed Barkley's request, although Leia did wonder how she was going to let the detective know when she was attached to a leash.

Barkley so wished he had a little dried sardine he could pop into his mouth to munch on, as it helped him to focus. He was thirsty, but his water bowl never looked inviting as it just accumulated leaves and bugs. Barkley looked up at the hole in the roof and saw a gray sky. His whiskers told him rain was on the way.

Returning his focus to the task at hand, Barkley turned the page.

'Matilda – this is yours.'

A gray tabby cat jumped down and stared at the page, licking the corner to see if any of the loveliness tasted good. There she was, playing in various poses. The historiated initial showed her leaping through the middle of the letter R and wrapped around the S. At the bottom of the page, Matilda was lying on what looked like grass but was actually writing that said 'Majestic Abundance Overall'.

*Run*
*Jump,*
*Soar*
*To the heights of being you.*
*Too much reflection stifles.*
*Spontaneously creative,*
*Creatively spontaneous.*
*Breath in,*
*Creativity out.*

Barkley glanced at Matilda, who sat listening quietly.

*Spontaneity*
*To allow myself to be in the moment, creating.*
*To take pleasure with my outcome,*
*To do away with the need to control,*

*To pack away fear.*
*To let the almighty Breath of Life in and watch it*
*gloriously and magnificently explore*
*Possibilities,*
*Giggling pleasures.*
*To dash across the Universe to a future place in time,*
*preparing to reap rewards.*
*To smile at the world and allow it to smile back.*
*To allow only my essence of creativity touch,*
*and remove judgement and criticism from the equation.*

'Florry, you were nodding throughout this, does this mean something to you?' asked Barkley gently.

'Yeah, he is the spontaneous one and I'm more of the quiet one. Although we do get up to some pretty spontaneous stuff,' said Florry, looking at Budge.

'Yeah, that's right. We were playing chasey outside and ran in to get a drink. Florry here noticed our muddy footprints on the floor,' said Budge, a twinkle in his eye.

'Then I got the idea to put our paws on the wall and make a pretty picture, like what Lynne does. So many times, we've walked over her paintings and been yelled at. We only wanted to have some fun like she does.'

Barkley ignored Florry and looked at Matilda inquisitively. Not once did she take her eyes off the page. She stood up, pressed her nose against all the words and returned to her spot amongst the scratching posts, looking proud and reflective. There she was in all her magnificence on the page with lovely words about stuff she could not even fathom. Barkley looked at her longingly. He so wanted to know what it all meant. Where was a sardine when you needed one? He sighed and returned to the book.

The door to Barkley's new school banged. All heads turned as they listened to the latecomer wince in pain as he moved through the maze to the front of the class.

'Storm!' announced Barkley, delighted to see his friend again. 'Where have you been?'

'Chasing a feline off your roof. I almost caught her three times, but she was way too quick and agile.'

Florry shrank. He had already had one altercation with the ginger giant and did not want another.

'What did she look like?'

'Black and white.'

'We were just talking about this feline!' said Barkley.

'Yes, that was who ran under your house, remember?' said Storm, jogging Barkley's memory. His muscles were sore again after the exercise of chasing the new neighbourhood cat down the road.

Leia and Peppu got up and informed Barkley they had better go home. They knew big rain was coming and did not want to be out when the loud bangs and flashes in the sky were going off, besides, they had been gone long enough. Barkley suggested they take Ponchoo and Coco and their newfound bones with them (he hoped they would not remember where they got them from as he did not want them coming back for more). From the back of the audience, Zenya's graceful body rose and also bid Barkley farewell. Barkley was sad to see her go.

'Florry, what's with you?' asked the detective, watching him fidget.

'Sorry, Barks. I had better go too. My head is telling me it's time for eating and sleeping,' said Florry, not wanting Storm to remember the recent embarrassing incident.

'Bye, Barkles,' said Budge as they all wandered out.

Storm, oblivious to Florry's fear, lay down on the floor on top of shreds of clawed paper. Inquisitive bugs, looking for some warmth from the cold concrete, tried to make their way into his ample fur.

Barkley felt frustrated. Who was this black and white feline? Was she the cat he saw in Rowan's front yard the other night? Was she Mao?

'Storm, this is you.'

Storm sat patiently. He had already heard it at Mrs Andrews' place.

*All that matters is held together with Belonging Glue.*
*Belonging creates an amplitude to feeling safe in*
*    crowded emptiness.*
*In darkness, we shine the light for others to see.*

*To belong*
*To know that we are One,*
*To understand I do not fit into life;*
*life fits into me.*
*To overcome the darkest of shadows*
*through knowing my existence matters.*
*To acknowledge my presence.*
*To honour being Seen and Heard,*
*Respected.*
*To be part of Humankind and all its kindness,*
*To say 'Yes!' to life.*
*To be supported in leaping,*
*To have strength to keep going.*
*To forgive the naysayers and me as well,*
*To know I am shining my best.*

Storm's page was decorated with white daisies. He had them at his feet, and one small painting had him lying sphynx-like next to an embossed golden 'A' with a crown of daisies on his head. 'My, how regal he looks,' thought Barkley. Underneath another small painting, large paw prints walked on what looked like grass, but it said ever-so-minutely 'Mystically Acquired Occurrences'.

Just then, Leia and Peppu re-entered the world of special words and asked Blackberry to show them the way home. Slowly, a twitching nose belonging to a black rabbit emerged from the back of the drawer, looked at Leia cautiously, jumped down and ran out. Barkley, Storm and Matilda watched in humorous silence.

'Matilda, don't you want to go home and stay dry? It smells like a lot of rain and thunder coming,' said Barkley, curious as to why she had not left. Barkley did not want to be out in the bad weather either, but he did not want anyone to know that the bangs in the sky made him nervous.

'Nah, I've never been afraid of thunder,' she responded, settling down to listen to more of the book.

Barkley gulped, 'Seeing as everyone has gone, Matilda, Storm, I think I will wait till they return before I continue reading.'

'Fair enough,' said Matilda and commenced giving herself a bath and chewing her toenails.

'Matilda, I'm off to collect more clues. I'll see you later, and if you can think about what your words mean, that would be most helpful,' directed Barkley.

Matilda looked at Barkley wide-eyed, her tongue sticking out but said nothing as she went back to bathing.

Barkley and Storm walked out, leaving Matilda to reminisce over what had been read.

'You going inside for a sleep then?' asked Storm, knowing his friend all too well.

'Yes,' replied Barkley.

'I think it's about time I went home and saw my family,' said Storm, who was ready to have his fur, ears and tail tugged again.

Barkley bid Storm farewell at his back door and watched the giant ginger turn right down the driveway. Realising the back door was shut, he quickly scouted around to the front door, which was also locked.

*If both doors are shut, why is the gate still open?*

There was nothing for it but to go back to his bureau and wait till the rain stopped. Barkley ran for shelter.

'Did you get another clue?'

'Huh?'

'Did you get your clue?' asked Matilda.

'Um... no. They weren't home. I'll go back later,' lied the detective, diverting any realisation that he was afraid when the sky banged.

Barkley sat, lost in his ponderings.

'Where's the book?' he asked Matilda in fear.

'Your neighbour came and took it,' replied Matilda.

'My neighbour? You mean Reg?' asked Barkley.

'Yeah, Reg. Black and white feline,' said Matilda.

'Reg is the dog next door! Was it a dog or a feline? That is the only bit of evidence I have so far!' declared Barkley, tormented with stress that this major clue had been stolen.

'I had my head down. When I looked up, I saw a black and white cat jump down from the hole in the roof and pick up your book.

She said she was your neighbour and was borrowing it for mastering, then left,' explained Matilda.

'MATILDA! We talked about this black and white cat! You said you had been visited by this feline! Why on earth did you let her take the book? Storm has just been chasing her. You could've nabbed her for questioning!' shrilled Barkley in utter disbelief and annoyance.

'Sorry, Barkley. She was here taking the book before I could fathom what was going on. She spoke in such a lovely, melodious voice and it all happened so quickly.'

Barkley sighed, 'What exactly did she say?'

'She said "I'm from next door. He will understand I'm mastering this," then left, ever so quietly.'

'Which way did she go?'

Matilda pointed upwards and looked at the hole in the roof.

Barkley wondered how a cat could get back through the top of the ceiling.

*She must be some sort of flying feline; no wonder Storm couldn't catch her!*

'She went out the door, jumped up onto the roof and then I saw her gazing at me through the hole. She gave me a quite lovely miaow,' explained Matilda, pointing to the hole.

Barkley watched the rain coming down. A waterfall fell into the bowl and swished the leaves and bugs around. What had started off as a fine mist, then drizzle, was now heavy rain. Barkley moved to higher ground and climbed inside one of the enclosures of a large cat scratching pole, where he huddled and waited for the rain to stop making puddles. He wondered if the book was safe and dry; he knew they were not just printed words on those pages, but drawn and painted by someone who had a very dexterous paw.

Barkley's whiskers shuddered every time he heard the sky bang.

Matilda squeezed into the enclosure with him, commenced licking his head and asked, 'So, why did you become a detective?'

'I decided to become a detective because of the things I heard. You remember the black cat with the white patch under his chin? He was a street fighter, one of the best, when he suddenly disappeared. You remember the time the two dogs being walked on a lead deliberately broke from their collars and ran inside to attack Snowy?

Or the little boy who killed every fish he was given? Well, all this happened and I was very upset by it. I had to do something.'

Rain pelted down, lightning flashed across the sky and thunder clapped. Barkley was nervous at first, but having Matilda bathe him and ask him questions took his mind off the torrential downpour. He prayed the book was being kept dry but had no idea how he was going to get it back. Pay a visit to Mrs Andrews? He did so enjoy the dish of sardines and milk she gave him.

'And the writing notes?' Matilda purred.

'I remember it was a hot day. I was fast asleep when I heard, "Where's the glue? I need the glue." I woke and watched my lady and Sarah at the table, cutting out pictures and sticking them down with a bottle of stuff. They mentioned something about show and tell and wanting a good mark. Later on, I paid a visit to the fish over the fence and saw a leaf stuck to the side of a rock and wondered if that was glue.'

'What's glue?'

'I think it's for sticking something to something else. This gave me the idea of scratching out letters and words from newspapers and sticking them down. I needed glue, so I make my own,' explained Barkley, pointing to an old paint lid that had on it stomach acid he had vomited up from eating grass. 'Then Titch gave me the idea of attaching a bone. So, from that I became a detective and have solved many cases, although this one is my greatest.'

'I looked very elegant in the book, didn't I?' purred Matilda.

'Yes, you did.'

'Are you in the book?'

'No, I'm not.' Barkley was a bit disappointed that he had not read special words about himself, nor had he seen a lovely picture.

'Whoever painted the book knows what we all look like, so they must be local.'

'That's true! Whoever it is, is very clever to be able to draw and write. At first, I wondered if a snake was doing the writing. Who else can hold a pen and write so neatly?' Barkley wondered.

'Where did the book come from?'

'From Mrs Andrews. Storm was recuperating there and heard her reading it to her grandchildren.'

'Do you think she made the book?'

'I don't know. I got no answer from her when I questioned her and gazed into her eyes.'

'Did you go inside?' purred Matilda, licking his ears.

'No, we met out the back.'

'Perhaps if you go inside and look for paint, pen and such, it might give you a start.'

'Yes, that's a good idea. I will go as soon as the rain has stopped. I need to get the book back and Mrs Andrews is the only place I know where to start.' Barkley wondered if he would get a plate of sardines again and some of that delicious milk that he never got at home.

Matilda finished bathing, curled up into a ball next to Barkley and fell asleep. The rain eased off and the thunder and lightning moved on to a new area of the sky. Barkley felt relaxed having Matilda keep him company while he listened to the receding thunder. It was good to be able to talk things through with someone who could ask coherent questions instead of listening to, 'I don't know, I can't read, can I.'

He loved Budge and Florry — they always brought such an atmosphere of fun and mischief with them. They were not like Titch, who wanted to be crowned King of the Street and saw beating everyone up as his way of getting there. Budge and Florry were too much into giggling and seeing everything as a good time.

Storm, on the other paw, was the biggest cat he had ever seen. Barkley had always been afraid of Storm, who till recently, never said anything to anyone. No matter how much you spoke to him, he would just stare back at you with those penetrating big green eyes. When he turned up that foggy morning, Barkley quivered fearfully. Now look — they had become best buddies.

Barkley knew Storm was incredibly strong but also that he really would not hurt anyone. Storm had been sat on, ridden and patted by toddlers for too long and had endured a lot of tugging and pulling. Barkley remembered Storm telling him one day one of the children got the scissors and cut his whiskers off, then proceeded to trim his fur. Storm thought that was enough, got up and walked out. That was when he met Mrs Andrews for the first time and they have been constant friends ever since. Storm makes sure he visits her on a regular basis just to say thank you for taking care of him and for respite from the screaming children. Dress-ups are a definite no for Storm. Once was enough, he was not going through that ever again, so a hasty retreat to Mrs Andrews' proved to be very fortuitous.

Snug with Matilda, Barkley found it comforting to have someone to sleep next to. It was nice listening to a fellow feline purr and the bath he got was excellent. His head did not feel like fog anymore. The comforting sound of purring made him yawn and fall asleep.

# Chapter Eight

'Ugh, not you again!'

Barkley woke to see Matilda get up and arch her back at Titch, who had returned.

'Oi, Barkles! I came to give you this and got kicked out for it!' yelled Titch, throwing a note onto the floor.

Barkley yawned and stretched, then jumped down from the warmth of snuggles. Bleary-eyed, he looked at Titch and asked him to repeat what he had said. An explanation in the language of muttering and grumbling ensued.

Picking up the note, he read:

*There is beauty to be had, but Heaven does not reside here.*
*Confucius of Mao*

Barkley looked at Titch and asked, 'Has your collar gone missing too?'

'No. Why?' asked Titch, looking frustrated and twitching with anger.

'Because this Confucius of Mao character is leaving notes and stealing collars,' responded Barkley.

'No, she's not. She's actually quite cute,' said Titch, calming down.

Barkley gasped.

'What do you mean *she*? Mao is a girl? So how come you've met him... her and I haven't?' demanded Barkley indignantly. Wasn't this his case? Wasn't he the detective of the area?

'I watched her slip through the Frenchie's cat flap the night you sat in her garden, as I was just about to do the same. She was probably going to have a feed, like me, when you raced inside. Then the night that hulk chased her down the street she came and took refuge in my garden,' explained Titch, scratching an ear.

'And you beat her up!' said Matilda.

Not wanting to feel intimidated, Titch turned in anger and retaliated with, 'What's it to you, Fluff?!'

'Titch,' said Barkley, patting the grump on the shoulder to get his attention, 'my head hurts all the time. This is very important to me. When did you first see this Mao?'

'At Miss Fi-Fi's, like I said, the night you were in her garden munching on those ghastly fish things you eat.'

'What does she look like?'

'She's black and white. She's got the sweetest voice you've ever heard; it's quite melodic. She's very gentle and nurturing and has a lovely smile,' he said, reminiscing.

'She's black and white? That's the same feline Storm chased today!' said Barkley.

This was not the description Barkley had formed of Mao in his own mind. The great cryptic note writing cat was a girl? Surely not?! And how come the local street fighter, who wallops anyone who passes his territory, has been talking to his greatest adversary?

*Why, oh why, did Mao not make herself known to me first? Am I not the smartest cat around these parts?'*

Barkley was feeling despondent.

Watching Titch scratch yet another flea, Barkley felt he too was itching all over and began to scratch.

Matilda, being curious and forthright, asked Titch, 'Why are you so angry all the time?'

'I DON'T LIKE MY NAME! OKAY? I wanted to be called something better than "Titch the Fearless" just because of the mark on my back!' he declared, turning to show them the exclamation mark. Barkley did not know what he was looking for.

'What would you like to be called?' asked Matilda, a gentle tone of caring and willingness to listen in her voice.

'Well, if you must know, I always thought Jonathan was nice. It means the Great King Cat in the Sky has been given a gift. My father was called Jonathan. He was a great magician and could make pieces of paper stuck to his paws disappear.'

Barkley thought this was amazing. This was also the first time he had ever heard Titch speak in a calm, normal voice. Matilda was doing a great job connecting with him.

'Titch, will you help me? I've been working on this case for many dinners now and it's just getting bigger and bigger, with no end in sight. Do you think this Mao just wants to muddle my brain so she can take over as detective in these parts?'

'I don't know. I'm going home to get some shut eye.'

'No, wait. Tell me, what's with all these notes? What did she say to you?'

'I don't know, why don't you ask her?'

'I would if I knew where to find her! How do I find Mao, Titch?' asked Barkley of the disappearing torn-eared cat.

'I don't know! She just sort of turns up. If you want to talk to her, come to my place. I'm going to get some shut eye!' and off sauntered Titch like he was about to enter a boxing ring.

'Goodbye, Jonathan!' called Matilda to the perpetual grump.

Barkley turned and looked at her with such indignation.

'Can you believe it? Titch has known this Mao character all along! Storm has chased her twice now – and she's been up on the roof and in here and taken the book! I've not even laid eyes on her, not even a whisker, yet she seems to be pals with the local grump! What does that tell you? Perhaps Titch is in on this and they are playing with me to give up being a detective so Mao and his... her sidekick, Titch, can take over and run the whole neighbourhood! No doubt this note is just a ploy to get me to look in another direction!'

'Calm down. You're supposed to be a detective, not a nervous wreck!' instructed Matilda.

'What?'

'Get a whisker! Show a paw! Obviously, you can solve this, otherwise you wouldn't have been given the task. Everyone comes to you to solve their needs. No one goes to, what's her name, Mao, do they? How is it that none of us have seen nor heard of Mao till now? Perhaps she's been kept inside all this time and has only just been let out? Perhaps she is new to the neighbourhood and wants to get to know us gently? Although writing notes and disappearing when seen is a funny way to make friends. Perhaps she's very shy? Maybe she can't speak the local lingo? Have you thought of that?' pondered Matilda, throwing ideas around. Now she thought about it, it was pretty odd behaviour to be stealing collars and writing notes. Why not just come and say hello and give a whisker to see what's what?

Barkley calmed down. 'You're right, Matilda. I'm just twitching because I've run out of sardines.'

'Oh, for Kitty Cavern's sake!' declared Matilda in frustration.

Barkley jumped down from his perch and got a piece of paper left over from the children's starship days; during that time, he was made First Mate (whatever that meant), when he ran around and chased them, especially when it was bedtime. Sitting in front of old newspapers, he started to search for the spelling he wanted. Sometimes he was lucky and found the word he was looking for, but mostly he had to claw out the letters he needed to spell out words. Slowly and methodically, Barkley stuck the letters onto the page with his special glue.

'Excuse me, Matilda. I'll be back soon.' Barkley went out into the garden to eat some grass, then returned and continued looking for the letters he needed. Eventually satisfied, Barkley sat back to admire his work.

Where did the book come from

'I will take this to Mrs Andrews. I no longer have a fresh bone to give her, so I hope this note will do,' explained Barkley, looking at where the bones used to be that now resided in the stomachs of the local dogs.

'What does it say?' asked Matilda, pressing her nose against the letters and sniffing. 'Yuk! What have you used to stick this down with?'

'I make my own glue,' replied Barkley evasively.

'With what?'

'It's a bit scientific,' responded Barkley, feeling a bit sick.

'How syentifik?' quizzed Matilda. She had never heard the word 'scientific' before and was not sure what it meant.

Just then, Barkley moved over to his old paint lid, adopted the vomit position and coughed up the grass he had just eaten so he had fresh glue.

'I thought that was called cleansing the stomach – but you call it syentifik? I'll have to remember that. Sy-en-tif-ik,' said Matilda, making sure she got the word right.

Just then, a strange man walked into the shed with a ladder and a tape measure, said hello, looked up at the hole in the roof, said, 'Ah, yep, classic case of tree versus roof,' then whistled his way out again.

Barkley jumped to higher ground, while Matilda walked out without saying a word of goodbye or anything.

A few contemplations later, the man reappeared, deposited a ladder outside in the wet, climbed up and took a sheet of the roof off, leaving a massive hole. The whistling disappeared again, then came back before Barkley could even fathom a way to defend his territory. The hole in the roof where the water flowed into his drinking bowl and fed the drowned bugs had now disappeared under a few bangs and a fresh sheet of galvanised iron. Like a flash of thunder in the sky, the ladder and whistling disappeared as quickly as they had arrived with a simple declaration of, 'See ya, Puss!'

To Barkley's surprise, he just sat wide-eyed and muttered 'miaow' to the man when he said goodbye, then jumped down and followed him out, miaowing all the way to the letterbox. Barkley watched him pack his car and drive off.

*What just happened? Who was that?*

Barkley jumped up onto the brick pier that housed the letterbox as he watched the car drive away. Then the postie came whizzing around the corner on his motorbike, stopped and delivered mail, patted Barkley on the head and took off up the street.

Now he knew why the gate was left open this morning.

*Still, it does not explain why everyone turned up to listen to the book when I have only just acquired it. How did they know they were even in the book when I cannot find myself there? Mao isn't in the book, is he… she?*

Barkley sat and basked in the sunshine that was drying up all the rain.

*It's very nice to have my office fixed. Now I can have invites more often.*

Barkley puffed up his chest with purring pride.

'Hello, Barkley,' said Sarah, stroking him.

Barkley followed Sarah inside, explaining the day's events with loud miaows. Sarah responded with a crunch of an apple, threw her shoes off and sat down to watch television. Barkley wondered why they did that. The person in the screen never seemed to respond to them, even when they yelled at it – it was not like there was someone actually there. Surely exploring the garden, climbing trees and fences, sniffing new smells, rolling around in possum wee, playing chasey and whiskering with others was way more fun.

# Chapter Nine

Barkley had a bite to eat, miaowed to be let out and quickly ran into his office to get the newly made note. Folding it up as best he could, he popped it into his mouth and made his way over to Storm's second place via Miss Fi-Fi's, which meant instead of going over the back fence he headed out the front, turned right and right again. He wanted to know if she had ever seen Titch, or a black and white cat, come through her door. He also wanted to see if she had delivered her kittens yet. Arriving at her back door, he looked around at the mess in the garden just as a flying piece of a clay pot whizzed past his head.

'You! Stop leaving notes and old bones at my door! Now get!' yelled Miss Fi-F's owner.

Barkley made a hasty retreat and ran and hid behind the shrubbery. Another piece of broken pot flew his way. Barkley jumped and darted towards the back fence, clay chards chasing him.

*It's difficult to run with paper in your mouth!*

Leaping up a tree, he stopped and quietly watched Shirley Longford tidy up the garden in frustrated disappointment. A large branch of a tree had fallen onto a glass shed that Barkley was sure was not there when he pulled the all-nighter to catch Mao. He sent Miss Fi-Fi another vibration through his whiskers to let her know he was there. He waited – no response.

*I'll retreat to the peaceful solitude of Mrs Andrews' garden as Matilda suggested and see if I can get inside.*

Manoeuvring his way from branch to fence, Barkley jumped down into a bunch of weeds and prickles that stuck to his fur. One lodged between his toes and he had to stop and chew it out. He could hear the yapping dog of the flying slippers barking; it sounded like metal balls being fired.

'Here 'tis,' he said and ran up Mrs Andrews' driveway to the back door and dropped the note on the mat.

'MIAOW? MIAOW?'

No answer.

The door was ajar. Cautiously, Barkley pushed the door and snuck inside to a warm house that smelled clean and tidy.

'MIIIAAOOW!'

Still no answer.

Barkley invited himself inside and began to roam around.

'If I wasn't a cat, what would I do with my curiosity?' was his response to questions of why. The kitchen table and benches looked pretty clean; no sign of paint and brushes there. The lounge room was tidy and Barkley smelt furniture polish on the coffee table. In one of the spare bedrooms, he climbed up onto a desk and poked into a pot of pens and pencils, but again, no clues. In Mrs Andrews' bedroom he discovered a neatly made bed that had a silky feel to it as he marched over it to get a look at the things on her bedside table.

The back door was open, yet where was she? Where was Mrs Andrews with the lovely sardines, special milk and perhaps paints and brushes? Barkley began to drool walking on the thick, soft bedcover, he could quite... happ-il-y curl... up and... have a good... sleep...

Too... many... clues... to... think... of...

'Oh, I know, Rosemary, but what am I going to do? It was here on Sunday as I showed it to Freda and Magnus. What am I going to say to her? "Sorry, I've lost the only art commission you've had all year!" It's taken her months of work and it's still not finished. You know her work is exquisite!' said Mrs Andrews, coming in the front door and putting her gloves down on the freshly polished hall table.

Barkley woke with a start, wondering whose voice was that, when he suddenly realised where he was and jumped down off the bed, raced through the lounge room, out the back to the mat, picked up the note he had brought, then marched up to her with full pride and dropped it at her feet. Beaming with anticipation, he waited.

He did not hear Mrs Andrews gasp in terror when she saw him run past her.

'Miaow?'

Mrs Andrews was too absorbed in her current situation to notice Barkley had dropped a piece of paper at her feet. Barkley picked up the note and followed Mrs Andrews to the lounge, where she had sat down. Putting the note in her lap, he gave her a nudge.

She picked up the note and read:

WeAr is 3ook from

'This cat has just brought me a piece of paper that I think says "Where is Three hundred thousand from?" I don't have three hundred thousand dollars! Is this some sort of ransom note? Pay up or else? Oh God, Rosemary, what am I going to do?'

'What? No, not Ginge. This is another cat who turned up the other day. No, I can't stay calm — not till I find her artwork! I've looked everywhere for it, even under the bushes out the front!'

'Huh? It says, "Where is three hundred thousand dollars from", although the spelling is pretty bad. It looks like a ransom note. Letters from a magazine stuck down on a piece of paper. The glue is still wet so they must be close by. How they got this cat to bring the note, I don't know. Perhaps I should keep him here with me till the owners come looking for him, although that could be days and Lynne is coming tomorrow,' she sighed in utter frustration.

'You want me to what? Okay, it's capital W, lower case e, then capital A, lower case r, then space, then the word "is", then the number three, two zeros or is that double o, the letter k, then a space, then the word "from" with no punctuation afterwards, no question mark or anything,' replied Mrs Andrews with a huge sigh of fear and frustration.

'Yes… Yes… What? I don't have time for this! You don't understand, Rosemary, this is Lynne's artwork! Where is the book from? You think so? You mean someone has her work and wants to know where it's from. What do I do, write a letter back and give it to the cat? You got a ransom note too? When was that?' Mrs Andrews' nerves were frazzled.

Barkley had been miaowing and purring the whole time Mrs Andrews was talking to Rosemary.

'What did it say? Something about Bruce's fleas? Yes, that's right. He's here now. You got a bone as well? How long did this go on for? A week? I can't wait that long! Look Rosemary, I've got to go. I've got to try and find Lynne's commission. I don't think Magnus or Freda took it with them on the plane back to Sweden. I suppose they could have but I didn't think they had any friends here to show it to, not unless one of the neighbours heard us when we were sitting out the back the other day and they took it. No, Ginge was here when I showed it to them, but he's gone home again now. I did see an exotic cat here the other day. I think she's pregnant. She didn't stay for long.'

Barkley kept purring and miaowing.

Mrs Andrews stroked him to calm him down.

'MIAOW,' said Barkley, eagerly putting his paws on her face.

'I should not have asked her to let me show her artwork to the grandchildren. It's just that I am so proud of her and her work is exquisite! Look, Rosemary, I've got to go. Bye.'

Exhausted, she sighed, looked at Barkley and said, 'Come on, I have to find Lynne's work or she'll never forgive me. You're a stickybeak cat, do you know where it is?' Barkley miaowed, jumped down from the lounge and ran to the back door, motioning to his new friend to go with him. Back he ran to her legs, tapped her ankles with his paws and motioned again for her to follow him.

Mrs Andrews looked at him and thought she might just as well. Maybe someone was hurt and needed to be rescued, as Barkley's persistent cries were not going away. Olivia put her coat on and Barkley took off out the back door, signalling her to follow. Should any neighbours have happened to see, they would have noticed a small Burmese cat running down the street with a practical-looking lady hurriedly following.

Mrs Andrews followed Barkley's miaows of, 'This way! This way!' Down the street he bolted, stopping every so often to wait for her to catch up, then crossed the road and ran up the throwing slippers driveway.

Puffing, Mrs Andrews said, 'So this is where you live,' as she marched up the drive, trying to get her breath. Barkley, who had waited for her, ran to the back fence, jumped up, glanced back at

Mrs Andrews and said, 'Come on, it's this way!' A grunt of disbelief sprang from the depths of Mrs Andrews as she uttered, 'I can't climb over the fence!' She turned and made her way back onto the street, hoping the occupants had not seen her.

'You keep your cat out of my yard!' yelled the elderly gent, then slammed the door shut.

Just then, Barkley appeared on the footpath, smooched her legs, miaowed and ran down the street, taking Mrs Andrews 'the long way round' to his place, down the street, around the corner and the next, then up a bit. Finally, he reached his letterbox and waited with excitement.

Struggling to put one foot in front of the other, Mrs Andrews stopped to get her breath before she pulled herself further. 'Hopefully this is it.'

Barkley ran up and down the driveway, urging his new friend to, 'Come this way, come this way.' Up the driveway she went, peering into the backyard, then with cautious hands, opened the small white picket gate that divided the house and yard from the garage and driveway. Barkley carefully swayed through the gap between the fence and house, marched across the backyard, down the side of the house and into his den, keeping an eye and ear on the ensuing fast breathing.

'Goodness, I hope there isn't anyone home!' gulped Mrs Andrews as she trespassed across the backyard and entered the disused shed. Winding her way around the stored furniture and scratching posts, all she saw was a diabolical mess of empty sardine packets strewn about, butchers' paper, shredded magazines and newspapers, crusty fur balls vomited up many moons ago and long since dried out and hardened, a bowl of bugs and leaves where somehow water had gotten into the area and soaked it all, not to mention the smell.

Barkley was proud of his office. This was where he did all his thinking and planning. He picked up one of his business cards and went to give it to her but it slipped out of his paws and he chased after it.

'Can I help you?' came a sweet voice.

Mrs Andrews turned and saw a young girl of around fifteen years of age. She had long brown hair, with a fringe that hung over her eyebrows and accentuated her big blue eyes. She was still in her school uniform and now had wet socks.

'It's a simple misunderstanding, you see, your cat came into my house and I followed him here. I thought...'

'Thought what? Look, I think you had better leave!'

'Yes, you are perfectly right. I'm very sorry to have frightened you, my dear,' said Mrs Andrews as she made her way through the labyrinth to the exit. Barkley sat at his desk watching, listening to the conversation in the hope that more evidence would reveal itself.

Sarah stepped aside to let Mrs Andrews pass and noticed Barkley sitting on top of the chest of drawers, looking eagerly at his guest. Pushing past the elegant lady, she asked, 'What is going on here?'

'Well, it's like I said, your cat came into my house and yes, that's right, he gave me this note and I, um, followed him here,' said Mrs Andrews, nervously pulling the note out of her coat pocket.

'What was he doing at your place?'

'I have no idea. I was out the front. When I went inside he ran out from my bedroom, bolted out the back door, then came back inside and dropped this piece of paper at my feet,' explained Mrs Andrews, knowing her face was now blushing.

'Not you as well! Mum and Dad were talking about this the other night.' Sarah opened the note and read 'WeAr is 3ook from'. Puzzled, she looked at Mrs Andrews and asked, 'What does this mean?'

'I am not sure. Some precious artwork was stolen from my place; I thought it may have made its way here. At first, I thought it was a ransom note for $300,000, then I wondered if the three and the "ook" might be a misspelling of book. You know how children love to play games,' said Mrs Andrews with a nervous giggle.

'What children?'

'Well, that's just it, I don't know. I just thought... you could tell me?'

Sarah shook her head in disbelief at Mrs Andrews' question. Looking around in dismay, all she could see was mess.

'What are all these packets doing here? There's my magazine I lost! What's with all this torn newspaper and what is that smell? There's the remnants of the electricity bill we've been searching for! What has been going on?'

'You said "not you as well". Are there others who have received a note?' queried Mrs Andrews anxiously.

'Huh?'

'When I told you about the note, you said, "Not you as well". There are others who have received a note?'

'Um… yes. Mum said Mrs Longford got one.'

'Do you know what it said?'

'Hey! Look at this, someone has written in the dust here "Welcome to my world". Who wrote that? It looks like it's fresh… Ahh, no, sorry. I don't know what it said. I mean, I can't remember.'

'Who is Mrs Longford?'

'She lives around the corner,' replied Sarah, pointing the way as she roamed around Barkley's work zone.

Barkley pricked up his ears. A clue? A major clue? How come I missed this? Quick as a flash, Barkley was up and sniffing the writing in the dust. Achoo! Achoo! Achoo!

'So, you have no idea what is going on either? Have you seen an A3 display book with spiral binding? It has paintings of cats with lovely writing,' queried Mrs Andrews, looking for facial signs of guilt and lies.

'No. Is that what you're looking for? Is it your work?'

'It's not my work; it's my daughter's. She left it with me and now it's gone missing.'

'When did you see it last?'

'Sunday. I showed it to my grandchildren.'

'Is it possible they took it?'

'No, the book was still with me after they had left.'

Sarah wandered around the paraphernalia, wondering what was going on. Where did all the packets of dried fish come from? She picked up the empty packets, bits of torn paper, her magazine and the electricity bill. Barkley started miaowing, following her around.

'DON'T TOUCH! I need all that. Leave the bone alone; I need that too. No, don't take that piece of paper; it's got letters specific to my case I'm working on. No, that's my freshly made glue! Leave it alone!' he miaowed urgently.

Sarah picked Barkley up in her arms and looked around the room in amazement. Barkley purred and reminisced about the days of fun he'd had here with Sarah, Beth and the children next door, riding around on their bicycles chasing aliens, then racing back to the 'Star Flip End Prize'.

Mrs Andrews watched the young girl with the look of total disbelief try to make sense of it all. Near the entrance, Mrs Andrews spotted the object leaning up against the leg of one of the stacked chairs, there was now a ribbon attached to it that had been used to drag it back to the Inquisitor's den; she grabbed it and hid it under her coat.

'Well, I must be going now. Lovely to have met you.' She turned and made a hasty retreat out of the den of dust and mess, past the massive gum tree, leaving Sarah to ponder on what had just happened.

Mrs Andrews walked home briskly in the drizzling rain with the artwork tucked tightly under her coat. She sighed with anger that it had gone missing but was also extremely grateful she had found it again so quickly. She began to wonder how it got there in the first place. No, too much. Best to just focus on getting it home, safely out of the rain, and make sure Lynne's artwork is okay before she gives it back to her.

Now home, she put her daughter's pride and joy down on the kitchen table, got out of her wet clothes and went to dry her hair. What she did not know was a small cat with a button nose saw her grab it and followed her in the wet back to her place, making sure he kept a few paces behind so he was not seen and shooed away.

'No time for a bath now. Gotta get more clues,' said the detective, sneaking in through the back door that had not been shut properly. One push with his nose and he was inside. He heard Mrs Andrews in the front of the house muttering, 'Dear God, thank you, thank you! How in God's name that got there I will never know!'

'To work, detective, where did she put the book? Where is it?' Barkley ran around quickly, looking for the portfolio of lovely words and pictures of his friends but could not find it. Then he suddenly remembered when his family come home, they put everything on the kitchen table. Up he jumped — and there it was — sitting next to a small vase of flowers. Puffing up his fur to stay warm, Barkley extended a claw, flipped the book open and starting reading once more, hoping for a pattern somewhere, a clue.

*Everyone is here except Mao and I!*

He did not realise Regie was not there but that did not count as he was only good for the odd bone to help with bribing.

Barkley's whiskers buzzed like crazy. This normally meant be alert, pay attention to what is going on, but he was concentrating so much on what he was reading and how the page was set out, the paintings and pretty letters, that he paid no attention to his whiskers or the vibration that was now in his paws. He sniffed as many words up his nose as he could and ran his paw over the pictures. Here were his pals – Miss Fi-Fi and Storm beautifully decorated and glowing in these wonderful pages with the magical words. Satiated with this information, Barkley sat on top of the book with his nose resting quietly on his giant mate.

'Good grief! Not you again?! What is it with you that this is so fascinating? Get down! Go on! Now get out!' yelled Mrs Andrews.

Barkley miaowed profusely in protest. 'You don't understand! You are in possession of a major clue to this almighty case I'm struggling to solve!' screamed the detective, trying to hang on to the book as much as he could while Mrs Andrews shoved him out of the way, grabbed the artwork and put it on top of the fridge, where she knew he could not get to it.

'Now go home! It's not for you! Go on, shoo!' she cried, but Barkley was not going anywhere. He scratched and tried to bite the lovely lady.

'I'M NOT GOING ANYWHERE TILL YOU TELL ME WHERE YOU GOT THE BOOK FROM!' Before he knew it, he was unceremoniously picked up and put outside to miaow as much as he liked. Angry and frustrated, Barkley head-butted the back door in defiance.

'Go home cat or I'll have to get your owner to come and get you!' Mrs Andrews' nerves were frazzled beyond belief. She was normally a quiet lady who enjoyed her garden, music, watercolour painting and the odd movie (her artistic abilities were nowhere near her daughter's level).

Barkley's whiskers were still buzzing. His stomach growling, he was desperate for a sardine to calm his nerves but was determined to stay with Mrs Andrews till he knew what was going on. So, he sat in defiant contemplation, till out from behind the plants a black and white cat appeared, calmly walked across the grass, looked at Captain B, then darted down the driveway.

'MAO!' With lightning speed, Barkley sprang up on his toes and took chase after the elusive cat of cryptic clues who ran lightly down the street like somersaults swaying in the breeze on a summer's day. Barkley bolted as fast as he could.

*Gosh, she is quick!*

Barkley whizzed down the footpath as fast as his legs could carry him, around the corner, then the next and down into – his place. Barkley did not stop once. He ran straight up the drive, across the yard and into his den, darting over scratching poles and kicking up torn newspaper as he leapt into his quarters, ready to do battle.

'I've got you now!' exclaimed Barkley, coming to a screeching halt.

*Huh? Where did she go?*

Barkley was dumbfounded. His first sighting of Mao and she had vanished.

'Can cats really walk through walls?' pondered the detective as he heard voices from behind.

'He's done a pretty good job, hasn't he? It must've taken him all of ten minutes to rip off that bit of iron and put up a new one,' said Sarah's father.

'Dad, have you seen all this?' queried Sarah, still in her school uniform as she stared and pointed at Barkley' s world of hidden clues and solved crimes.

'Hmm? I thought that was you and Beth from when you played spaceships with the kids from next door.'

'No, Dad. I found the electricity bill here that Mum had been looking for, and my favourite magazine. Hey, look! There's my alphabet reader and my favourite book from when I was in Grade One. I loved that book! It's been here all along. I was so sure mum had thrown it out.' Sarah bent down and picked up her long-lost treasure.

'MIAOW! MIAOW!' cried Barkley, trying to get the book back.

'Good grief! There's my best tie! How did it get in here? And there's another! What is that? It's a bone! My best tie is wrapped around a bone!'

'MIAOW! MIAOW! MIAOW!'

'What on earth have you and Beth been doing in here? You'd better have a good excuse for all this!' said Tom. He was angry now and upset that his best ties had been abused and ruined.

'MIAOW! MIAAOW!'

'Dad! Can't you see? Shirley Longford was right. Look at this! Barkley has been writing notes. Why else would all these letters be scratched out?'

'MIAOW! MIAOW!'

'And look, here's one...'

Change duss piet or she dets it

'What can it mean?'

'What are you doing? Blaming the cat for your own mistake? He's a cat, Sarah! Cats can't read and write. They eat and sleep – that's all!'

'Dad, you're not listening!'

'MIAOW! MIAAOW! MIAAAOW!'

'Oh, yes, I am! You're delusional, thinking the cat can make this mess! I'm surprised at you! Can't you come up with something better than that? Huh? It's about time you took responsibility! You and Beth can get in here on the weekend and clean this place up! It's smelly!'

'MIAOW! MIAOW!'

'But Dad!'

'And you can put those scratching posts out on the footpath for hard refuse!' yelled her father, stepping over the array of paper to get his ties to show his wife. In a flash, Barkley leapt over and grabbed the tie with the bone in it and a tug of war ensued.

'GET OFF!' the button nose growled. 'I've gone to great lengths to get that ready for Mrs Andrews. Now leave it!'

'CRAZY CAT! LET GO! LET GO!'

Barkley growled, bit into the tie and dug his feet in. 'Let go or it will be goodnight with a Band-Aid!' yelled the detective.

'This cat has gone mad! GET OFF!' Tom yelled, then tugged all he could. Barkley let go, lunged forward, grabbed Tom's hand in his paws and scratched him, whereupon Tom let go of the tie and Barkley grabbed it, held tight and growled at him to keep off.

'Ouch! God dammit! Flaming cat!' Tom marched out without responding to Sarah's pleas of, 'Dad, are you alright?'

'GET THIS PLACE CLEANED UP!' was the only reply coming her way.

Sarah watched her father storm out, heard the back door slam, then turned and stroked her cat, wondering what was going on.

'Barkley? What has gotten into you? Hey? Barkles? Is this you making all this mess?'

'Mess? This happens to be my office. These are my clues; this is my thinking zone. You are trespassing. I'm on my greatest case yet and you are taking up my valuable time,' said the greatest detective ever in a matter-of-fact voice.

Sarah started gathering up the empty packets of dried fish and occasionally picked up one of Barkley's attempts to write a note, some of which he had gotten right, others had obviously been challenging. The latest one, 'Change tich to Joinaythin' made no sense to her, nor did 'Were iz dock from' or 'No god or quss gets it'.

Sarah sat looking at the old butchers' paper and remembered how she and Beth drew planets and stars on it of where their home planet was. Now it had letters badly scratched out and half stuck down with some sort of glue that seemed to contain grass.

'You mean "No dog or puss gets it". It's a ransom letter. Is that what you've been doing? You're writing ransom letters and the payment is a packet of dried fish? Heh, Barkley? Is that what you've been doing? And I thought you were an ordinary cat,' said Sarah in quiet astonishment.

'Zarzar. Dinner,' said Sarah's little brother Corey from the labyrinth's doorway.

Sarah sat with Barkley, who continued to hold onto his prize. He was angry with them for invading his office and letting Mao slip through his paws. Now the coast was clear, Barkley dragged his tie with bone into one of the hidey-holes inside a cat scratching post before heading inside for dinner. Tom glared at him, his hand covered in Band-Aids. Barkley glared back with, 'Serves you right! I gave you fair warning!'

Sarah tried to explain to her mum that Mrs Longford was right but her dad would not have a bar of it and shut her down quickly, emphasizing that she and Beth would be cleaning up the mess on the weekend and there would be no visiting friends till it was done.

It was dark now, the fire was on and Barkley, who wanted some warmth, watched Corey snuggle up to his big sister to keep her company through the evening's upset. Barkley knew the weekend was when the family were all home but just exactly when that was, he had no idea.

# Chapter Ten

Olivia Andrews rose in the morning, put the kettle on and opened Lynne's portfolio. There, sitting on top of one of the pots waiting to come in, was Barkley.

'Good grief! Not you again! What is it with you and Lynne's work?'

'Miaow,' he declared sweetly.

Olivia turned and looked at the artwork on the table, then looked at Barkley.

'You want to be painted and on display? Is that it? You want to be on the bedding?' she asked.

'Miaow!' said Barkley, stretching up and putting his paws on the door. 'Yes, yes. That's it, my dear. I want to be on display, now let me in and tell me all about it.'

Olivia had her breakfast and re-read the artwork, while keeping an eye on the small Burmese cat at the back door. Each turn of the page was met with a miaowing plea and a rattle at the door.

The doorbell rang. He watched her open the door.

*Do I have time to run around the front and come in that way?*

Before Barkley could decide, the door closed and he saw the two women embrace and kiss.

'Hello love.'

'Hi Mum. How's things? Have you had a chance to look at my work? What do you think?'

'It's exceptionally good, my dear. All your work is good.'

'Yeah, thanks Mum, but do you think they will like it?'

'They'd be mad not to! I don't see why you doubt yourself so much,' said Olivia, putting the kettle on again.

'Well, it's been a while since I had a commission, besides – who's that? Have you got a new cat, Mum? You didn't tell me!'

'Oh, that's a crazy cat called Barkley. He first turned up here a few weeks ago. He seems obsessed about things.'

'What happened to the ginger one?'

'He's still around. He's gone back to his family, but he'll come again. He stayed quite a while last time, longest ever. I thought he'd been hit as his back leg was sore for quite some time. He had a limp but it got better and then he went home again. It was nice to have him here though,' replied the mother with a glint of affection in her eyes.

Lynne got up from her cuppa to go outside and greet the intense gaze staring into the coffee area.

'No, Lynne! Don't let him in! I don't want him inside!' stressed Olivia.

'Oh Mum, why not? He looks cute. Doesn't bite and scratch, does he?'

'No, he's just mad, that's all.'

'Come on, get your coffee and we'll have it out the back,' said Lynne.

Olivia sighed and stood up like the weight of the world had suddenly appeared on her shoulders again.

With much fuss-making, Barkley jumped up onto the table. Lynne stroked him and he reciprocated by purring loudly as the two women sat and chatted about Allan, his gorgeous Swedish wife Anikka and their two children, now that they had returned to Sweden. Olivia missed her son, but knew she had to let her children live their own life their own way. It was nice to spend time with her grandchildren, Freda and Magnus.

Barkley basked in his own glory as he listened to words of praise like, 'He's cute. He's got a lovely nose. He has a nice soft purr that is so relaxing. His coat is healthy. He looks wise, and there's also a huge amount of mischievousness about him.'

'When will you hand in your work to the client?' asked Olivia.

'I've got a fortnight from next Thursday.'

The sun peeped through the clouds and for a few moments, beamed onto the table and warmed up Barkley as he sat looking resplendent, taking in every word.

'I must admit you have really captured Budge and Florry well. You can see their personality and how playful they are.'

*Budge? Florry? You mean you're Lynne? Artist Lynne? Budge and Florry's nurturer?*

With a thud, a small ginger bear jumped up onto the table.

'Are you waiting for another plate of sardines and milk?' queried a deep voice Barkley knew well.

'Storm! Pal! How are you? It's Lynne! Fudge and Borrie's carer! Mrs Andrews is mum, is mum and she ron't let me lead the pook!'

Storm squeezed past Barkley and did a belly flop on the table between the two ladies, purred loudly, rolled over onto his back and put his paws into Tai Chi waving clouds. Lynne and Olivia laughed and rubbed his belly. 'Oh, what a delight,' whiskered Storm, waving his tail at Barkley to sneak away.

Barkley took his cue and quietly slipped off. Creeping inside, he stood on top of the table, extended a claw and opened his most precious clue once again. He loved looking at the pictures and passing his paw over the gilded letters. Admiring the magnificently presented pages, he also noticed that the sequence started with Miss Fi-Fi, a new mother caring for her young.

All the lovely pictures with beautiful words spelt that there is no right nor wrong way to anything, it's all about how you perceive yourself in the moment, and we as special carers to our nurturers hold a vital key – but what was it all for? Who was it who wanted this type of beauty? Then he remembered Lynne was handing over her work to someone on a Thursday.

*What is Thursday? I must find out who or what this Thursday is; must be someone important.*

He found the paintings of the brothers that he had not yet read. Looking like they were about to pop out of the page and start chatting to him, Budge and Florry wandered around the two pages playing. There was Budge, black and white, lying on his back watching a dragonfly while Florry, white and black, was tossing a ball into the air. At the bottom, the two brothers were curled up together, fast asleep. The adjacent page was splashed with paw prints covered in paint that then saw the brothers painting a wall. Then they walked side by side like they had their arms around each other and looked straight at you; a small smile giving away their mischievousness. Barkley laughed, remembering the story they had told as he passed his paw over the page like he wanted some of this magic to enter into his own feet. Barkley carefully read the magnificent words that decorated the pages:

*The only cure to being lost*
*is to teach your heart to sing.*

*In a Kingdom not far from me,*
*Is a world where I can be.*
*Here there is no stress,*
*Just being at my best.*
*Of potential ready to speak,*
*Come, dive in and take a peek.*
*Creativity dawning*
*On this beautiful morning,*
*Shining upon my face*
*In this glorious place,*
*Packed full of ideas,*
*Found under blankets of fears.*
*Look up and see a full cup,*
*Of joy that could be breathing.*
*Instead of what you are seeing,*
*Come and see what's inside.*
*This curtain of love you so hide,*
*In a kingdom not far from me,*
*Is a world where I can be me.*

Barkley sat purring ever so loudly. 'In a kingdom not far from me is a world where I can be me,' he sighed. 'That means curled up asleep by the fire instead of being shut in the laundry, staying out late on hot nights and when the wind blows, chasing leaves but most of all it means eating as many sardines as I can get!' daydreamed the detective as he scratched another imaginary flea.

'Hey! Puss cat! What are you doing? What are you up to? That's not a plaything. You come away from that! I don't want you ruining my work,' scolded Lynne as she came inside and prized a cute cat away from her artwork. 'This is precious work, Puss. Look but don't touch,' she explained to her new furry friend.

Barkley looked up at Lynne with his cute face of innocence and purred even louder, miaowing and motioning her to turn the page.

'See, this is my work I've been doing. It's very important,' and with that, one of those things that people stare at and occasionally talk into appeared out of her pocket, pointed at Barkley and made clicks, then quickly disappeared again.

Barkley motioned her to turn the page, turn the page, turn the page. 'I have to report back to Titch what his one says!'

Lynne stood up and moved to pick up her portfolio.

'But I was just – wait!' purred Barkley as he stood up on his hind legs, front paws stretching up to her. Lynne, unable to resist a purring cat, picked up Barkley instead, hugged him in her arms and took him back outside to her waiting mother who was busy stroking a giant ginger belly.

'Do you want another coffee?' she asked as if her worldly purchases were now complete in the purring she was cuddling. The response was no. The two women continued to chat about family, whether Lynne had heard from her ex, impending travels, the garden, a new bakery that had opened and a black and white cat that had been lurking around. While Lynne and Barkley smooched, Olivia stroked Storm's belly – from whiskers to tail he would have stretched almost the entire length of the table.

'Storm,' whispered Barkley while he rubbed his nose on Lynne's chin and purred like a lawn mower. 'I need to know what it says for Titch. He has come by and I'm to report back.'

'It talks about the ideal and being grateful for what you have.'

'Really? Are you sure? How… How can you remember that? Do you remember all of them?'

'I remember bits and pieces.'

'Goodness! Even I can't remember who got what. Are you sure?'

'Go check.'

'What? I can't go in there again. I've already been told off enough. I don't want a smacked bottom. Oh, Lynne smells nice, you know,' whispered an extremely smooched cat.

'I will create a diversion. Watch this.' Storm got up and boxed Barkley's ears and growled at him. Barkley miaowed like he was frightened and ran off. Storm stuck himself in front of Lynne and demanded that she stroke him and they nuzzle together. Olivia complained to Ginge that his behaviour was not very friendly, particularly when last time they played so nicely together. Lynne patted him, remarking that he wore no collar. The sun continued to shine on the conversation held at the outdoor dining table in Mrs Andrews' backyard with Storm basking in the warmth and delight of all the attention. After a while, Olivia got up and took the cups inside to be washed.

Barkley was now hiding on one of the dining chairs tucked into the table. He had read the elegant words and seen Titch looking cute with a small smile of innocence, which Barkley and all the other cats and dogs in the neighbourhood knew was not true. He was pictured climbing a tree, leaping into a pile of leaves and sleeping on top of cushions.

*He who lives through the ideal, lives in sorrow.*
*He who lives with gratitude lives in peace.*

*There is beauty to be had*
*but Heaven does not reside here.*
*There are dreams to fulfill but do not take the ideal.*
*Sorrow, Sadness,*
*Grateful Gladness.*
*Are all lessons based on trust?*
*Friendship is the greatest gift.*
*Only through gratitude are the eyes to the heart opened.*
*Only with gratitude do the whispers of greatness come to be.*
*Peace is the harvest.*

As it started to rain, the women moved inside. Olivia put the fire on in her recently decorated room and suggested to Lynne she heat up some soup and serve it with crusty bread. Knowing he would not be welcome, Barkley whiskered to Storm if he could remain with them and listen to what was said and report back to him. His giant friend got up and wandered in the direction of fresh heat and conversation. Even though Barkley loved a warm fire, he stayed out of sight.

The door closed and the conversation became muffled, so Barkley hopped off the chair and ran up the corridor to listen to what was being said.

'Magnus and Freda are growing up fast, aren't they?' said Olivia. 'Gosh that tastes good! Just the right amount of spice!'

'Well, they are to us. We only see them once every two years or so,' replied Lynne through a mouthful of bread. 'This soup is so good! You know, I used to rave to the kids at school about how good your cooking was, is. I even got into a fight one day with a boy over it. You remember Samuel McMahon?'

'Of course I do! You brought him over for dinner and he would invite himself over about three times a week! I had to budget for extra food just to feed him!'

Lynne laughed and took another bite of her buttered bread. Barkley listened to spoons clatter against bowls, Storm purring and imagined if he were actually there, he would have seen crumbs covering the carpet.

The chat continued about new plants Olivia wanted in her garden so she could paint the flowers in summer, admiration of a garden on one of her walks and what was the name of that rose she found?

'Come on! I'll make us some tea and you can try some of my blueberry jam and scones,' said Olivia, standing up to take the tray with empty bowls back to the kitchen. Barkley heard the movement so ran into the room opposite and hid.

After two cups of tea and three scones, Lynne decided to leave. 'Don't forget your work,' reminded her mum. They kissed each other goodbye and as they embraced, Barkley emerged into the corridor, scampered out the front door and hid. He watched Lynne get into her car and drive away, then made his way home via the back fence instead of going along the street.

# Chapter Eleven

Barkley sat on a shelf, gazed out the small window at the garden and wished he had a dried fish to munch on. He could think better with a sardine in his mouth. Storm made his way through the labyrinth.

'What did you find out?' asked Storm.

'You were right about what Titch's one says – it speaks of the ideal, while Budge and Florry's talks about being in a kingdom where you can do as you like. That's my kind of kingdom! You had all the luck! How was it staying in front of the fire all afternoon listening to their conversations? Did you find out anything?'

'Nothing more than what you heard through the door. Although Mrs Andrews did comment on tiny writing that appears as grass where all the words started with M.A.O,' said Storm.

Barkley looked wide-eyed at his pal.

Storm continued, explaining, 'M.A.O. spells Mao.'

Barkley jumped down from the shelf and went to his desk, where all the pieces of paper were laid out. They were all signed Confucius of Mao, which Barkley read as 'Confused us of Mao'. He thought all the notes were to confuse him into thinking one thing and throw him off the actual trail of clues that would allow him to win the case. He was having an awful time trying to piece everything together. All his other cases had been quite simple up till now, such as who killed the budgerigar; that dog has attacked a cat, he needs a lesson; why did the rabbit die so unexpectedly; this cat does not like its tucker, get the owner to change it. This case was something completely different. He had seen his arch-rival once when he chased her down the street but she ran into his den and disappeared, to where he did not know. Perhaps she leapt up into the ceiling and went through the hole, just like Matilda said she had.

Storm continued, 'That means Lynne must know Mao, or at least have some sort of contact with her. No doubt Budge and Florry must have seen her about. Perhaps Mao is leaving notes for Lynne like she is for you? I don't know, but it's worth looking into.'

'You're right, Storm. I thought I'd go see Lynne myself, only I am not exactly sure where she lives. Budge and Florry come over here, but I've never been to their place. I thought the only thing I could do was to stay here and wait for them to turn up.'

'Yes, or you could ask Miss Fi-Fi if she knows where they live. She gets around a bit.'

'I did stop by there yesterday on my way to Mrs Andrews', but she didn't come out. Her lady saw me, threw things at me and yelled at me to get away. She doesn't want any more of Regie's bones and definitely no more notes.'

'How is Regie, anyway?'

'Barking at shadows, as usual! Sometimes he keeps me awake all night with his barking. The possums run along the fence and he goes nuts. I keep telling him if he wants to have a tail that curls around at the end I will arrange it for him. You know Storm, I'm extremely grateful that you come over here to help me. It's getting on for my dinner now, so if you don't mind, I will go and greet my family and hopefully get something scrummy-rum to eat.'

'Fair enough. I'll see you tomorrow,' Storm bid his friend goodbye.

'Best not come over. If I get nothing from Miss Fi-Fi, I'll wait here till Budge and Florry come.'

'You don't want me here when they come?'

'Florry is frightened of you. Ever since you growled at him when he deposited at Mrs Andrews', he is afraid you will beat him up.'

'I've never beaten anyone up. I don't need to. Standing up and looking them in the eye works for me. I don't need to say anything, they know; however, I shall leave you to await their arrival. If you find out where they live, I am happy to go with you to see Lynne.'

'Thanks, Storm. You know, I used to be petrified of you. The day you first came over with your note I couldn't even speak properly to get my words out I was shaking that much,' admitted Barkley to his pal.

'Oh well Barx, you're not the only one. Just be grateful you've gotten over your fear and found a friend instead.'

Barkley looked at him with such gratitude and admiration.

# Chapter Twelve

Sneaking in through the back door, a tired detective looked to see what his family were doing. He got a glare from Tom, whose hand was still bandaged. Barkley ignored him with a flippant, 'Serves you right,' and miaowed for his dinner. He tried opening his cupboard with his paw so he could see what was available, then moved to the oven to see if he was getting what they were having.

'What are you having for dinner? Can I have some? It smells nice!' he sniffed. 'MIAOW!'

Sarah appeared in the kitchen, stroked Barkley, then quickly fed him.

'Don't forget, Sarah – you and Beth are cleaning up the shed tomorrow and there will be no going out till it's all done!' reminded her dad.

'Yes, I know,' she responded sadly.

'What has she gone and done now that I need to be punished for?' demanded Beth, who had come to set the table or she would get no pocket money.

'It's alright, Beth, I'll explain later,' said Sarah, trying not to remind her dad of his sore hand.

Barkley had planned on basking his belly on top of the heating duct all night, till he had a horrible realisation.

*Tomorrow, Sarah and Beth are tidying up my office! That means they're going to see all my clues!*

'QUICK! LET ME OUT! MIAOW! MIAOW! GOTTA GO OUT!' he cried at the door, feigning a bursting bladder.

Barkley darted outside into the cold, dark night, jumped over the fence and ran as fast as he could to Storm's place, only where was he – at home or with Mrs Andrews? There would be no way she would let him inside! Barkley thought he would try his first home to see if he was there.

*So much for keeping my belly warm for the entire evening and having delicious sleeps.*

Barkley grumbled.

*Why couldn't they have just left things as they are? They've not set foot in the place for years and I've got myself all set up. Everyone knows where I am, and now they're going to take all my solved crimes away, take all my clues and ruin everything! I will have to start from scratch!*

Barkley was angry and panicking.

*I need reinforcements to ward them off!*

Barkley wished he could growl as meanly as Titch. At Storm's driveway, he saw a man holding a bag emerge from a car. The man looked at Barkley and thought nothing of it. When he shut the car door, Barkley ran to the opposite side of the car and dashed up the drive, then as the man approached the front steps, Barkley crept out and stayed just behind him. As the man opened the front door, Barkley jumped out and ran inside into the lounge room. There, hidden amongst the toys that lay strewn all over the floor, was his enormous pal, stretched out in front of the fire. The latest addition to the family sat next to him, patting him like he was some sort of bouncing ball.

'Hey! What are you doing? Get out!' cried the man.

'Greg, what is it?' came a female voice.

'Some cat has just run inside!' he yelled.

'Oh, poor thing! He's probably hungry,' replied the woman, entering the scene while drying her hands on a tea towel. Peering over her husband's shoulder, she gazed at Barkley.

'Oh, he is cute! See if he has a tag.'

Two boys who looked the same appeared in the lounge room and pointed their toy swords at Barkley, said something, then ran off. Barkley wondered if they, too, were playing starships. The man bent down to look at the cat's tag but Barkley was having none of it and hid behind one of the lounge chairs.

'STORM! STORM!'

The giant ginger lifted his head, wondering what the commotion was about.

'Must be important for you to come tearing in here. What's up?' he asked.

'Storm! Sarah and Beth are going to tidy up my office tomorrow. That means they will see all my clues, all my evidence and possibly (gulp) throw everything out. I can't let that happen. This case is too big for me to start again,' explained Barkley. 'I've already had a fight with Tom. I need reinforcements to stand them off and attack if needed. Can you rally around for me? Get Matilda and Zenya, although I don't know where she lives. What about Titch, do you think he would come? He is about as grumpy as they get and I'm sure would be happy for a fight,' said Barkley, out of breath and still panicking.

'Hey Albie, is this a friend of yours? You got a visitor, isn't that nice?' commented Greg.

'Maybe that's where he goes when he disappears for days on end. Maybe he is at his place? Did you get a look at his tag?' suggested the woman.

'No, he wouldn't let me near him.'

'Well, dinner's ready. Shall we feed him?' she asked.

'Yeah, that's an idea,' he responded, watching the two cats chat. Most of the chatting was done via whisker vibration, with the occasional miaow.

'Okay, I'll see what I can do,' Storm responded. 'Would it be easier to put your clues away somewhere?'

'Where? There isn't anywhere safe anymore. It's all going tomorrow. All my scratching posts are being thrown out. I used to have such fun in there playing spaceships with the children. I won't have much of an office left after tomorrow – and what if they take all my things for making notes? Felidaes if they take the bones too! What shall I do?'

At that point, a plate of food was presented to Barkley.

'Thanks, I've no time to eat, maybe next time,' replied the detective who was always ready for a good feed. 'Why do you get Mrs Andrews to feed you when your meals are so nice here?'

'Going to Mrs Andrews is not about the food; it's about respite from the noise. Come on, I'll come with you and we'll figure something out.' Storm and Barkley went out the front door that had remained open thanks to Greg's surprise at seeing a strange cat march into his house.

'Hey, Albie! Where you going, mate? Albie! You come back here, come on!' called Greg, standing at the front door watching two cats converse like some sort of business deal was going on as they made their way down the driveway. 'Huh! Well, I'll be!' he said and went back inside to tell his wife Carla that Albie had just left with some cat and that something must be up.

'Do you think we should follow them?' she asked.

'Okay, you look after the kids and I'll go see which way they went,' he responded, putting his coat back on and proceeding to run down the street looking for which way the business deal was taking place. Fifteen minutes later he came back, out of breath, and declared he did not know where they went and that he had looked everywhere, even up driveways. Having never seen the other cat before, they wondered if he was new but that would not explain all the occasions Albie had gone off to be fed somewhere else all these years.

'Well, it must be serious if that cat has come all the way over here to get him and they left quickly together. I hope his owner is not hurt. Do you think we should wait up for him?' wondered Carla.

'Wait up for him? It could be days before we see him again!'

'Yeah, you're right. Come on,' she said, hugging her husband, 'come and eat.'

With a twinkle is his eye, he hugged her in return and went into the dining room for his dinner. Ten-month-old Evelina was already in her highchair playing with her food. The eldest, Nick, was in his bedroom slogging over his homework; he was a studious young man who wanted good grades. Five-year-old Samantha was trying to put a large baked potato into her mouth.

'Just a minute, sweetie. I'll come and cut that up for you,' said her dad.

Samantha's gravy-covered face nodded excitedly.

The twins, Lucas and Joshua, were still running around playing sword fights.

Carla entered the room and put Greg's dinner down for him.

'Come on boys, dinner time now or the big green Brussel sprout will get you!' said Carla, grabbing her giggling nine-year-olds and tickling them to the table with hugs and kisses.

Greg sat down and fed Evelina while he ate his own dinner. Carla coaxed the boys to calm down and eat amongst their laughter and antics, while calling Nick away from his studies to come and eat. Nick bolted down the stairs with two books under his arm and ate his dinner while reading both of them.

Meanwhile, Barkley and Storm marched into the soon-to-be-cleaned office. Storm picked up all the notes and told Barkley to go and put them under the house.

'What about the bones, my notes and glue?'

'I'm thinking about that and haven't got an answer yet. Can you put those under the house as well?'

'Perhaps. We're going to be at it all night, aren't we?' asked a forlorn looking button-nosed detective.

Storm motioned to his friend to get a move on. Barkley marched out, his mouth stuffed with small, folded pieces of paper and wondered why it was that when he looked into Storm's eyes he went all gooey and could not think straight? He was sure that for all the times he was dragged on holiday with his nurturer family to the salty smelling house that there would be no difference between Storm's eyes and the ocean.

It took some pushing and wriggling for Barkley to get his body through the gap and under the house. He could not hold all the notes in his mouth at the same time and heave himself through, so he put his head through the gap, dropped the notes, then squeezed the rest of himself under the house. Gathering all the pieces of paper, he put them in what he thought was a dry spot, away from anyone being able to see them.

*Will they be safe there though? What if Mao comes through and takes them away?*

Storm heard Barkley re-enter his office and turned to tell him what his plan was, then broke out in giggles – Barkley's ears and face were covered in a large collection of dust and spider webs. He flicked his head to get rid of them but only made it worse.

'Hold still,' said Storm and pulled the sticky construction off.

'Thanks,' said Barkley.

'Okay, let me tell you what I've done. All the empty packets can go, you don't need them anymore. They will probably clean out all the drawers and let's say all the scratching posts are going. However, I have found this cupboard here that seems to have some garden tools and things in it that I think they will keep, so let's put your bones, paper and things in the bottom here and hope for the best. Fortunately, it's cold at the moment so there aren't many flies around to attract attention. We can put this old woollen thing on top to make it look like it has been here all along,' suggested the giant solutionist.

'Okay, great. Paws and whiskers that they don't notice a thing. What about all my clues from my old cases?'

'Put them in the cupboard too, under the woollen thing. Have they seen any of this stuff?'

Barkley nodded. 'Sarah and Tom were in here inspecting where the hole in the ceiling used to be and saw everything. He became angry when he saw one of Regie's bones and wanted my special thing I use to carry it around with but I wouldn't let him have it. He had taken it off and left it there, so I made use of it. Anyway, we had a tug of who was going to win and I told him to let go or it's goodnight with a Band-Aid.'

'And he went to bed with a Band-Aid?'

'Of course he did! What does he think this is? I am way faster than he is and I can fight better than he can! If only he would learn it's a cat's world!' retorted Barkley, getting het up again. He felt indignant that his world was being taken away from him when it had taken him years to establish himself. 'Where else is everyone going to find such a good detective around here?'

'Come on,' said Storm, surveying the place and seeing that dust was settling again. 'We might just get away with it.'

Barkley looked around at his office and as way of saying thanks, smooched his friend and purred loudly. When Barkley stood next to Storm, the tops of his ears reached the massive muscles in Storm's front legs. If he ducked just a little, Barkley could walk right underneath him.

Storm bid his pal goodnight and said he would be back in the morning to see how it all goes, then jumped over the fence and made his way up his own driveway, back to the warmth of his fire and a prayer that the children would be in bed so he could warm himself in peace without being pestered. Barkley miaowed and banged the front door to be let in.

*Hopefully I can stay inside in the warmth and not be chucked into the laundry for safe keeping!*

Apparently, Barkley made too much noise at nighttime, he ran around too much and his nails made scratching noises on the wooden floors, so said the mother of the house. Barkley disagreed. He wondered how they could hear him moving around when he listened to them snoring all night and even, on occasion, talking in their sleep. One night, when the house was quiet, Barkley was looking to curl up on Corey's bed when he heard, 'Oh, hello! How are you? I haven't seen you in a long time,' and went to investigate. Into the large bedroom he wandered, to hear the mother speak again, 'Two of those and one of those. What? No, send them,' then giggling and snoring as she rolled over. Barkley waited days for the parcel to arrive but it never did. Perhaps she was ordering more snoring?

'Finally! Do you know how cold it is out here?' said Barkley as Beth opened the front door and he ushered himself in, looking pleased that his office of clues just might be saved after all.

# Chapter Thirteen

Slowly, the sun rose. Barkley woke from a wriggling Corey, jumped down and marched into the laundry to get a snack before breakfast. No one was up. What to do now? The heating had gone off, he was hungry and he needed to visit the bushes.

*I'll go wake Sarah. No, I won't. That means her and Beth will be in my office early and I don't want that. Can't wake Corey, he sleeps through most things. Jean? Shall I wake her? No point in waking Tom, he'll just throw me off the bed.*

Barkley had a few of his biscuits that were next to his water bowl and pondered how to stay warm. Perhaps he should go back to Corey's bed and snuggle up? Just then, he heard a bang at the back door.

'Barkley? Barkley, you there?'

'Yes, who is that?'

'It's us. Matilda, Budge and Florry,' explained Matilda. 'We've come to help you ward them off.'

'They're not even up yet,' Barkley explained.

'That's okay. We'll wait in your office,' replied Matilda.

'Okay, I'll be out as soon as I can get someone to open the door,' said Barkley. 'Where's Storm?'

'He's coming. He's gone to see if – what's his name? Budge, who has Storm gone to get?'

'Was it George? I don't know. Flor, where has Storm gone?'

Barkley shuddered at the sound of George's name. Surely, he hasn't gone to persuade that massive brute to come and fight for him?

'He's gone to get Leia and Peppu, hasn't he?' said Florry.

'Thank Felidae for that! I am so lucky to have such good friends,' sighed Barkley. He sat at the back door to wait, knowing all would be well shortly, and even better when he could stop holding onto his bladder.

'Do I hear movement? Someone is up? Yes, they are! Quick, pester! Pester! MIAOW! MIAOW! MIAAOOOW! MIIAAOOOOW!' cried Barkley, prancing up and down with his tail between his legs.

Loud yawning appeared in the kitchen and coffee cups emerged from the cupboard.

'MIAOW! MIAOW! MIAOW!'

Tom opened the back door and Barkley ran out to do his business.

*What a relief! Now I'll just pester again to get a quick bite to eat.*

As he approached the back door, he heard the key turn and the bolt slide over.

*Fine! I'll go and see my friends then.*

Barkley knew Tom was still angry that his whatsit was being used to cart bones around. 'At least I know they're having a lazy sleep in, which gives me more time,' thought the greatest detective in these parts, manoeuvring his body through the narrow laneway in the shed till he reached the opening where he did all his thinking.

'Hi everyone! Thank you so much for coming to my rescue,' Barkley greeted his friends, explaining the dilemma.

*Dilemmas — at the ultimate outcome I will still be loved and cared for. Yes, but I want all this looked after, not thrown out. How can I provide a good service with no office? Yes, I shall say that to them. I shall say I need to provide a good service and I cannot do that unless I have the proper equipment!*

'Morning Barkles!' chorused Budge and Florry. 'We've been here a few times, haven't we Flor,' Florry nodded, 'only you weren't here, so we went home again. We thought of leaving you a calling card, only we don't have any fur balls,' said Budge, pleased to see his detective friend again. 'We've been wondering how it's all going with the case?'

'Actually, I'm glad you're here. I've been at Mrs Andrews' place a lot and it appears Lynne is the one who made the picture book of you all,' explained Barkley matter-of-factly.

'Yeah, that's right,' said Budge. 'We've seen Mrs Andrews at our place loads of times, haven't we?' Florry nodded. 'She comes every so often. That's Lynne's mum. Lynne painted us a while back and has these other pictures of other felines on her talking whatsit.'

'WHY THE HECK DIDN'T YOU SAY SO? You could've saved me a huge amount of bother! I've been working on this case for ages, to the point where Mrs Andrews will no longer let me in her house!' screamed Barkley in exasperation.

'You didn't ask, did you?' responded Budge.

'What else do you know that I don't know? Who is Mao? Have you seen her yet? I suppose you are in cahoots with Titch on all this?'

'What's Titch got to do with it? Look Barkles, like we've said before, we're cats. We eat, we sleep, end of story,' said Budge, looking at Florry like, 'What's his problem?' Florry shrugged.

'Okay then, who is it who has asked Lynne to do all this work, to paint all these lovely pictures?' demanded Barkley.

'That would be Athena at the design place. What's it called, Flor?'

'Dunno. They're making bedding stuff for children. We're hoping to get a bed of our own, aren't we Budge,' said Florry.

'Yeah, we're going to sleep on the lovely words, plus, we want to see what it's like to sleep on top of ourselves,' said Budge.

Barkley put his head into his paws and sighed.

'I don't believe it! After all this time, you knew all along and didn't say anything! Do you know how long I've been looking for this Mao character? I could've gone straight to Lynne, but no, the two felines who knew everything all along chose to keep their mouths shut!'

'Now see here, Barx, you've been looking for this Mao character. You didn't say anything about Lynne's painting,' said Budge, trying to reason with the detective.

'Yes, but when we brought the picture book here into my office from Mrs Andrews' place, you said nothing!'

'Because we wanted to hear what was said about us! We can't read, can we. Not like you! We wanted to hear all the lovely things said about everyone so we could be proud of our display when it goes on show. This is for bedding, for sleeping and staying warm, cosy in the lovely words and pretty pictures. It's nothing about our collars going missing or this Mao character,' said Budge. 'Flor, you tell him!'

'That's right, Barx. So many times we wanted to be in Lynne's pictures, so we trod over everything. She would get so cross with us and then one day, we were being painted. Then other felines were being painted. We came to you because you could help us with our collars going missing and the little bits of paper with the funny writing. We had no idea it was all the same thing,' said Florry, trying hard to explain things properly.

'You're right. I'm sorry boys,' said Barkley, calming down from feeling he had been betrayed.

'You're the greatest detective we know. Who else are we going to ask?' said the brothers in unison.

'Okay. Look everyone, they're going to be in here soon taking all this stuff out. What I suggest we do is stand our ground and attack first, then ask questions later,' said Captain Barkley, feeling better about his conversation with Budge and Florry.

Storm appeared and told Barkley that Leia and Peppu were not coming. He told Matilda to stay outside and let him know when the girls were heading their way. Budge and Florry were to sit inside the cupboard on top of the paraphernalia. 'Whatever happens,' explained the giant, 'remain seated and don't let them look under what you are sitting on.'

Although Florry was shaking in his fur again with Storm being in such close proximity, he did as he was told and sat in the cupboard with Budge; at least he would not be able to see the giant, so might not have to run off in a bundle of nerves. 'What is it with those big green eyes he has?' mumbled Florry as the cupboard door closed behind them.

'You alright, Budge?'

'Yeah, you alright?'

'Yeah, better now the door is shut.'

In silence, they sat waiting. Barkley sat on top of his desk, gazing out the window. Storm sat under a dining table next to the exit. If worst came to worst and they happened to nosey in the cupboard, he could shut the door and not let them out till they handed over Barkley's prized possessions. Mind you, they would have found Budge and Florry first, who would help cause a distraction. Maybe a bit of hissing could get them out and away from the hidden clues.

Two young voices, belonging to Sarah and Beth, still in dressing gowns and slippers, appeared in the shed and made their way into their old spaceship where they had drawn star maps, rode around the neighbourhood on their bikes and won and lost battles with the children next door. Sarah explained to Beth that they had to clean the place up and get Dad's tie and put it in the wash. She asked Beth what she made of all the empty packets of dried fish and the pieces of butchers' paper that had letters stuck down on them in attempts to make words, only the words were indecipherable.

'What does this mean to you?' she asked her young sister, holding up one of Barkley's notes that she found stuffed down the back of the desk.

'I don't know. I just want to get this done so I can meet Julia. Dad said we're not allowed out till it's done, so stop your whining and get on with it. The sooner it's done the quicker we can go out,' responded the blonde-haired thirteen-year-old.

'We did have some fun in here when we were young, didn't we? Do you remember the time we dragged those two large cat climbing things back here on our bikes? They were already filthy but we didn't care and how we made Barkley captain of our spaceship?' giggled Sarah.

'Yeah, I remember,' Beth was trying not to engage in the conversation.

'Have you seen Dad's tie yet?'

'No. What's it look like?'

'It's the one we gave him for Christmas.'

'Oh, that. Dunno.'

'It was here the other day, wrapped up in a bone,' said Sarah.

'A bone? Are you crazy? You must have been seeing things, there are no bones here,' said Beth emphatically.

Slowly the office of unseen clues grew space. Scratching poles for climbing on and hiding in were taken outside to the curb for council pick up. A dirty old water bowl full of bugs and dead leaves was emptied, with the bowl then put in the rubbish. Throughout, Barkley sat gazing as nonchalantly as he could over the morning's relocation of dust particles and former possessions. He tried ever so hard not to cry out when they picked up his old water bowl but then, he never used it. Hiding under an antique dining table with chairs stacked on top, a large ginger face watched attentively.

'Are we done now?' asked Beth, stuffing paper and the remains of the empty sardine packets into a bag ready for the bin.

'We need to find Dad's Sunday best tie. Barkley wouldn't let go of it the other day. He's probably hidden it somewhere,' said Sarah, looking around.

'A cat has hidden Dad's tie? You mean the one we gave him for Christmas? The same tie that was wrapped around a bone? Notes the cat has written? You have finally gone loopy-loopy, you know that, don't you?'

'Why is it you never listen to anything I say?'

'Probably because it's not worth listening to!'

'Beth, you don't mean that. You are my lovely sister who is smart, kind and intelligent,' Sarah looked straight at Beth.

'Yeah, okay. I'm sorry. I get irritable when I haven't eaten.'

'Come on then, we'll get this done and you can jump in the shower and I'll make us breakfast, how's that?' suggested Sarah.

'Okay,' Beth smiled, screwing up the piece of paper she had just picked up and jokingly threw it at Sarah. 'Ya dork! Talking cat indeed!'

'He doesn't talk. He writes letters to people. Ransom notes,' explained Sarah, holding a terribly spelt one up. 'I think I might get this one framed. See, it's one of our star maps with Barkley's bad spelling on top.'

'If it will make you feel better, go ahead,' laughed Beth, making loopy faces at Sarah.

*'Bad spelling? Am I really that terrible? Can't anyone read what I've written?'* pondered Barkley, becoming depressed.

Tom came in to inspect the area and asked if they had his tie. They both responded with 'Not seen it.' Tom nodded and said he did not want it back anymore, not now the cat had used it.

'Come on,' he said, 'get cleaned up and we'll go out for breakfast. What about pancakes at the café?'

Excitedly, the sisters looked at each other and ran inside. Tom surveyed their work, then left the place with an echoing sneeze.

'Phew! That was close!' said Barkley. 'I thought they were going to go through the cupboard!'

'Not so fast,' directed Storm!. 'Everyone get back in your places.'

Matilda had whiskered that a man was coming. Just then, Tom appeared in the shed again. This time he started looking around, opening drawers and an old wardrobe. He nearly stepped on Storm's tail when he squeezed himself around the old dining table to look inside the writing bureau that was wedged up against the wall.

'Hello! What are you doing there?' he asked Storm.

Storm did not know what to do. 'Shall I emerge and purr loudly or race out looking frightened?'

Barkley miaowed and watched, ready to leap over the newly laid dust and take action to protect his best friend.

'Come on, out you come. I won't hurt you,' coaxed Tom.

Storm hissed and backed away further under the table, making his way to the door.

Budge and Florry heard, 'Come on, out you come,' and emerged from the cupboard.

'Is it all over then?' asked Florry. 'I didn't think I was going to breathe anymore.'

'Nah, me neither... oops!' said Budge, looking at Tom, who had spotted the cupboard open and saw the brothers emerge. He saw Storm make his exit out the door and declared, 'Gosh, that is a big cat!'

Barkley jumped down from his perch, hissing at Tom to keep away. Budge and Florry followed suit. Not knowing what to do, they started making loud cat wailing noises and marched past Tom and out the door. Barkley thought this was a good idea and followed suit, miaowing as loudly as he could, like he was ushering them out of his area. Tom stood and watched in amazement, then looked inside the opened cupboard, lifted the woollen jumper and found his tie.

Pleased he had gotten his possession back from 'the crazy cat', he picked up the old paint lid and sniffed the 'glue', then bundled up all the magazines and scratched bits of paper, took the bone that his tie had been knotted around and threw it all in the bin, along with the bird's skull, rabbit's foot and Simone's tail. The jumper also went into the rubbish but not the tie – that was going into the wash.

'Gosh, that was the biggest cat I have ever seen,' were the last words the dust heard that morning.

# Chapter Fourteen

arkley followed Budge and Florry home to their place, which was in the opposite direction to Mrs Andrews'. Instead of going over the back fence, they went out the front, turned left, crossed over, then up the street quite a way to a house that seemed to be covered in trees and bushes.

*Certainly not clean and tidy like Mrs Andrews' place.*

'You live here?' asked Barkley.

'No, this is just the way we go,' explained Budge. Up the driveway they went, past the geraniums and out the back to the vegie patch. Florry told Barkley to stick to the path and not walk on the garden or there would be hell to pay. 'They don't want paw prints in the garden,' he explained, then squeezed past the rake that had been left leaning for months and up and over the fence.

'This is us,' said Budge.

'Lynne'll be out the back, painting,' said Florry, following Budge into the room attached to the back of the house. This was her painting studio, where the boys had gotten into trouble many a time dabbing their paws into her work and traipsing it inside.

'Miaow! Miaow!' said the brothers to Lynne as they walked into her studio, followed by Barkley, who was wide-eyed, looking at everything.

'Hello, you two, where have you been this time?' quizzed Lynne, looking up from her work.

Budge and Florry sat near Lynne. 'Miaow,' they said. Lynne bent down and gave them a pat hello, then saw Barkley staring at a large canvas painting she had done years before.

'Just the cat I need,' said Lynne and picked up Barkley and put him on her worktable. 'Sit there, Barkley,' she instructed, stroking him but the visitor was having none of that. Barkley miaowed and marched around her desk, treading on everything.

'You've got all these lovely paintings!' he miaowed, roaming around.

'Come on, sit down so I can paint you,' coaxed Lynne, putting some cat biscuits down on the table. She figured cats would stay put if there was food around; they'd eat, purr, then sleep.

'Paint me? What colour are you going to paint me? I had my toes painted once,' he reminisced about the time Sarah and Beth painted their toenails and then did his.

'She's not going to put paint *on you*, Barkles, she's going to paint your picture,' explained Florry.

Barkley finished munching on his biscuits, looked at Lynne and asked, 'You haven't got a sardine, have you?' then got comfortable and sat with the best air of grace he could muster.

Lynne giggled. 'Yes, that's it. Stay there, but don't look so serious. You're not a serious cat, are you? You're a fun-loving cat.'

Barkley purred, 'Did you hear that, boys? She said I'm fun-loving. I thought I was a detective.'

'Yeah, she says the same to us,' said Budge.

Barkley sat contentedly, watching Lynne form a picture of what he looked like. There he sat, looking straight at Lynne through the page. Down the bottom she drew him in pencil playing with a ball of string, then began to fill it in with a brush. At the top of the page, she quickly drew Barkley side-on, looking down at the artwork, just like she had at her mum's place. Barkley sat, amazed how with a few strokes of a pencil and brush he suddenly appeared on the page, looking resplendent.

'What about the fancy words?' miaowed Barkley, wondering if someone else was doing that bit. Lynne ruled up a few lines on the page and out came a funny-looking pen. Letters started to slowly appear right before his eyes. Barkley turned himself around so he could read what was being written.

*Dusty shadows*
*Let me go forth,*
*Let me be unstoppable,*
*Like the flow of a river,*
*As I gather all that is required and smooth ruffles.*
*There is no such thing as fear,*

*Only the unknown,*
*And that is for exploring.*
*'I am' does not always equate to true self.*
*Let me breathe and leap,*
*Into the unknown,*
*Where excitement and discovery lie.*

On the other page she wrote:

*Look after my greatness,*
*For I am the only one.*
*I am strength that abounds and conquers all.*
*Excitement endeavours*
*To reach out and touch the void,*
*Of the unknown particle that already exists,*
*Exploring riches designed in mastery,*
*While forgetting trepidation*
*and swimming forth.*

Barkley sat patiently, watching the page come to life. Lynne peered into the funny rectangle thing that people stare at, then painted a bit more. Barkley stretched his neck, craning to see what she was looking at, and saw a picture of himself when he was sitting on the dining table at Mrs Andrews' place.

'That's me! That's me in there!' he miaowed excitedly. 'How did I get in there? Budge, Florry! I am going to be in the book! She is painting me into pictures and writing lovely words about dusty shadows and looking after greatness. I didn't know shadows could be dusty.'

*How do you clean a shadow? I must give myself a bath when I get home.*

Budge and Florry were fast asleep in front of the fire. Barkley purred loudly and licked Lynne's head to say thank you. He was so pleased he was going to be in the picture book. 'I will be on show,' he thought while he looked into Lynne's eyes as she stroked him. 'The greatest detective in these parts is going to be on display. Everyone will see how cute I am!' he chuffed, then lay down on the table and watched Lynne's pens and brushes flourish drawings and words across the pages. The ball of string he was chasing wrote across the page with 'Making Answers Obvious'.

What got to Barkley was that Budge and Florry never took anything seriously. For them, it appeared, laughing and having a good time was the only way. Barkley often wished he could giggle like they did, but he took everything too seriously. 'Detectives don't giggle; I must uphold appearances,' he would think to himself.

Yet he thought nothing of playing chasey with the children at bedtime, running around the house and hiding under Corey's bed. Before that, he used to hide under Beth or Sarah's bed, whip out a paw and tag them on their feet before returning to the darkest corner. When they were in bed, he would lie on his back under the bed and his paws would flick at their bed covers till the giggling stopped.

When he knew they were asleep, he would climb onto their bed to stay warm. It was better than sleeping in his own bed. Granted, that was where his food, water and toilet were, but he did not like using his tray as it was opposite the back door and he liked his privacy, especially if a client was coming over. Barkley was beginning to feel cold and a little tired and wondered if he might join his two pals. They looked so comfortable sleeping in the warmth of the fire.

'Just a minute,' said Lynne, giving him a pat. 'I just need one more look into your eyes... okay. Thanks, Barkley.'

Barkley jumped down and went looking for a spot around the pot belly stove that jutted out away from the wall – it was ever so warm.

Lynne kept painting her new recruit for Athena's project. She closed the studio door to keep the heat in as nighttime approached. Eventually, she put her brushes down and went to go inside.

'Budge, Florry! Dinner time! Come on, you two.'

Slowly, two sleepy-eyed cats yawned and followed Lynne inside.

As Lynne turned off the heating, one of her paintings shuffled against the wall and out popped Barkley, bleary-eyed.

'Barkley! I thought you'd gone home! Go on! Time for you to go home now! Off you go! Thanks for the visit,' said Lynne, patting him goodbye.

'See ya, Barx,' said Budge, standing at the back door.

'Yeah, see ya, Bergulz,' said Florry, unable to form words properly while half asleep.

'Night Budge, Florry. See you tomorrow,' said Barkley through yawns. Making his way home in the dark, he was glad when he jumped over their fence that the white camellias gave some semblance of light and acknowledgement that he was going the right way. It was odd seeing his hidey holes for keeping safe when the 'sky is banging' out on the footpath. His play friends were growing up and the days of Thunder Ada and Captain Dark had long since disappeared. Barkley did wonder if Corey was going to take on the spaceship, but he was more into playing over at his friend's house.

# Chapter Fifteen

The following day, Barkley visited the bushes, had a bite to eat then marched off to his office. He thought of writing Lynne a thank you note for allowing him to stay and not be shooed off. Eagerly opening the cupboard to bring out his prized possessions, to his horror, he found they were no longer there. Everything had disappeared, gone, vanished.

Barkley was so furious he could barely speak. He marched inside and looked at his family – the children were lounging on the couch watching television, Jean was gathering clothes for the washing machine and Tom was reading the paper online. Barkley miaowed the loudest he could miaow. He wanted to fill the living area with as much disdain as possible to let everyone know he was not happy. The only person who looked his way was Sarah; everyone else was engrossed in their activities. Another miaow and still no one moved. No one asked him what the matter was.

Barkley jumped up onto the dining table, glared at Tom and said, 'It was you, wasn't it?!' Tom yelled at him to get down, but Barkley was not going anywhere. He had made sure he was just beyond Tom's reach for being knocked off with a single push of the hand. Tom continued to tell Barkley to get down, standing up to pick him up and put him on the floor but recoiled when Barkley hissed at him.

'Can someone come and get this cat off the table? He's hissing at me!' yelled Tom.

Barkley jumped down, not wanting to be touched, stroked or patted. One final glance at his family and he turned and walked out the back door. If they were not going to respect his work, why should he remain there? Furious and indignant, Barkley's anger took him out to the street.

He thought a visit to Miss Fi-Fi would be nice. It would calm him down, plus he had not seen her for a while and he wanted to know how many kittens she had had; however, the thought of a piece of clay pot coming his way deterred him. He was not aware where he was going till he found himself at Storm's place, sitting on the verandah out the front, breathing in the fresh air and watching the bees buzz around the lavender bush. He saw a small boy ride his bicycle down the street, then a lady with a pram walked past, staring into the 'square thing'. Barkley did not know what those things were but he did know there was less talking at home, less playing games, less laughter and less spontaneity. Everyone seemed to be so fascinated by those things, as they stared at them constantly. Even Lynne had one, as he had seen himself in it. He wished the games in the 'star flip end prize' out the back had not come to an end. Storm's front door opened and Carla emerged with Nick.

'Do you need anything from the shops, honey? Oh, look! There's that cat again. Hello, Puss. He must be lost, you know,' she said, bending down to stroke Barkley who was having none of it. 'Okay, well, maybe next time. Come on, Nick, let's go.'

Barkley listened to Carla explaining to Nick the time when he barged into Storm's place, only yesterday, when he was looking for help with his possessions in the shed. After her car drove off, peace and quietude resumed for a second till he heard laughter and feet thumping on the wooden floorboards.

*It certainly isn't this loud with my family.*

'Hello, Detective,' said Storm, approaching from around the back.

'Morning, Storm, I'm staying with you from now on,' said Barkley, a look of disgust on his face.

'Have you not had a good morning?' asked his giant pal.

'They have… (sigh) they have taken everything we put in the cupboard. The woollen thing, my glue, paper, letters for scratching and Simone's tail is gone. Bob the Bunnykin's foot has disappeared, as well as Patch's skull. The thing I used to drag my bones around with has also gone. It's all gone. I can't stay there anymore. They don't respect my work and the efforts I go to. I'm moving in with you. Thank Felidae you have excellent tucker!' said Barkley, still surveying the surrounds.

'That is very disappointing. I thought we'd covered all bases. What are you going to do? How are you going to write your notes?'

'I'm not making any more notes! I'm staying here. I'll run my office from here.'

'Well, if you do decide to stay, be prepared to be run over by toys, stabbed by swords and have your tail pulled on a daily basis. If you're lucky, the boys will throw you a bit of sausage when they have that for dinner. I'm not keen on the mashed potato it comes with and the sauce is not to my liking either. Apart from all that, make yourself at home.'

Barkley said nothing.

'What about all your clues from Mao, are they still under the house?'

'I presume so, I haven't looked,' replied the detective, too indignant to summon any enthusiasm for solving the case.

'Shall we go and have a look? I'll come with you,' suggested his friend with the deep, calming voice.

Barkley said nothing but continued to look around, absorbing his surroundings as the sun slowly rose in the sky. Storm smooched his friend silently, then went around the back to finish his breakfast, leaving his pal to his thoughts so he could calm down and allow rational thinking to return.

*Lovely day, but I cannot think with all that racket going on!*

Suddenly, the front door burst open and out popped two giggling swords, which pointed at Barkley, yelled, 'Waaaaahhhhh!' then ran back inside, leaving the door open. Barkley could feel the warmth from inside the house escaping and wondered if he should find a place in front of the fire or somewhere nice and cosy, when a small girl in a pink dress looked out and shut the door.

The notes under the house were bugging him.

*Are they still there? What do I do if they aren't?*

Curiosity getting the better of him, he made his way home to investigate.

*I really will leave home if the notes are all gone!*

Squeezing himself through the gap, Barkley allowed his eyes to adjust to the darkness under the house. Looking around for all the notes – there they were, where he had left them. Phew! What a relief!

*Wait a minute! I can smell perfume.*

There, scratched into the dirt was:

*When the moon is full,*
*meet me under the lemon tree*
*Mao*

*A message from Mao! Does she know I don't know how many letters there are? What lemon tree? When is the moon full next?*

Barkley had not paid any attention to the moon of late as he was too busy working on this case that was taking too long to solve. Neither did he know if the sky would be clear enough to see what stage the moon was at. There was only one lemon tree that he knew of and that was two doors up. Barkley calmed down and decided he could rest now. He was finally going to meet Mao. She would tell him what he wanted to know and hopefully help him with his alphabet and spelling, like how to tell the difference between 'b, d, p and q' and what is the difference between that funny looking 3 and B?

Barkley made his way to a sunny spot in the garden for a sleep.

*All is well now. Mao will answer my questions and the case will be solved.*

Barkley sighed as he drifted into dreamland. The imagined warmth kept Barkley asleep all day, till a giant shadow came over and a deep purring sound penetrated his slumber. Barkley woke and stretched.

'I thought you had moved out of home?' queried Storm.

'I came back to check if Mao's notes were all there.'

'And?'

'Yes, they are, and she has left me a note saying she will meet me under the lemon tree when the moon is full. Would you come with me? It might be good to have you as back up should anything happen,' explained Barkley.

'I doubt you'll need me, but yes, I'll come.'

'Mao is going to tell me how many letters there are,' said Barkley, still thinking of his dream he had.  Soon it will all be over, case closed. 'Do you think I need to be aware of anything?'

'No, I don't think so. Besides, so far, we have no evidence that Mao is an unsavoury sort. I will come with you. Should anything go wrong, my presence alone should put a stop to things,' said Storm. Barkley sighed, relieved that all was now working out well.

'She is friends with Titch though, so she might be unsavoury. She might bring him as back up,' contemplated the small Burmese with the cute nose.

'Yes, that's true. Is she referring to the lemon tree that everyone visits?' queried giant whiskers in return.

'I think so. At least, that is where I'm going.'

The lemon tree in front of the flats a few doors up from Barkley was popular, as everyone in the neighbourhood discreetly stole a lemon here and there for cooking and drinking purposes.

'At least you'll be on neutral ground,' said Storm.

'I was thinking you could hide in the big tree or on top of the roof where they put their cars. What do you think?' asked Barkley, negotiating vantage points with Storm.

'Okay, I think on top of the roof would be best. That way I can stay back a bit and keep an ear out, then if things start to take off, I can jump down,' he suggested.

'Excellent idea!' said Barkley, continuing to bathe his belly in Storm's shadow.

Storm watched his mate arch onto his back and stretch his paws up to the sky, then with a smile said, 'Well, I shan't expect you for dinner then,' and went home.

Barkley, like most cats, loved sleeping in the sun. It was great to have some natural warmth on him. He thought about going back to sleep, but decided instead to fetch all of Mao's notes from under the house and lay them out once again on his desk in his now tidy office with no running fountain when it rained.

Barkley did not like crawling under the house, only because it was a tight squeeze and when he tried to get out there was nothing to push off from as the ground was lower. Scrambling and wriggling through the gap, he always ended up falling face-first till he got his front legs through and managed to break his fall. It was not easy doing this with things in your mouth either, and trying not to drop them or put teeth marks in them would leave his saliva dripping.

Barkley made three trips under the house to get the small pieces of paper, then took them to the old wooden shed, only to find that he could not get the door open. He miaowed and stood up at the handle, scratching and pawing at it. To no avail, the door was not going to open; the new padlock was not going to let him in.

This had been his office for years! He had done all his thinking in there, received clients, and in summer slept there, listening to the possums and bats make their racket all night long. From here he had gone wandering around the neighbourhood, peeped here, sniffed there, made deposits in other people's gardens front and back and found refuge when he needed quiet time from his family after the days of playing spaceships.

This was just the place for a small detective with an exceptionally cute nose, only now it was locked and the chance of entry had been permanently denied. At least he still had the notes from Mao and could keep working on his current case – but now he had no work zone, no office, nowhere to munch on the dried fish his clients brought him as payment for his services.

*Oh, for a sardine!*

Barkley gathered the notes again and slipped them through the wood slats that skirted the house.

*What to do now? Where do I run my office from?*

Barkley suspected it was the father who had put the lock on. He could speculate and was pretty sure he would be right, but what to do?

*Perhaps Sarah will assist me in opening the door. Yes, she might be able to help me. She seems to understand my needs more than the others.*

The dappled sunlight and warmth on his body had made him very sleepy. Even though Barkley would normally be stomping angry, he was still half dazed from his joyful slumber in the sun as he had not slept well in a long time. The thing with working on any case is it gnaws away at you constantly till it is solved and the end result is brought to fruition.

*Perhaps I should move in with Storm? Wait a bit, what if I move in with Mrs Andrews? No, she is fed up with me now. Move to Budge and Florry's place? Lynne seemed to like me. I am in a dilemma of what to do. How is anyone going to find me now that my office has been forcibly taken away from me? Felidae! Felidae! Felidae! Miss Fi-Fi knows about dilemmas. I will go and speak with her.*

Off Barkley trotted to see the new mother, thinking discussing kittens would be a good excuse to ask her about how to overcome being in a dilemma.

The sun was low in the sky and the warmth of the day had gone when he left for Miss Fi-Fi's. It seemed pretty quiet when he arrived there.

*Shall I risk it and slip through the cat flap and make my way inside?*

Barkley hid behind the glasshouse, kept an eye on the back door and sent Miss Fi-Fi whisker messages that he was there and hoped she would emerge.

No response.

He tried a small miaow to alert her, then a louder miaow. The pot-throwing lady appeared with a mop, looking like she was ready to attack anyone who came near. Barkley decided not to take any chances and went to leave. Just as he approached the car parked in the driveway, he watched Mr and Mrs Longford get in and drive away.

*Now is my chance to sneak inside!*

Barkley ran around to the back door and pushed through the cat flap. He knew where Miss Fi-Fi was as he had been in her room before. She had a whole room to herself, not like Barkley, who only had a small space in the laundry. Turning left into the kitchen, Barkley's eyes boggled as he saw notices on all the cupboards – 'le pain', 'les assiettes', 'coutellerie', 'les tasses', 'les verres', 'casseroles et poêles', 'plateaux de service', 'pommes de terre', 'le journal', only he could not understand any of it.

*I can't read any of this! They must be bad at spelling, like me.*

Down the corridor he found Miss Fi-Fi's bedroom and read another sign on the door that he could not make out 'Chambre de Fi-Fi'. He pushed the door open and miaowed.

'Miss Fi-Fi? Hello?' Quietly, he crept in and saw his French friend asleep in a basket with five little kittens nuzzling her belly. Barkley gushed. He was so proud to see the little ones and that his friend was doing well. Out he tip-toed without disturbing them and made his way through the cat flap and into the garden.

'She's doing alright, isn't she?' said Budge.

'Budge! Florry! What are you doing here?' asked a startled Barkley.

'Same as you. We've come to see how the little ones are. We come every week around this time.'

Barkley pondered what on earth time was and how do you know when it's about?

'That's when they go out and we come in,' Budge explained, with Florry giggling in agreement.

'Has she seen you come in?'

'No. Not yet. We are VERY careful not to be seen, aren't we?' said Budge.

'I mean Miss Fi-Fi, has she seen you yet? Have you seen the kittens?'

'Oh yeah, we saw them a couple of days after they were born,' said Florry.

Barkley sometimes thought that Budge and Florry were so akin to each other if you squinted just a bit, they would turn into one giant cat with two heads and would answer each other's questions.

'Is she awake, then?' asked Budge, his head at the cat flap, ready to push himself through.

'No, she is fast asleep with her kittens,' said Barkley.

'So, how's the case going, Barkles?' asked Florry.

'Not bad. I'm meeting Mao on the full moon,' he said.

'You're going to meet Mao? Can we come?' asked the boys in unison.

'If you want. Storm will be there.'

'Oh. Well, you know what? I think I need to have a bath then. Sorry Barx. I'm busy. I'd like to come, but you know, a cat has to do what a cat has to do,' said Florry, looking at Budge for confirmation.

'Yeah, well, he will visit Lilly and make himself sick on her tucker, then gets the trots after, won't he? Why do you have to keep seeing her?' asked Budge.

'I don't know. I think she likes my company,' replied Florry.

Budge looked at Barkley and nodded his head in Florry's direction as if to say, 'You can't help them, can you?'

'Well, I'm going home for dinner now. Bye Budge and Florry. Oh, and before I forget, they've locked my office, so I won't be able to receive guests till the problem is solved,' said the detective matter-of-factly, trying to hide extreme disappointment in his voice.

'What? What are you going to do now they've taken your office away?' asked Florry.

'I don't know. I'll think of something,' said Barkley, feeling the pain of no longer having a place to call his own.

'You want us to get you some paper and a bone so you can write them a letter?' asked Florry.

*Why didn't I think of that?*

'Yes. That would be wonderful, and some letters as well. I will need letters to stick down. As I have nowhere to work from, could I do it from your place? Perhaps from Lynne's work room, or do you have a shed I could use?' asked Barkley, getting excited that he could have a chance to communicate with people again.

'Gosh, don't know, Barx. We'll have to think about it, won't we Flor? Lynne locks her room after she is finished for the day,' said Budge.

'It keeps the possums out,' responded Florry.

'Okay, well, see you,' said Barkley, not wanting to talk about the fact that his business was crumbling. The thought of returning to being an ordinary cat was too depressing when you can have so much excitement, even though this case was the hardest he had ever taken on. Before leaving, he watched the brothers squeeze their thickset bodies through the cat flap. Even though they were not as huge as Storm, they had large feet and square shoulders, unlike Miss Fi-Fi, who was as slender as they come.

Barkley returned home, ate dinner and sat next to Sarah for the evening. He thought if he paid her some attention and spent time with her, he could call her to come and open his office for him. Then, whiskers willing, all this nonsense of blocking his lucrative business would be forgotten about, otherwise he would have to resort to another episode of Band-Aids at bedtime.

The household slept well that night. Barkley stayed inside and made sure he slept on Sarah's bed, something he would not normally do, and even though it was Corey's turn to 'feed the cat', he miaowed for Sarah to get his breakfast, imagining afterwards he would urge her to go outside. What he did not know was it was now a school day, so everyone was up early and off to wherever they went, leaving a bored cat sleeping and waiting till they came home.

That night, just after dinner, Barkley watched the moon slowly rise in the sky.

*Almost full, not quite. Tomorrow, I meet Mao.*

It was like being in limbo – the excitement of meeting your greatest adversary and getting your questions answered all at once.

*What shall I say to her? Should I be nice and pleasant or be serious and ask questions first? Shall I tell her if she misbehaves she'll have me to deal with me first and Storm second? Shall I play aloof, turn up late and suss her out first before I show myself? I think the first thing I should do is give her one of my cards, only I don't have any and making one this time of year is… is… yes, well.*

*I don't want to appear too eager to know how many letters there are in the alphabet and I can't show her my letters I send to people as I no longer have any means of writing. Besides, her spelling is probably impeccable; it would have to be, her writing is so neat. She has probably never put a paw wrong in her life! Where does that leave me?*

*The nincompoop of the neighbourhood – can't spell and can't detect! I must ask her why the Great King Cat in Kitty Cavern is a girl. I must also ask her why she was stealing everyone's collars.*

*So many questions! I hope I get answers, otherwise I am not worthy of being called Detective Inspector.*

# Chapter Sixteen

**Mao Day**

Barkley had eaten all his breakfast and was pestering for more. He figured if he filled his belly up he would sleep all day, be well rested, have time to give himself a bath and be ready to meet Mao at the appointed rising full moon. As he began to doze under the sofa, he wondered if he should ask Mao what time is.

*Time, ty-em, toom, tiemm – how do you spell it? One more question to ask. Do you think she would give me spelling lessons?'*

Barkley pondered these questions as his thoughts turned into gentle breathing and a peaceful sleep in a quiet house with everyone out.

'Barkley! Barkley! BARKLEY!'

'Huh? What is it? Who's there?'

'BARKLEY! It's us! Storm, Matilda – and Titch is also here,' called Storm, miaowing from the back door.

'What's wrong?' Barkley asked, making his way to the locked door.

'You tell him,' said Titch, with his usual furrowed brow.

'Titch says Mao said you are to come on your own. You are not to bring anyone with you,' explained Storm, his deep voice easily penetrating the wooden door for Barkley to hear him.

'Oh, bother! I felt safer knowing Storm was going to be there,' he sighed. 'Okay, I will go alone. Hang on a minute, how does she know I was going to bring someone with me?'

'Because she said she knew you would do that,' said Titch, talking as loudly as he could through the door.

'How does she know? Why is she sending you as her messenger?' asked Barkley, now peeved he had to meet her on his own. If it turned nasty he would just have to try and box her ears as best he could.

'Oh Barkles, you don't know what she knows but you'll soon find out, and don't you go mashing her up, either. She really is a cut above the rest of the felines around here,' said Titch.

'You miaow for yourself!' said Matilda. 'If you want a cut above the rest of us felines, I'll give you one!'

'See what I mean? And you wonder why I'm grumpy all the time!' Titch glared at Matilda.

'I thought you were grumpy because you want to be called Jonathan, son of Magician.'

'It means I am son of the Great King Cat in the sky!'

Storm moved himself between the two of them and told them in his deep voice to calm down and focus. Titch was having none of it and stomped off home, reminding Barkles to 'Watch it, or else!'

'Someone's home, I'll get them to let me out,' said Barkley on hearing the front door open.

In came Sarah and Beth, home from school. On went the telly, off went their shoes, bags flung on the floor. Barkley miaowed to be let out but no movement occurred, so he pranced at the front door like he needed a wee, then jumped up onto the coffee table and miaowed his loudest to get their attention.

*Tsk! Finally! The effort I have to go to just to get some attention around here these days! Oh, how I miss those days of playing in my office and dodging spaceships everywhere! At least we had fun, laughing and giggling, playing outside. Now it's just like talking to your teddy bear and getting no answer.*

The front door opened and Barkley ran out, through the gap between the gate and house and around to the back door to see his friends.

'Hello,' he said.

'I'm happy to wait in the garden next door, Barkley, if you need any help,' suggested Matilda, who did not want to be left out of any excitement.

'Thanks Matilda, but I think I had better do as Mao says. I have many questions to ask her and if she suspects anything I might not get my answers. I need to get her to trust me before I can rely on any assistance,' explained Barkley, now nervous that when the sun began to set and the moon began to rise, he would be meeting his greatest adversary yet.

'Hey, Sarah! Come and look at this!' said Beth.

'What is it?'

'It's that giant cat dad was talking about. You know the really big one he saw in the shed the other day? He is standing over Barkley like he's going to beat him up or something. Look how big he is! I've never seen a cat that big. Wait, I'll get my phone – I want to get a picture!' Beth ran from peering out the kitchen window to get her phone.

'Hey! That looks like Nick's cat, Albie!' declared Sarah.

'Who's Nick?'

'He's a boy in my class. His cat went missing. He showed me a photo. Looks just like him,' said Sarah, then opened the back door.

'Hey Puss! Whatcha doing? Hey? Albie, come here boy! Come on! I won't hurt you!'

Matilda scarpered as fast as she could. 'Not hanging around here!'

Storm stood wide-eyed, wondering what to do. Beth appeared and took photos of Barkley and Storm standing next to each other.

'Look how big he is! He towers over Barkley!' said Beth.

'I think he must be friendly as he doesn't look like he's going to beat him up. Albie, come on, Albie. Come and say hello,' coaxed Sarah.

'Wait, go and get some cat biscuits and throw a few down. Maybe he'll eat them,' suggested Beth, taking as many photos as she could.

'This is my cue to say goodbye, Detective Inspector. I will see you tomorrow if I don't hear from you before. Good luck tonight!' said Storm as he ran for the back fence and jumped over it, taking one last look back to see if anyone was coming.

'Did you see how quickly he made it to the back fence? Three leaps and he was there! Gosh, that must be some cat!' declared Beth. 'I'll send you some photos so you can show Nick.'

'Thanks!'

Barkley watched the two sisters and wished they were that excited to see him every day!

'Barkley! Come on, come inside,' said Sarah, in the process of shutting the door.

From Barkley's back door you walked into the laundry which housed the washing machine and dryer. Under the shelves on the back wall, behind the door, was Barkley's area. To the right from the entrance was a sliding door that took you into the kitchen, where there was a breakfast bar that came around to the sliding door. On the other side of the kitchen was the dining area, and all this overlooked the lounge room. When Barkley was young, he would climb onto the dining chairs, hop up onto the table, then jump onto the kitchen benches because whatever they were making smelt so good he wanted some too. All he got was being yelled at, a smacked bottom and shoved into the laundry with the door shut.

Barkley got up and lazily walked inside, had a drink from his water bowl and decided to cuddle up on Sarah's lap. Some gentle stroking would help calm his nerves about meeting Mao in a few hours, also, he still wanted her to open his office for him. Eventually, Barkley began to calm down and slowly nodded his head into a gentle doze.

The noise of the front door opening with Jean and Corey coming home woke him up. Corey never came straight home after school; he stayed at Will's place till Jean picked him up. Out flew the orders, 'Beth, feed the cat. Sarah, peel the potatoes and both of you put your school things away. Corey, you too. Put your things away and get in the bath so you're ready for bed.'

Barkley was too nervous to eat his dinner.

*What if it all goes wrong with Mao? I'll be all on my own.*

Feeling panicked, he did his best to stay calm.

*Another drink of water will help calm my nerves.*

Barkley pestered to go outside. Off into the bushes for a wee and a deposit, then to the designated meeting place. He climbed the wattle tree that grew next to the lemon and waited till the glow of the moon started to rise in the sky, then came down, sat and waited.

*What do I say when I meet her? I can't give her a business card; my office is locked and they probably were all thrown out anyway. What was that?*

Barkley startled on hearing rustling behind him.

*Possums! I shall wait. What if she doesn't turn up till the moon is high in the sky?*

Waiting… waiting… then he heard the sweetest voice he had ever heard.

'Good evening, Detective Inspector Barkley Button Nose. I am Mao, Master of Academic Observances.'

Barkley whizzed his head around to the direction of her voice.

Finally, he faced Mao for the first time. The last time he saw her was when he was chasing her down the street and had not been able to see her face, now here she was, a black cat with white belly and legs, lovely blue eyes and a warm smile. She smelt nice too.

Barkley swallowed. 'Good evening to you, Mao. I am Barkley, Master of… Button Noses,' he replied, stunned by how sweet she was and not really knowing what else to say.

Mao giggled, 'Yes, I am aware of who you are. I have been enlightened and entertained by your detective service. You seem to have a knack for following your nose, probably why it is so cute.'

Barkley blushed. Here was the great Mao, a master, paying him a compliment.

Mao continued, 'Perhaps you would like to extend your knowledge into greater fields and see where it takes you?'

*Knowledge? Me? I can't even spell properly! What are you going to do, tie me down till I learn the alphabet once and for all?*

Was Mao going to yell at him for not knowing how to spell and tell the difference between the letters that gave him trouble? Then he asked, 'Why all the secrecy? Why couldn't you just come and say hello like everyone else?'

'I did come and say hello, every time you dozed in your office. You didn't hear me. I spoke to you quietly and you did not respond, so I tried a different tactic to get your attention, one that I thought would last for a long time,' she replied.

'You came and said hello when I slept in my office? I don't remember hearing you at all. Why not come during waking hours?'

'I came at different times; did you not hear me purring?' she asked.

'Are you going to tell me how many letters there are in the alphabet?' Barkley plucked up his courage and asked her more questions, 'Are you wanting to move into my place with me? And what's with all the notes you've been leaving around the place?'

'There are 26 letters in the alphabet, just as Miss Fi-Fi told you. I am not moving in with you. It is a pity you've lost your office, but for now, let me help you with your letters. B is for belly,' she said, drawing a line down her back and a round part for the belly. 'C is for cat and f is for feline, which is the same as cat or f for Felidae. D is for dog,' she motioned, again drawing a line down her back but putting the round part behind her with her tail.

'G is for goodnight,' she drew a round shape over her belly and hooked her tail around while making a snoring sound. 'P is for people because they have long legs and their head is up there. Q is when you are questing for answers, which is what you have been doing. You have been questing to get your questions answered,' she explained sweetly.

'How do I know which is which when they change shape?' asked Barkley, beginning to understand. He liked the way she explained belly and dog; he could use it as bait next time he tormented Regie.

Mao giggled and drew two circles around her belly and motioned 'bell-ee' but added it was difficult without any letters or drawing tools to show him.

'We can go to Budge and Florry's place. They have drawing tools. They are supposed to be bringing me paper and… and letters for me to scratch out,' said Barkley, looking forlorn now as he could not write fluently like Mao.

'I will sing you a song, you follow.' Mao jumped up onto the branches of the large wattle tree and began, 'A, b, c, d, e, f, g… h, i, j, k, l, m, n, o, p… q, r, s, t, u, v,… w, x, y and zee.'

Barkley laughed, 'I remember that now. The little-uns used to sing that when they came home from school. I still don't know how to tell the difference between some of the letters. They change shape and I get confused.'

'That's okay, if you will allow, I will help you along the way and then the letters will come all by themselves,' responded Mao.

Barkley thought for a second and asked, 'What does that mean and how do you know that these letters are the ones that give me trouble?'

'Because when I was learning how to read and write, I had the same issue.'

Barkley looked wide-eyed at Mao. 'You had to learn how to spell too? I thought everything came to you perfectly!' Barkley continued with another question, 'Why were you stealing everyone's collars?'

'I did not steal anyone's collars. I suggest you look elsewhere for that answer, perhaps somewhere closer to home.'

'Does that mean you know who it was?'

'This is your case, Barkley; I respect that you are the one solving the crimes. As I said, I suggest you look closer,' was all Mao said.

*Why the heck does she speak in riddles? I've waited long enough for all this and now I'm not getting any answers. I can't be bothered. I think I might go home and seek advice elsewhere. Lynne knows stuff, maybe she can tell me where Athena lives.*

'I am not being difficult. I came to create knowledge with you, important knowledge. The stealing of collars is irrelevant, isn't it? When was the last time a collar was stolen?' asked Mao like she could read Barkley's thoughts.

'That's true. No one has had their collar stolen for ages. In fact, only Budge, Florry, Miss Fi-Fi and Zenya, have had their collars stolen. So, all the cryptic notes you wrote? Where did you get them from?'

'I did not write them. They came from a place much higher than I could imagine,' explained Mao.

'You mean the Great King Cat in Kitty Cavern gave them to you?' asked Barkley, gasping in disbelief. 'You've met the Great King Cat? And? Is she a girl like Budge and Florry said?'

Mao giggled again; this was too funny.

Barkley had so many questions he began asking them before Mao could take a breath and gather her thoughts to answer the previous one. 'Why is Miss Fi-Fi in a dilemma? Why does Storm need belonging glue? What is belonging glue? Why do Budge and Florry need to sing? Why have you befriended Titch, the street grump? Am I not a better friend than he is? I don't go around beating everyone up like he does.'

Barkley looked at her with such anticipation, expecting all the answers to come flying back at him as fast as he had spat out his questions. He knew his nerves were getting the better of him. He wanted to appear grand in Mao's eyes, yet here he was letting his fears get at him again.

'My dear Barkley, shall we take a breath to a paw? There is plenty of time for me to answer all your questions. Perhaps it would be better if I told you a little of myself? As I mentioned, I am Mao. I am one among many who have been trained in the art of Academic Observances. I met my Master when I was a kitten in the Temple of Little Ming. I was a disciple in learning the art of measuring the way forward. It was a most fortunate time for me and I think it would be good for you too, hence I am passing on what I know.'

'And you want me to be your next dis... dis-y-ple?' asked a wide-eyed cat full of 'I can't believe this is happening!'

'You are already a disciple. I merely want to extend your repertoire,' said Mao, puffing up her fur to stay warm, which made her sweet perfume waft around the trees.

Barkley did not know what to say. He felt proud that the Great Mao was telling him that under her guidance he would be greater still. Instead of openly accepting the invitation, he responded with yet another question.

'I have not seen you before. You must have recently moved into this area?'

Mao was looking directly at Barkley, waiting for a response of either yes, that would be wonderful or no, not my thing. She had to pause a moment to answer his question, but decided to deflect by saying, 'The family I am with have been here for some time now.'

'Yes, but where do you live?' asked an eager button nose with whiskers.

'If you will allow me, I will take you there,' said Mao, standing up in readiness to go.

*Go to Mao's place? See where she lives? It could be a trap. Then again, she could be legitimate. Just think of the clues I could find!*

'Okay, I'll come with you,' responded Barkley, wanting to prove he really was the detective of the moment.

Down the street they went, around the corner past Miss Fi-Fi's place, then over the road where he would normally turn to go to Titch's place should he have the need to see the street fighter (though highly unlikely). They kept going down the street.

*Is this some sort of trick. How far is she taking me? Has she got a friend called George who is going to eat me alive or something? Is she going to finish me off for good and take over my business?*

They ran through a small park with children's play equipment and on into the next street. Mao stopped at the third house along, 'This is me.'

Barkley felt a long way from home. He had never been this far before, except when he was put into the car, under protesting miaows of, 'I don't want to go! I don't want to go!' Trying not to look scared and wanting to run home, Barkley puffed up his chest like Storm had shown him and marched up the driveway like he was a king in the making of Mao's discipleship. Mao watched him saunter and giggled yet again.

Barkley sat by the back door and listened. He could hear loud talking, lots of laughter, giggling, music playing, TV going, small footsteps running on wooden floorboards, glasses chinked, cutlery clashed and plates were splashed under a tap as the dishwasher was loaded and the go button was pressed. The voices then faded away into another room. The backyard, Barkley observed, was not tidy like Mrs Andrews' place was but was laid out with beds decorated with garden stakes. It all seemed pretty bare, except for one which was lush with beans. A spade and rake leaned against one empty garden bed. A pair of gloves covered in mud looked like they were gnarled and needed to stretch out to rid themselves of a hard day's work. Barkley watched a possum run up one of the trees, then turned and looked at Mao as if to say, 'Now what?'

Mao escorted Barkley to the back of the yard, where she climbed the branches of a tree, up into a treehouse. Using his claws to steady himself, Barkley followed, high into the sky.

*Perhaps this was what she meant when she said the words came from a higher place? Perhaps the tree told her? No, she has befriended a possum that can miaow! It would be more pleasant than the grunting noise they make! Maybe she has a snake for a friend and this is where he lives? Thus his ability to write so neatly! Snakes are supposed to have great wisdom.*

Mao sat and listened to her family talking and having fun. She enjoyed it when they were laughing and joking around. Suddenly, Barkley could smell something he had not smelt in a long time.

'Dried fish?' asked Mao, pointing to a packet of what Barkley called sardines.

Unable to help himself, Barkley eagerly said, 'Don't mind if I do!' and hooked in a paw and pulled out a fish.

*Ahh! The sweet taste of salty fish to chew on! This is the life! Up here in the treehouse tucked away from everyone, full moon, clear skies, sardines. All I need now is some of that milk Mrs Andrews gave me.*

Barkley felt he had come home. 'You get sardines as well?'

'No. I snitched them from your office,' Mao replied.

Barkley looked at her like 'What a cheek!' and took another, continuing to munch on what he considered to be his payment for services rendered.

'Did you know, from up here you can see the moon better?' asked Mao, gazing through one of the windows of the tree house that was normally used to spy on approaching imaginary enemies. Barkley did not respond. Sardine in his mouth, he just looked at Mao, at the moon, and continued listening to the frivolity in the house beyond the non-existent vegetable patch.

'Your family seems very nice,' said Barkley, commenting on how well they all played together.

'Yes, they are. The Ming Temple gave me an aptitude for resilience with children when they are learning to walk and talk,' said Mao.

'You should talk to Storm about that. He has had his fair share of having his fur pulled, tail tugged, being ridden like a horse and being run over by scooters up and down the hallway. I don't know how he does it, but he takes solace at Mrs Andrews' place, and just as well. He has her to thank for looking after him and feeding him that delicious tucker she has,' said Barkley, drooling for some yummy milk.

'Yes, Storm certainly is a giant character, isn't he?'

'I know you've been dropping your notes at everyone's door. Would you like to meet them face-to-face instead?' asked Barkley, looking directly into her glistening blue eyes.

'Yes, that would be lovely,' she said. 'I will follow your…'

Just then, two possums emerged into the small enclosure from the branches above, then continued down the trunk to the ground to forage for food. Barkley was taken back a bit. He had not been that close to a possum before. Mao just sat quietly and the nighttime wildlife passed through without noticing two cats being dusted in moonlight.

'You know, I thought you were trying to take my business away from me. I thought that was why you turned up and left all those cryptic notes, so you could outwit me and take my clientele away,' said Barkley, being honest with his new friend.

'Well, I thought I'd bring you up here first, tie you up and then take your business away from you,' said Mao with a straight face, then burst out laughing.

Barkley froze for a bit, before realising she was joking.

'Well, thank you for bringing me here. If you don't mind, I think I would like to retire for the evening,' said Barkley, wanting some warmth.

'You are welcome to stay here. Your office is now locked and you have no way to write your ransom notes, so you can stay here if you want,' suggested Mao.

Barkley found her voice so sweet and relaxing he could have asked her to read him the writing on the packet of sardines over and over as he indulged himself in a salty morsel and had Mao's sweet voice in his ear.

'You mean sleep up here all night? I think…'

'No, I mean sleep here with me,' said Mao. 'It's up to you, but you are most welcome.'

'Won't they wonder what you're doing bringing another feline inside? Won't I be shooed away?'

'No, not in the slightest. Come on,' said Mao, jumping down out of the tree and making her way across the garden. 'What are you waiting for? Come on curious Barkley Button Nose!'

Barkley sighed, jumped down out of the treehouse and followed Mao.

*Is this when she ties me up?*

Mao made her way not inside the house but through a door slightly ajar and to the left of the back entrance. This was a separate room that housed a washing machine and dryer that kept the place warm pretty much all the time; towards the back was a small bed, food, and to Barkley's delight, a clean water bowl.

'I get shut in the laundry too, only your place is way nicer than mine!' he sighed.

*I think I could really get used to living here in the lap of luxury!*

'Help yourself to anything you want,' offered Mao and sat down to have a bath.

Barkley had a drink of water, which he noticed was nice and cool. He never dared drink from the bowl in his office, but he did like to sit and watch the bugs swim around in circles till they either managed to climb out or became part of the decomposing muck. Barkley decided he would also have a bath and sat on the floor to give his new friend space on her bed. When she was finished, she curled up and went to sleep. Barkley edged himself onto the bed and listened to her soft purring. He was certain he had heard her purring sound before but was not sure where.

The dawn chorus commenced and after the sun was well and truly in the sky, Barkley woke to the laundry door being opened with a pile of clothes to be washed. Startled, he jumped up and ran out, not even stopping to see who was carrying the basket or the astonished look on their face. Mao woke, stretched, then went back to sleep. Barkley made his way home as fast as he could.

*Can I even remember the way? Is it out to the front or over the back fence?*

He went out to the road to get his bearings, turned left, slipped through the playground and ran up the street, clinging to the fences all the way. Up the drive to the front door, 'Miaow, miaow.'

Bang the door.

Round the back, 'Miaow, miaow,' at the door. Bang the door, 'Miaow, miaow.' No one was home, so no breakfast for him this morning.

# Chapter Seventeen

Frustrated, Barkley made his way to Storm's place, hoping to get something to eat. No answer came.

*Where is everyone? Why isn't anyone answering my cries? I'll go and visit Budge and Florry; at least there I have not worn out my welcome.*

'Morning, Barkles! What brings you here so early?' asked Budge, having just come outside through the cat flap, Florry close behind him.

'Hi boys. I am wondering if… if… I have not eaten yet and everyone at my place has left for the day. Do you have any spare tucker for me?' asked Barkley, looking hungry and forlorn at the same time.

Budge looked at Florry, who had just finished gorging himself and was still licking his whiskers.

'Sure. Flor here was just about to go visit Lilly so he can make himself sick again, weren't you, Flor? You'd better go inside and a feed,' said Budge, motioning to Barkley that he would need to squeeze through the cat flap.

'So, how was your meeting with Mao last night?' Florry asked.

'Oh yeah, Barkles. Tell us how it was. What's she like? How long did the meeting last?' Budge was eager to hear the response.

'It went really well. She is extremely nice and sweet. I have only just left her place now. That is why my family are all out and I am very hungry,' explained Barkley.

'You were there all night? What did you do? Where does she live?' continued Budge, while Florry burped after eating too much.

'Yeah, do tell!' said Florry enthusiastically.

'Well, she is extremely sweet and smiles all the time. She lives in a nice house, way down the way in the next road. She took me up into a tree house and I had some sardines, then spent the night next to her in her room,' explained Barkley, looking hungry.

'Looks like you got a twinkle in your eye, Barx! Looks like you got a twinkle!' said Budge, looking at Florry and laughing.

'Where's Lynne? Will she mind if I come in and eat?'

'Nah, she's gone to the shops, hasn't she,' said Florry.

'Okay, great,' said Barkley, then pushed himself through the cat flap onto a wooden floor with high ceilings and Victorian architraves and corbels.

Budge took Barkley to their eating area and allowed him to eat what was left of their breakfast and have a drink of water. To Barkley's surprise, their tucker was not served in the laundry like his and Mao's. They had their own area in the corner of the kitchen, next to the dining table. On the wall above was a small, gold-framed painting of the two brothers walking along the footpath – they looked so sweet, the best of chums, with a laugh just about to emerge.

'Thanks boys,' said Barkley, feeling better. 'You sure do have a nice place here,' he said, roaming around and having a good look. He could see why the boys liked to decorate the place with their muddy paws; he would do the same given the chance. The hallway he entered was wider than his own, had wooden floors and paintings hung on the walls on both sides; he presumed done by Lynne herself. There were more paintings in the kitchen, lounge room, and two large ones in the dining room.

'It sure is sumptuous here, and to think you have the run of this place all to yourself,' said Barkley, with a look in his eye of *I'm moving in here! I can get paper from Lynne and set myself up in the corner of her art studio, glue my letters down, she can help me with my spelling and I'm still running a business! All I have to do is tell everyone I've moved office!*

'Yeah, it's pretty cool here and Lynne looks after us well, doesn't she, Flor?' responded Budge.

'Yeah, she does,' agreed his brother.

Florry noticed one of their ping pong balls on the floor and flicked it over to Budge, who flicked it to Barkley. They had a lovely time chasing the small bouncy ball around the floor, flicking it here and there and tossing it into the air. Barkley had never had so much fun.

'Hey, do you want to hear our song we've been singing?' asked Florry.

'Yes, please!' said Barkley excitedly.

*If you are ever in need of a chat,*
*Just come and see us cats.*
*I'm called Budge,*
*He's called Florry,*
*Together we make Fudge and Blorry!*

The boys sang together, giggling their heads off.

Barkley laughed and laughed. He could not believe how much of a good time these two had together.

'Where do you two sleep?' asked Barkley, wondering if they had a bed in the laundry like he did.

'Most of the time we sleep with Lynne,' said Budge, showing Barkley the big bed they slept on.

Barkley was amazed.

'You get to eat in the kitchen and sleep with Lynne? I don't get any of that. I eat in the laundry away from everyone, and if I'm lucky, I sleep on the heating duct or on one of the children's beds, otherwise I'm shut in the laundry for the night.'

'Oh, you need to play more. Budge and I play every night, don't we? And we snuggle up with Lynne when she's watching stuff,' explained Florry.

'I play with the children, I play chasey with them; although the more they grow the more subdued the playfulness has become.'

'You need to play with everyone. That way they'll appreciate you more,' said Florry, chasing his tail around in circles, jumping on Budge and proceeding to have a play fight. The pair then sang their song again and Barkley joined in with much laughter.

'Oh, you two really do have a good time. You make my heart sing. You make my heart want to sing out loud and take in all the joy and laughter. If only I could spread this around my family. If you ever need to chat, just come and find us cats, one is called Budge and the other is called Florry, together they make Fudge and Blorry,' giggled Barkley, dancing around and wiggling his tail.

'Yeah well, you see Barx, you decided to be a detective, didn't you? That's not us. We can't do that. We're more into going with the flow and seeing where it takes us,' explained Budge, continuing to play with Florry.

'Yeah, like if Lynne didn't get so angry, we'd be painting in her studio and doing the same stuff she does. Only we muck up her work, then she has to start again and we get yelled at. Otherwise, we'd be painting all the time. We love to go exploring with her paints,' said Florry.

'You could paint your own paintings and maybe put them on display somewhere, or what if she were to sell your art and that could buy you your tucker?' suggested Barkley, wide-eyed with excitement.

Budge and Florry looked at each other like that was the ultimate dream – to paint and have their paintings make enough to buy their own food.

'I wouldn't have to see Lilly anymore,' said Florry.

'You don't have to see her now!' said Budge.

'Come on! Let's go and see what paints she's got!' said Florry, running out the bedroom to the door.

Budge and Barkley followed, pushing themselves through the cat flap and over to the adjacent door that housed Lynne's work.

'How do we get in?' asked Barkley, pressing his nose against the door in the hope it would just open.

'We don't. Lynne keeps the door locked now. It keeps the possums out,' said Budge.

'And us as well,' Florry looked downhearted.

'What about a song then?' asked Barkley, trying to divert their attention to more fun. 'Do you have a song I can sing?'

'What is a berk when it is not a bark? A button nose!' giggled Florry, then looked at his brother and they both began to sing.

*Detective Barkley, Detective Barkley,*
*Has the cutest Button of Noses.*
*Detective Barkley, Detective Barkley,*
*He knows where his nose goes.*
*You might see a paw here and there,*

Barkley sat with a look of total amazement on his face. 'Where did you get that from?'

'We made it up the other day, didn't we?' said Florry. Budge nodded.

'Yeah, we were mucking around and it just sort of slipped into our heads,' said Budge.

'Do you always make up songs just like that?' asked the dumbfounded detective.

'Nah, we've only just started. Things just sort of have a way of popping in,' said Florry.

'And they didn't before?'

'Nah, it all seemed to happen after our dream we had,' said Budge, with Florry nodding in agreement.

'What dream?'

'The one where he was being chased by a wombat and the wombat was laughing at him because he couldn't laugh and run at the same time,' said Florry. 'Then I had my dream just before waking where this wombat kept wanting to cuddle me and I wouldn't let him. Eventually this wombat, who called himself Ma... Mastering Anything, he said, ran off to find someone else to cuddle and that was when we found the note, in the morning, near our breakfast bowls.'

'Good grief! Were you asleep on Lynne's bed when this happened?' asked Barkley, just about unable to speak or fathom what he had just heard.

'Nah, the heating was still going so we slept next to the fire till it switched off,' said Florry.

'Did you... did you get a sense of what this wombat looked like?'

'Only that he was big and cuddly,' said Florry, with Budge nodding in agreement again.

'This is so hard for me to take in,' said Barkley. 'I have to go and see everyone...' then an absent-minded cute cat left and went to walk down the driveway.

'Barkles?'

'Huh?'

'It's that way,' said Florry, nodding towards the back fence.

'Oh yes, thanks.'

Barkley did not know which way he was going or whose place to visit next. Storm was not home, probably at Mrs Andrews' place, pity he had worn out his invite with the lovely lady.

*Matilda, I shall go and visit Matilda.*

Barkley made his way down his street on the opposite side, jumping back in fright when he got to the corner – there was Regie and his owner coming back from a walk. 'Woof! Woof! Woof!' Regie lunged towards Barkley but was quickly jerked along on his lead. Barkley, feeling exposed out on the street, said nothing, but made a mental note to torment him later.

Barkley put out his senses to make sure there were no cars coming, then ran over the road to Matilda's place. He knew where she lived as he had seen her sitting out the front numerous times on the occasions he had managed to spend nights outside. Barkley found a spot in Matilda's front garden to sit and sent her regular vibrations through his whiskers to say he was there. No response.

*She is probably asleep, which is what I wish I was doing right now, only I have no office to sleep in anymore!*

'Barkley,' said Matilda, yawning from a deep slumber. 'What is so important?'

'Matilda,' said Barkley, looking around but not seeing where she was.

'Well?'

'Where are you?'

'I was asleep in bed till you turned up,' she said, emerging from a small round cat bed on the front verandah.

'Oh, there you are. Good morning. Have you had any dreams about wombats?'

Matilda stared at him. 'What? You got me out of my sleep to ask if I have had any dreams about wombats? No, I can't say I have.'

'You said you had a funny dream but couldn't remember what it was. Have you had any other funny dreams?'

'I have lots of dreams; none of them mean much.'

'Such as? What type of dreams?'

'I don't know… chasing mice, smelling flowers, watching a butterfly, being as big as Storm, climbing the massive tree out the front.'

'When you came to my office and saw yourself in the book with the lovely words, you said you'd had a funny dream. Any chance you remember what that was?'

Matilda thought for a bit. 'No, sorry. Only that I had a feeling that I was flying.'

'Has anything changed since you had that dream?'

'Not that I can tell. What's all this about, anyway?'

'Does the name Mastering Anything mean something to you?'

'No, sorry, it doesn't.'

'Have you seen or heard anything odd?'

'Now that you mention it, the other night I watched this feline from the window. She was running around the garden like a mad thing, playing and chasing things, jumping from this pot here to that pot there and back again. I pestered to go out so I could shoo her off, but I wasn't allowed. Why, what does all this mean?'

'It means the words in the book are changing us.'

'Oh yes, I know that.'

Barkley stared at her in astonishment. 'How do you know that?'

'Because I have suddenly discovered flicking leaves into the air till they land in the swimming pool is so much fun! The leaves float around and make pretty pictures in a way. It really is the most fun! Come on and I'll show you,' said Matilda, excited that she now had the chance to show someone her new pursuit. Barkley followed her to the pool area and watched her pick up a dead leaf and toss it in the air. She flicked it here and there till if fell into the swimming pool, then stood and watched it float across the water.

'Come on, you try,' she said, getting another leaf.

Barkley picked up a leaf and tossed it into the air, grabbed it again, then threw it as high as he could, then flicked it here and there till it went in and floated across the water. Both stood watching, mesmerised.

'Come on, get another one,' said Matilda.

They played 'toss' till they had flicked the dried leaves into the swimming pool and watched them float across the surface.

'See now, if you look at it from the other way,' she said, running around to the other side of the pool, 'sometimes it makes a completely different picture. See how some of them come together and others float away? Then you look at the leaves like the stars in the sky and make a picture, like this one looks like a... a giant mouse! See – head, ears, body and tail.'

'Oh yes, I see. My, that really is very clever, and nice of you to show that to me. Thank you, Matilda. You've made my day. I enjoyed that immensely,' said Barkley, looking directly at Matilda so she knew his gratitude was genuine and heartfelt.

'You're welcome, Barkley. Anytime you want to come over and play pretty pictures in the pool, let me know. We could make a picture each.'

'Thanks, I will. Good day to you Matilda, and thanks,' said the departing detective.

'Bye, Barkley.'

*Who shall I go to next?* wondered the detective, making his way to the footpath.

*Titch? Ugh! I hope I don't get beaten up! Okay, here I go. As Storm says, chest out, Barkley! Show them you are not afraid and go and see Titch.*

Barkley marched along the street like he owned the place, ran across the road when it was safe and up the next corner to Titch's place. Taking a large gulp of air, he made his way up the drive.

'Titch! I mean Joinaythin!'

No response.

'Titch!'

'If you bellow like that one more time, I'll box your ears! Oh, it's you Barkley, I'll let you off,' said a cross-looking cat with fresh scars decorating his ears and missing fur in places. Titch always slept out the front so he could keep an eye on who came past and if needed, beat them up.

'Who have you been fighting with this time?' asked Barkley, trying to look menacing.

'All you cats around here are so placid, I have to go down to Shadow's place to sharpen my claws. What do you want? I was asleep!'

'Have you had any dreams about wombats or mastering anything? Have you noticed if anything has changed?'

'Have you completely lost the plot this time, Barkles? Who dreams of wombats? No, I have not noticed that anything has changed, should it? Dreams of Mastering Anything? No, but Mao and I have had long discussions about mastering things.'

'Really? Like what?'

'Well, as you know, I want to be a magician and call myself Jonathan and… and…'

'And what?' asked Barkley gently so he could let Titch speak freely.

'Mao says he who is grateful wins – and I want to win every time.'

'That is very interesting. What else does Mao say?'

'Only that one day you'll get the hang of it. By the way, that note I gave you, what did it say?'

'Oh, um, let me see if I can remember. It said something about fulfilling dreams and being grateful and to not be sad. Does that help? You are very lucky to spend time with Mao.'

'She's alright, you know. She's smart. I can have a good conversation with her.'

'Yes, you can. She is very smart. One day we will all be as smart as she is.'

'Unless you want something else, I'm going back to sleep. Don't bother me again!'

'You know Titch, I really don't understand why you play tough all the time. Why can't you just say, I want to be called Join…. Joinay…. Joinaything from now on and then practice being the magician you want to be. Why make it so hard? You know, you would make a great magician but who is brave enough to come and see you perform your tricks not knowing if they're going to be beaten up? Hmmm? I would gladly watch you do your magic and so would Matilda, but really, the invite needs to be sweet, otherwise no one will come.'

Titch sat scowling at Barkley and scratched one more imaginary flea.

As no response was forthcoming, Barkley left Titch to his itching and wondered who he should pay a visit to next.

*George? Oh, I can just see it now! Hello, George, remember me? Just wanting to know if you've had any dreams about wombats and have you mastered anything lately? No? Oh well, I'll be on my way then. Bye.*

Barkley suddenly thought he would go and visit Zenya. He had a vague idea where she lived but was not sure. He made his way back towards his place and crossed the road, went down Mr Rowan's driveway and hopped over the back fence.

*Is it this one or the next?*

Barkley jumped down into the yard and started exploring and sniffing for cat scents, which he found. He also found the scent of a dog. Did Zenya live with a dog? Not wanting to have another episode with snarling teeth, Barkley thought he had best stay near a fence so he could jump to safety.

'Zenya?' he whiskered. 'Zenya?'

'Barkley? I'm over here,' came the response from the next fence.

Barkley jumped over and saw Zenya on the back porch. Sitting next to her on a large bed was a massive Bernese Mountain Dog. Barkley gasped in terror as the dog lifted his head and made a gruff sound at him.

'Hi, Barkley. You needn't worry about him, he's harmless,' said Zenya. 'Puffy, this is Barkley. Barkley, this is Puffy.'

*Puffy? What sort of name is Puffy?*

Barkley wondered if he should make his way home now. Puffy put his head down and went back to sleep. Cautiously, Barkley approached, but kept his distance just in case.

'You're welcome to come and sit on the bed if you like. Puffy creates a lot of warmth.'

'Ahh, thanks, but I think I'll stay here,' answered a trepidatious detective on a mission.

'What can I do for you? It must be important for you to come and visit me,' said Zenya.

'Yes, I am wondering if you've had any dreams.' Puffy moved and Barkley jumped but continued to ask his question while keeping an eye on the sleeping mountain. 'Any dreams about wombats and/or mastering anything?'

'I haven't, but Puffy here was chasing something in his sleep the other day. He was twitching and barking at something in his dream. That might've been a wombat. Puffy, who were you chasing the other day in your dream? Was it a wombat?' asked Zenya. Puffy stood up, got comfortable again on the bed and went back to sleep.

Zenya looked at Barkley as if to say, 'There is your answer for you'. Barkley, was just about to ask why the enormous dog was called Puffy, when Zenya interrupted his thinking.

'Have you met... what's her name? You know, the feline you've been chasing about the place.'

'Yes, I met her last night.'

'Was she able to help you with your case you're working on?'

'Yes, she was. I asked so many questions, probably too many; she didn't have enough time to answer them.'

'Well, I'm sure she will answer them all at some stage. Did you know that if you just sit and be, you can discover a myriad of things?'

'Really? Like what?' asked the curiosity of a cute nose.

'I can't explain it to you. You have to give it a go yourself. Come on, I'll sit next to you and we will just be,' said Zenya, getting up from the bed she shared with her companion to sit opposite Barkley. 'Now, close your eyes. Go on, close your eyes. Puffy won't hurt you, besides, you can hear him coming from a mile away.' Reluctantly, Barkley closed his eyes. 'Now just listen to what is going on.'

'What am I listening for?' asked Barkley, hoping he would be given clues, perhaps even answers to his many questions.

'You are listening to inner knowing. You are listening to your heartbeat. You are listening to the spark that exists between you and the ground. You are feeling all these things, and although you are sitting quietly, there is a lot going on. Can you feel this sort of beat, the rhythm that connects everything together?'

'Yes, I can.'

'Well, listen to that. What does it say?'

'It says that although I have many questions and this is my hardest case yet, I will get there because there is this inner knowing that I will succeed. It sort of believes in me and... and...'

'Yes, exactly! See, this is where you get your strength from, where we all get our strength from. This is where you find the gumption to keep going and ask your questions. The answers might not come all at the same time, but they will come. Some of them might not need to be answered as you'll have figured them out by then, which means you got the answer anyway.'

'Goodness, Zenya! You're right! All the headaches and sleepless nights I've had – when all I needed to do was sit and listen. Thank you so much! You've been a great help. That's why your picture in the book spoke of meditation.'

'I don't know what you call it. I call it sitting in the inner spark.'

'How long have you been doing this for?'

'Don't know. I've always done it. I taught Puffy how to do it; he's pretty good at it now.'

'Goodness me! Zenya, you have enlightened my day! Thank you!'

'Not a problem, Barkley. Anytime.'

Barkley left feeling exhilarated and ready for his next discussion; however, he was still not up to talking to George.

*Perhaps I could get a message to Blackberry? How do I do that? Make a trail of lettuce to get him out of his hutch so I can talk to him about George? Excuse me, Blackberry, would you mind asking George if he has had any funny dreams, perhaps involving wombats? Has he managed to master anything yet? No? Oh, pity. Well, thank you, Blackberry, I must be going now. I can hear my fleas calling me.*

Barkley was roaming aimlessly, thinking about all the conversations he had had that morning, when he looked up and found himself outside Miss Fi-Fi's place.

*Their car isn't here. Perhaps this is an opportunity to sneak inside and see how she is?*

Taking a risk, Barkley dashed up the driveway, listened out for any talking or movement inside, then snuck around the back, went through the cat flap, turned left into the kitchen (all those words stuck on the cupboards were still there) and ran into Miss Fi-Fi's bedroom.

'Miss Fi-Fi?'

'Ooohh, Monsieur Nez, how are you? I have been wondering how you are going with your investigation?'

'I am making progress, Miss Fi-Fi. More importantly, how are you? How are your little-uns? I see you have five of them. I did stop by a while ago, but you were fast asleep, so I left you to it. I know Budge and Florry have been past to say hello.'

'Yes, it is true, they have come by a couple of times. Do you like mes enfants, Monsieur?'

'Oh yes, they look very fine indeed! Just lovely, Miss Fi-Fi, just lovely!'

'And how is Mao? Have you made your peace with her yet?'

'Yes, I have. She is really very lovely.'

'Ohh, that is great, Monsieur Nez. I am so pleased!'

'More importantly, how are you, Miss Fi-Fi? How are you getting on being a mother?'

'Oh, it comes naturally to you. I did not think it would, but it does.'

'And the poopee never turned up?'

'No, he did not. Thanks to you!'

Barkley blushed. 'And the dilemma you were in got sorted all by itself?'

'Sorry, what dilemma?'

'Oh yes, you were not there to hear what the picture book said about you. It was all about being taken care of and that at the end, all dilemmas will work themselves out. I think I've got that right, if I can remember it correctly.'

'Is that what the book said? That I was in some sort of dilemma?'

'No, remember the note you brought me?'

'Uh-huh'

'That said... let me see... that said, "...at the ultimate outcome to all dilemmas I will still be loved, heard and accepted". Then the picture book said that being cared for and caring for others is the ultimate respect you can have. You see, Miss Fi-Fi, it has all worked out exceptionally well.'

'Yes, it has. I feel very proud to be a mother. It is very rewarding. I love my children and they love me!'

'Miss Fi-Fi, I know you are very lucky to have this experience. Not many of us are, so well done to you! By the way, any funny dreams of late? Like dreaming of wombats or mastering things?' asked Barkley, shaking his head like he did not think she would say yes.

'Sorry, what is a wombat? I have not had the funny dream, as you say,' responded the new mother.

'That's okay, I didn't think you had. I will be going now; I will come again when you are up and about.'

'Okay. Monsieur Nez? Do I need to be careful of this, how do you say... wombat?'

Barkley giggled. 'No, you will never see him. You might have a cuddly thing in your dreams, but you will never see him.'

'Oh, you mean the cuddles at night?'

Barkley stared at her. 'You've seen the wombat?'

'I have seen Mao. She comes and visits me sometimes. She has such warmth and grace. She climbs into bed with me and makes me feel safe with her presence. She has given me strength and I feel stronger every day.'

Barkley was dumbfounded. 'Miss Fi-Fi, I do not know what to say. You are very lucky, very lucky indeed. I will say goodbye now.'

'Okay, thank you for coming.'

Barkley smiled and made his way out through the kitchen and squeezed himself through the cat flap and into the garden. He felt totally overwhelmed that Mao should be such a lovely cat to offer support to others without them even asking.

*Look at Titch, for example – he would rather take some fur off you than come and help, yet here is a feline, till now unknown in these parts, who suddenly starts helping other felines to remember how lovely they are within their own self, what their strengths are and how to enhance those strengths into something bigger and better.*

Barkley thought about the writing for his own picture, 'Look after my greatness and not to be afraid but to go exploring.'

*Does that mean if I am exploring, I am automatically looking after my greatness? I am a cat, so I am naturally curious; perhaps that's why we have nine lives? Take Budge and Florry – in a kingdom not far from them is a world where they can be who they want. Where is that kingdom? Is it at Lynne's place? Does it mean they are to be something other than making up songs and wanting to join in Lynne's painting? Perhaps none of us have found our true potential yet and need to explore other avenues? Mao is teaching not only me but everyone else, including the brute George, to be as beautiful and as graceful as she is, which means she knows that we can reach the potential she has already passed.*

Barkley was too tired to keep thinking about things. He needed to sleep and allow all this information to settle before he contemplated anything further.

*Where to go? Mao's place? Storm's place? My own place, even though I am currently shut out? Dilemma, dilemma!*

Barkley headed home. It was time to try and find a warm spot and have a sleep.

# Chapter Eighteen

The winter sunshine that kept Barkley warm in his slumber had moved on and dappled light now danced over his winter coat. Slowly, he began to stir from his sleep, wondering if anyone from his family had come home yet. He needed something to eat and to continue his rest in a warmer place, but the house still looked empty.

*Surely Sarah or Beth will be home soon?*

A large presence with emerald eyes jumped over the fence and greeted him.

'Hello, Barkley.'

'Hello, Storm,' smiled a sleepy cat, still curled up. 'I came over to your place this morning but there was no one home. I thought you'd gone to Mrs Andrews'. Unfortunately, I am no longer brave enough to visit her.'

'I was asleep. Everyone had gone out for the morning, so I took advantage of the peace.'

'I met Mao last night.'

'Yes, how did it go?'

'Purrs cannot express how lovely she is.'

Storm raised an eyebrow in astonishment as Barkley continued, 'Did you know she has been creeping into Miss Fi-Fi's place and cuddling with her at night to give her strength in being a mother?' Again, Storm looked astonished.

'Did you know Budge and Florry have taken to creating their own songs?' Storm laughed at that one. 'Did you know Zenya lives with a huge dog called Puffy?' Storm shook his head, no. 'Budge and Florry each had a dream about a wombat. I have visited almost everyone else about it today to see if they have had a similar dream – no one else has. You know, she really is the most amazing feline I have ever met!'

Storm looked amazed, as Barkley kept sharing.

'She took me to her place and we sat up a tree in a cubby house and watched the moon. Then, believe it or not, she invited me to stay and have something to eat. I ended up sleeping next to her all night, till this morning, then ran home and missed my breakfast. She has this lovely area in the laundry which is outside. It's very warm in there and she can come and go as she pleases. I am feeling rather exhausted with it all. Have you had any funny dreams of late? Noticed if anything has changed at all? What did your picture say about you again?'

'It spoke of belonging.'

'Oh yes, that's right. Has anything changed for you?'

'Not that I am aware of.'

'No, I am not aware that anything has changed for me either.'

'Should it have?'

'Well, it has for Budge and Florry, Matilda and perhaps Zenya. I'm not going to go and ask George if he has changed,' said Barkley with a shudder.

'No, I wouldn't go up there. It has taken me too long to recover from the last visit. Could we get a note to Blackberry somehow?'

'Can he even read? Maybe we could throw him lettuce to get him out of his cage and away from George, then ask our questions.'

'And if he doesn't know and has to watch George's behaviour for us, we will have to go back again,' said Storm.

Barkley wondered if two trips to see Blackberry was worth the effort to collect the clues he needed. 'Perhaps I could ask Mao instead? She has been up there and not had a beating. Maybe she knows when the opportune moments are?'

'Yes, that's an excellent idea. Do you remember what the book said about George?'

'Um, let me see. Something about being gentle and nurturing thoughts.'

'I wonder if he has become gentle?'

'It would be good if he had! No more being attacked!'

'I agree with that! So, I take it you are in the picture book now?'

'Yes, I am! Lynne painted my picture when I went over there with Budge and Florry. It was quite amazing to see myself appear on the page so quickly. I thought someone else was going to write the lovely words but she did that too. I asked Mao where the words came from and all she said was from a higher place; I don't know what that means. Higher than the tree house she took me to? A couple of possums came down from above. Maybe she got the information from them? She certainly wasn't scared.'

Storm giggled, listening to Barkley telling him of his adventure. 'So, Budge and Florry's nurturer has been creating the pictures. What did your writing say about you?'

'Oh, something about not being afraid to go exploring and looking after my greatness. I wondered does that mean when I am exploring, am I being great? I don't know. I threw so many questions at her; I gave her no chance to even get a whisker to answer me. I dashed out this morning without even saying goodbye.' Storm raised an eyebrow. 'Someone came in and saw us there so I upped and ran home as fast as I could. I had to go to Budge and Florry's for breakfast as everyone here was out,' said Barkley, tipping his head towards his house.

'Where does Mao live, anyway?'

'Oh, way down the way in the next street. I was a bit frightened to go that far from home. I haven't been inside, but her family seem nice,' said Barkley, pointing the way.

'Is Mao in the book as well?'

'No, she is not, which surprises me! You'd think she would be one of the first to be painted. Budge and Florry have, to my knowledge, not seen her around their place, although I do think the dream they had about the wombat laughing was really Mao coming to visit them. They and Miss Fi-Fi are the only two I know of who have a cat door.'

'What do you think the book would say about Mao, were she to be in it?' asked Storm, sitting down.

'Oh, probably something like no amount of information is too great for me or something along those lines,' said Barkley, standing up and stretching. 'What I don't get is why is she so elusive? Oh, one thing she did say was she wants to train me to have more knowledge. Yes, I am remembering now. She said she did her training at some place called Little Ming. Have you heard of it?' Storm shook his head, no.

'And she wants to train me in the way she was taught. I think she is training all of us. Do you know what MAO stands for? Now what did she say… Master of… Academic… Observances. That's it! Mao means Master of Academic Observances.'

'What did you say to that?'

'I said I am Master of Cute Noses!'

Storm laughed. 'Well, she can't deny you that title!'

'No, she can't, and she can't deny you the title of Master of Giants! I did offer to introduce her to everyone properly and she said she would like that. Why on earth she didn't just come and give a whisker like everyone else, I don't know. I did ask her, but I didn't get a response. Oh, no, sorry, she said she came to say hello when I was asleep in my office but I did not wake. Anyway, it doesn't matter now, I have officially met her.'

Just then Matilda turned up and said hello to them both. She was eager for them to go to her place and have a go at throwing leaves into the swimming pool to see if they got the same picture she did. Once there, Matilda explained that the cool air moved the leaves together and made a funny picture of what looked like a wombat to her.

'You know how you asked me if I had had any dreams about wombats. Well, there's one there,' she said, nodding to the leaves moving over the water in formation. 'Normally they don't stay together like that, they sort of do their own thing but don't you think that looks like a wombat?' she asked excitedly. 'Come on Storm, get some leaves and toss them into the water and see what picture you make. Barkley, come and give it another go!'

Matilda went and got another fallen leaf, chased it into the swimming pool and let it land on the surface, then fetched another one, then a few more, till she had a new picture. 'This one looks like a giraffe!' she said. 'What does yours look like, Barkley?'

'I don't know yet. I'm waiting for the leaves to come together…' responded a detective having fun. Barkley wondered if he too would see a wombat on the water.

'What about yours Storm, what does yours look like?' asked Matilda of her giant friend.

'Mine looks like a butterfly.' Storm liked butterflies. To him, there was nothing better than lying in the sun on a summer's day watching the butterflies dance around the garden. He always hoped one would land on his paw. One day, he lay on his back with his paws in the air, wishing one of the butterflies flittering around the flowers would come and land on him. Matilda looked up at Storm and smiled, for she too liked butterflies.

Storm turned around and ran up the tree in the middle of the garden to get a better look at the floating pictures. He thought it was amazing how things looked different again from up there. 'Look, Barkley, your one is merging with mine. Now it looks like my butterfly is visiting a flower. Now they have become one and it looks like... looks like... a monster! Grrr!' said Storm, laughing as he jumped onto the adjacent branch so Matilda and Barkley could run up the tree and look at the artwork from on high. Matilda wished she was as big as Storm so she could jump from branch to branch like he did.

'Thanks, Matilda. That was fun! I really enjoyed myself,' said Storm. 'If you are throwing leaves into the swimming pool, what happens to them afterwards?'

'Either Roger or Lucy clean them out. They get that thing there and sweep it across the water and it catches all the leaves.'

'Pity that he disrupts your artwork!' said Barkley.

'No, not really. It means the next time I can start fresh and make new pictures.'

'Like having a fresh page to put paint on!' said Barkley, having watched Lynne paint.

'Yes, that's right,' replied Matilda.

'Matilda, do you have a cat door to let yourself in and out?' asked Barkley.

'Well, sort of. I now have a window that is open for me to jump in and out of.'

'When inside, have you ever been visited by another cat?' asked the detective, unable to let his whiskers rest.

'Once, I thought there was someone inside eating my food. I went to investigate but saw no one.'

'When was that?'

'A while ago now. Roger had just started his new job, so many moons ago.'

'Before Mao turned up?'

'Yes, way before then.'

'Okay, thank you, and thank you for the experience of creating paintings with leaves. I must tell Budge and Florry. They are desperate to paint with Lynne's paints but are banned from making a mess! This way they can have fun and Lynne won't be angry.'

'Well, send them over! I am happy to make pictures with anyone.'

'Okay. Goodbye Matilda, and thank you for this wonderful opportunity,' said Barkley.

'Yes, thank you Matilda. I have had enormous fun!' said Storm.

'Thank you for coming. It was very nice to spend time with you both,' responded Matilda.

'And you!' said Barkley, with Storm agreeing.

The detective and his giant friend made their way back across the road to Barkley's place, where hunger pangs were beginning to aggravate the detective. Storm too was getting peckish, so bid his pal farewell and went home to get something to eat, reminding Barkley to tell him what Mao says. Barkley said he would, but did not let on he was nervous about going that far in the dark again on his own.

Barkley sat and waited by the back door for someone to come home.

*Why can't they leave a window open for me to come and go as I please? That would be a great help. Then I can sneak out when I need to and come in when I'm hungry. It would be better than having to stay outside in the cold! Perhaps I will write a note to Sarah and tell her what I want. I wonder if she would do that for me? Better get Mao to help me with my spelling first!*

Barkley sat quietly waiting, listening to his stomach growling, wondering what he was going to have for dinner.

'Movement? Someone is home?' 'MIAOW! MIAOW! MIAOW!' called Barkley, banging at the back door. 'MIAOW!'

Silently, the door opened and Barkley ushered himself in. 'Thanks Beth,' he said, smooching her legs to tell her, 'Feed me! I'm hungry!'

Barkley ate with gusto then curled up on the sofa next to Beth to show his appreciation. Slowly, the rest of his family arrived home and Barkley retired to sleep at the back of the sofa, where he knew he was safe and out of harm's way. He listened to the activities and conversations throughout the evening. Every so often, he woke. At the smell of dinner being cooked he thought about doing a Titch and sauntering out, demanding, 'I'll have some of that, thank you!' but he knew it would not work. He had tried it so many times before, and been left feeling his family did not understand nor appreciate him.

*Who was it who solved the case of the missing sunglasses last summer? Who was it who leapt about the garden and ran around like a mad thing last spring when Jean was out the front planting? Who was it who unravelled the ball of string and who found the spare key? Were it not for me, the detective of the moment, you would all still be searching for your lost items and you would not have enjoyed your time in the garden so much!*

Barkley wondered should he go now, as the sun was setting, or should he wait till the moon was up, knowing that after it was full it did not emerge in the sky till much later, roughly when Jean was getting everyone's lunches ready for tomorrow. If he went at dusk, he might be seen running down the street and that was a danger zone for any cat. They might be attacked by another feline, or worse, a dog. Every feline knew it was best to wait till dark for any necessary wanderings to occur.

As the usual evening rituals started to come to an end, Barkley got up and pestered to go outside just before the doors were locked. The moon was already up, but the trees hid the light. In a few moments, Barkley would be able to see his way in the dark as he ran down the road to Mao's place.

*Right, off I go.*

Around the corner then down the street he dashed, as fast as his legs and nervousness could carry him.

*There's the playground.*

Under the swings, turn right and the third house along, up the driveway and out the back. Barkley called out to Mao – no answer. He sent her a whisker to say, 'I am here.' No answer. He went into the laundry to see if she was there – she was not.

*Perhaps she's in the tree house?*

Barkley climbed the branches to the first floor of a young pirate's adventures. No Mao sitting there, no possums either, but there were fresh deposits. Barkley did not know what to do – go home or sit and wait?

*If I go home, I will probably have to stay outside all night.*

He slipped into the laundry where the whirling of the drier kept the place nice and warm and sat on Mao's bed, had a bath and waited for her return.

The dawn chorus commenced and Barkley woke with a bursting bladder.

'Good morning, Barkley,' said Mao, who had been curled up asleep behind him. Barkley stared at her with big eyes. 'Where did you come from?' he wondered aloud.

'I went to your place last night to further our discussions. I waited for you, then came home to find you here, waiting for me. I didn't want to disturb your slumber, so I crept in and slept beside you,' she explained.

'I do beg your pardon Mao, I did not hear you come in,' said Barkley, hoping his bladder would not burst.

'No, I entered very quietly. You were fast asleep in dreamland. I take it you slept well?'

'Yes, one of the best sleeps I've had in a long time,' said the detective, getting up and making his way to the door.

'You're not going to run off again, are you?'

'Um, no. I thought I heard a snake in the bushes out there and I think I had better investigate...'

Mao giggled. 'If you go to the top of the garden behind the big tree, there you will find what you are looking for.'

Barkley sighed and made his way to the designated area for leaving deposits and relieved the bursting feeling. 'Ahh, that's better!' he said to himself and made his way back to Mao's warm enclosure. He was hungry now, but did not want to eat all of her biscuits. 'Sardines! There's a packet of sardines up in the cubby house!'

Mao looked at him in the same way she always did, like she understood what was going through his mind. 'You are welcome to some of my biscuits,' she said, knowing someone would come soon with her breakfast.

'Thank you, that is very kind of you. I could not impose,' said a starving Barkley, who had decided to jump straight into asking his questions. 'Mao, I have ascertained that the writings in the book are changing everyone. For example, Budge and Florry's picture spoke of teaching your heart to sing and they have taken to making up songs.

Matilda's spoke of spontaneity and creativity and she is now making pictures with leaves in the swimming pool. I would normally go and see George, but one encounter is enough. Do you know if he has changed at all? How come you did not get a beating from him? Also, why are you not in the book?'

'My dear Barkley, all in good time. These things are not to be rushed. If you are going to enter the School of Mastering Academic Observances, you must be patient. I cannot tell you all you want to know. That would defeat the purpose of my contacting you. Like you, I have worked hard in watching you solve this case. I have left many clues. You have followed some and not seen others. I know this is frustrating for you; however, a bit of ingenuity and tenacity will hold you and everyone in good stead. I am not playing any game with you. I am showing you the way,' said Mao in her usual calm, melodic voice.

Barkley was frustrated. He wanted answers to all the questions that had been dripping down the walls of his now shut office. Questions on the tip of his tongue, ready to be fired one after the other, now had to wait, suspended in silence. It was hard to lose patience with Mao. She was always so calm and gracious. He could not yell at her at the top of his lungs like he did with Mrs Andrews. That would have resulted in another, 'My Dear Barkley, all in good time.'

*Might just as well go home then and get some breakka if it isn't too late to be fed.*

Yet again, Mao read the look on his face. 'You're not going home now, are you? There is much to be done. We must keep moving forward, Barkley. Now is the essence of putting yourself against the tide. Rise up and show them that you can do it! Come on!'

*What? Where did this fighting spirit in this calm demeanour come from?* he wondered, looking at Mao like he thought he knew her.

'What do you want me to do?' sighed the worn-out detective.

'After breakfast, I need you to write a note that you and I will take to the lady who looks after Sebastian and George,' explained Mao.

Barkley gulped. *George? You mean I am to visit that brute of a monster who could have killed Storm and me? I can see now that you are a few whiskers short on your lovely face, probably why your discerning skills are currently loopy!*

Mao waited for a further response from her hesitant student, then continued with her explanation.

'I understand your office is locked. Do you have means to produce a note?'

Barkley nodded. 'Budge and Florry said they would get me some paper and letters to scratch out. I am nervous about my spelling though. I don't want to hand you a note with bad spelling. What do you want the note to say?'

'The note will say "No more dressing Seb in dolls' clothes",' Mao smiled.

Barkley quickly ran the letters through his mind to make sure he remembered what to write. How to spell Seb was going to be a bit of stumble, but he would give it a go. Mao's smile made Barkley feel better.

*It feels good to work together. Perhaps we can become the two most formidable cats in the neighbourhood and hand out our own business cards. Markley and Bao, Bar and Maokley. Barkley and Mao. Mao and Barkley…*

A grumbling stomach was stopping him from thinking clearly.

'Okay, I'll meet you after breakfast at the lemon tree one sleep from now, is that enough time for you?' Mao asked.

There was that word again.

*Budge and Florry are just learning how to tell the time. Perhaps they could teach me too?*

Barkley was not sure that would be enough time. He needed to talk to the brothers, as well as find a place to stick the letters down onto paper, and that meant eating grass so he could produce some glue. In his desire to go and get breakfast to stop his stomach from making noises louder than the crows, he said yes and left Mao's company. He wondered if she was going to have breakfast and then have a nice sleep for the day, something he wanted to do. Perhaps she was going to hide and watch him figure out the spelling by himself, then emerge at the last minute to tell him he had gotten it all wrong.

All the way home, Barkley recited the note so he did not forget the words – No more dressing Seb in dolls' clothes. No more dressing Seb in dolls' clothes. He was glad to get home and find his family still there.

*Breakka, here I come!*

'Barkley! Where have you been? We've been worried about you! You stayed outside all night and weren't here this morning. Where have you been?' asked Sarah as she put some food down for him.

Barkley was glad to see his family and know the familiar smells that made up his house were still there. He smooched Sarah's legs and miaowed in appreciation, then ate all his breakfast and said he was still hungry. Sarah fed him again, then left for school. Barkley, who wanted to curl up on someone's bed and have a good sleep all day, instead ducked out the back door and made his way to Budge and Florry's place. Now that he no longer had an office to sleep in and ponder about things, it was difficult to action anything. If he was going out, it meant staying out all night – no sneaking inside for warmth or even sneaking out in summer on a hot night. It was like everything now had to be planned in advance, which meant no more spontaneously dropping off a note with a bone to someone's back door for a week in the hope they got his message loud and clear.

'You alright there, Berk? You want some breakfast again?' asked Budge as Barkley approached the brothers' door.

'Morning Budge. Mao has given me a task of writing a note, so I am in need of paper and letters. I am wondering if you've managed to procure anything for me yet?'

'We got this the other day,' said Budge, pointing to a pile of newspapers and catalogues that sat in a cardboard box under the porch. 'You'd better be quick. Lynne normally puts that stuff in the bin.'

Barkley was excited! They had not forgotten his request. All he needed now was paper.

'That's great, Budge. Thanks very much! And the paper?'

'That's in there,' Budge pointed into Lynne's studio. 'It's at the back of her desk.'

Barkley gazed into Lynne's studio and saw her sitting there painting. Too curious to stay out, he wandered in and miaowed 'hello' till Lynne turned around and saw him. She said hello, asked what brought him over here and gave him a pat. Barkley jumped up onto her desk and spied the packet of paper that sat at the back.

'Miaow,' he said, smooching Lynne and walking over her fresh painting.

'Careful! Don't step on my work. It's almost finished,' she said, holding up two paintings of a black and white cat with big blue eyes, sitting there looking resplendent. On one paper the cat was sitting, looking straight at you and the words appeared above her head. On the other, the cat took up the whole page and the words appeared over the top of her. She looked beautiful. Her blue eyes seemed to penetrate right through you, like a love story, where you know whatever happens, all will be well. There was a loving warmth about her. She just seemed to glow. At the bottom of the page were paw prints with the words 'Mastering Anything Occasionally' written underneath.

Barkley was boggle-eyed. 'Where did you get that from?' he miaowed, wondering how on the Great King Cat's paws did she end up being painted by Lynne. He put his paw onto Lynne's arm so her hand rested and he could read the fancy words properly. 'MIAOW!' he cried.

*Trust gives power to*
*'Everything will be okay'.*
*Through trust we become One.*
*It gives clarity to Awareness and*
*Allows acceptance to speak.*

*Embrace you,*
*For without you there would be no brilliance.*
*The universe is here to shine, and shine it must.*
*You, my friend, are here to see that this happens.*
*The world is your oyster and you are the key,*
*Till you open, the universe will never know the depth of*
*your magnificence.*

'Do you like them?' asked Lynne, proud of her work.

Barkley took a deep breath. He needed to allow the lovely words to sink in and shower over his body.

*The universe wants to know how much I shine, and shine I must! The Great King Cat in the sky will be so pleased with my brilliance!*

Barkley remembered his own words 'Do not be afraid, go exploring into the unknown.' Barkley turned and looked at Lynne with a smile, smooched her again and gently miaowed and purred. Lynne laughed and stroked him saying, 'That's it now, Barkley. I have finished. All I have to do now is take it to Athena. I hope she likes it.'

Barkley purred even louder. 'Like it? I love it! I love all of them! Except for George, but that's only because I'm frightened of him.' Barkley suddenly twigged that here he was being afraid of George when he was supposed to be exploring the unknown.

*George is not the unknown though. I know him. I've had an encounter with him and it was not pleasant. Why would I want to put myself in harm's way again?*

Just then there was a tap at the studio door and a voice called out, 'Knock, knock. Anyone home?'

'Athena! Come in! I've finished. I'm just waiting for the paint to dry,' said Lynne.

'That looks lovely! I love her blue eyes and how you've really captured her personality,' said Athena.

'When are you getting them all made up?' asked Lynne.

'Oh, not for a while yet. I've brought you one of our first prototypes,' she said as she dived into her bag and pulled out a parcel wrapped in paper, opened it and showed Lynne a mock version of what was yet to come. There were Budge and Florry on both sides of a duvet with their words of wisdom embroidered to make them stand out. Barkley sat looking at the brothers that appeared in the picture book now on display, something that you could run your paws over, snuggle up on and purr loudly. He wondered what his one would look like and how it would feel sleeping on himself.

*Would the lovely words finally sink in? Would I then be able to look after my greatness and swim forth? I'm not particularly keen on water, but if I am already great, what is there to look after — exploring my riches designed in mastery? The only richness I know is a good meal and a lovely sleep!*

'When do you leave?' asked Lyne, proud to see her work coming to fruition.

'We fly to Copenhagen in the middle of July.'

'It all sounds very exciting, doesn't it?'

'It has been a lot of hard work and sleepless nights. Still, we think we are prepared and that our displays will look good.'

'I'm sure they will. Can I offer you a cup of tea or coffee?'

'Thanks, I'd better not. I've got to dash. Thank you so much for all your work. It really is exceptional. I like the way you have incorporated our lettering into the grass and leaves. Hopefully it will give people a chance to remember us,' said Athena, reaching out to pat Barkley, who was having none of being stroked by this lady.

Barkley was not sure what to make of the force of energy that had just come into the studio. Athena was a tall lady whose thick, curly blonde hair tumbled down to her shoulders. She had a big smile with a small gap in her teeth, rings on all her fingers, numerous bracelets and a long necklace that jangled as she walked. She wore jeans with boots and a cream-coloured turtleneck jumper with a well-worn long brown cardigan that went down to her knees. A strong, forthright person, she knew where she was going. Her decisive nature was punctuated with a big laugh, huge smile and vivacious bright green eyes.

Barkley watched Lynne's portfolio of work gather into Athena's embrace and wished he could go too. He just wanted to be with the magic of his painting, of all the paintings and where they were going. This was the end – no more watching Lynne's pens and brushes create a page of excitement, no more lovely pictures to look at and fancy words to read. The women bade each other farewell and Barkley watched a whirlwind disappear out the door with, 'I'll be in touch.'

Lynne sighed and stroked Barkley, who suddenly remembered he was supposed to be getting paper to write a note. He turned, stuck his claw into the opened packet of paper that sat at the back of Lynne's desk and managed to toss the packet onto the floor so Lynne had to pick it all up. This gave Barkley an opportunity to jump down and sit on top of a few sheets and miaow profusely. Lynne said, 'Get off,' but a determined cat was not going to be outdone. Instead, Lynne went inside to make a cup of tea and Barkley grabbed the paper in his mouth and put it in the box outside with the local newspaper and other junk-mail, ready for gluing later.

Barkley waited for Lynne to return but then heard her on the phone and wondered if she was talking to Olivia.

'Budge! Budge! Wake up! Where's Florry?' asked Barkley, wanting some attention.

'Gone to see Lilly.' Sleeping resumed.

Curious, Barkley wondered where Lynne had gone. Wandering out of her studio, he stuck his head through the cat flap to see where she was and heard the front door shut. He figured she had gone to Olivia's place and probably would not be back for a while, so went to the recycling box and started looking for the letters he needed and scratched them out to make the note Mao had requested, 'Stop dressing Seb in dolls' clothes'.

'Right, now for some glue,' said Barkley as he wandered around Lynne's garden, looking for some long grass to eat. He then returned to his work area outside the studio and vomited. Carefully, he placed the letters down on the paper with his special glue, let it dry for at bit, then folded it up as best he could and carried it home in his mouth. He wished he had a bit of string or something to pull it along behind, as that would make jumping fences easier.

Now that he was home, where was he going to keep the note till he needed to give it to Mao? He decided under the house with the other notes he had collected was the best place. He pushed the piece of paper through the slats of wood then wriggled his way into the dark and put it with the others. Walking away, happy with his decision, Barkley had a thought, turned around and went back, waited for his eyes to adjust to the lack of light and re-read all the clues he had collected.

*To know at the ultimate outcome to all dilemmas,*
*I will still be loved, heard and accepted.*

*He who lives through the ideal lives in sorrow. He who lives with gratitude lives in peace.*

*Too much reflection stifles.*

*In quietude there is silence, yet much talking is done.*

*All that matters is held together with belonging glue.*

*Gentle loyalty.*

*Through trust we become One.*

Barkley thought about all of these and concluded that they were for everyone.

*Zenya got the one about meditation because she has already learnt how to meditate. Although… if it is quiet when you meditate, who is doing the talking? Storm got the one on belonging because he belongs with two families. Matilda got the one about reflection being stifling because… because… hmmm, don't know. Titch got the one on gratitude because he is such a grump and he could do with being grateful. It might cheer Joinaythingamy up! George got the one about gentle loyalty, because as Blackberry said, he would tear the washing off the clothesline and he is a brute. Miss Fi-Fi got the one on dilemmas and being loved because she was in the dilemma of becoming a mother with a dog in the house, but now there is no dog, so she is still loved and accepted.*

*I wish I was loved and accepted. I wish I had a room all to myself where I could come and go as I please.*

*Budge and Florry got one on teaching the heart to sing. Why do they need to sing? Could you imagine Budge and Florry singing all the time? I wonder what Lynne would make of that?*

*I got one on not being afraid, and let's face it, I need to give up being scared. I mean, when has there ever been a monster under the house?*

Barkley looked up to see if there were any monsters around but found none.

*Mao got the one on…. on… in trust we become One. Why do we become One when we trust? One with what? What are we trusting to become one with? What does Mao need to trust? She is already awesome, so knowledgeable, and nothing seems to phase her, so what does she need to trust? Who is she becoming one with? Maybe it is something she did not learn when she was at Little Ming? I'd love to go there and have a look around. I wonder what they would say to me? Welcome, oh Great One, we have heard so much about you. You are the Great Detective who can solve any crime… except this one has taken me beyond the emptiness of a packet of sardines!*

Barkley emerged from under the house and decided, seeing as he had finished his request from Mao, he would do the same thing she was probably doing and have a good sleep, only yet again there was no warm spot, no shelter, no den, nor anywhere to accept any visitors.

*I have a reputation to uphold. I can't do that without an office.*

With that thought, Barkley curled up next to the decomposing sign 'Detective Inspector Barkley Button Nose' at the entrance to his former den of hidden clues.

# Chapter Nineteen

'**M**y dear Barkley, you just don't get it, do you? How many times? The b goes this way, the d goes that way. See the stem goes up. With the p and q the stem goes down,' said Mao, purring like she was singing a song written just for her.

*If you would just listen to the sound,*
*You would come along in leaps and bounds.*
*B is for Barkley,*
*D is for diary,*
*P is for permission,*
*Q is for question.*
*You see it really is quite easy,*
*Once you place the b before the d.*
*Before you came dancing through the door,*
*I had a permissible pass,*
*To question all that was 'afore,*
*To query to the end.*
*What is the difference between bend and pend?*
*To wonder what is a query in a diary,*
*And a look in a book is all that it took,*
*Yet my question was not there.*
*When I came to compare,*
*The stem of the p is different to the d,*
*The dictionary called out my name.*
*It said, 'don't be a pain,'*
*Look and see how the b is before the d,*
*Yet dab is as important as slap or slab.*

*So, to answer your question, it is really a matter of quietly and quickly querying where does the stem go to make the letter you already know?*

Barkley swished his tail in time to the music and began to sing, 'B is for Barkley, d is for diary. It really does depend on the stem. P is for permission, q is for quick questions. A duck quacks. A dog barks. A possum makes an awful din. And q… and q… is for phew, I have no more work to do!' he purred.

*No more work to do! No more work to do. I still have to go with Mao and deliver the note to George. Is that when she pushes me off the fence and I get eaten and Mao wins the case of what happened to the greatest detective around these parts?*

*Can you tell me what you know of the whereabouts of Barkley Button Nose?*

*Why no, Your Honour. He was here one minute and gone the next. I just happened to see him jump into the jaws of that giant monster of a dog what ate him good and proper. Your Honour, is it okay now if I resume taking over his current case of the missing dog bowl? There is also a matter of my fee, one packet of sardines is owed to me. One packet of sardines is owed to me…*

'What are you dreaming about, Barkles? You were having a nice dream. You were singing a song. How does it go?' asked Budge.

'Huh? What?' said Barkley, startled. 'Budge, Florry. My boffice is dozed. What… What was your bestion?' asked a sleepy detective who had just had an alphabet lesson from Mao.

'You were singing in your sleep. We've come to see you because you nearly cost Florry here a trip to the doctor!'

'Huh? What doctor? Florry, you are probably sick from eating Lilly's tucker, go home and rest,' said Barkley, too tired to wake up fully.

'Dee-tective Barkley, you made a mess at Lynne's studio. Torn paper everywhere and vomit near her door. She thought it was me who made the mess. She nearly called the doctor and was going to take me to see him. I don't want to go to the doctor. We got you the paper – next time clean up or we'll have to say no more,' explained Florry, with Budge nodding in agreement.

'Vomit? What vomit?'

'Barkley! Wake up!' said the brothers in unison.

'Huh? Sorry boys, I have had such a good sleep, the best in ages. Florry, you were saying you went to the doctor? What did he say?' Barkley was awake now. The song and his lesson from Mao were slowly drifting out of his head and he could no longer remember what he had learnt.

'I didn't go to the doctor. You and your mess almost took me to the doctor! Next time, don't leave a mess. Lynne is neat and tidy and we have to keep it that way. We've been in enough trouble as it is, painting her doors and stuff. Don't make a mess and leave it there!' said Florry.

'Oh gosh! I hadn't thought of that. I wish I still had my office to run as I like. Do you want me to come and apologise to Lynne?'

'No, it's alright,' they said together.

'Okay, well, I am very sorry. I was too eager to get the note ready for my meeting with Mao.'

'When are you going to meet her again?' asked Budge.

'Tomorrow morning, under the lemon tree.'

'What was the note for?' asked Florry.

'It's for Sebastian, the kitten who lives with G... G... George. Mao and I are taking the note to the lady.'

'What does it say?'

'It is to stop the little girl dressing the kitten in dolls' clothes.'

'Really? That is very interesting. Can we come?'

'No. It's not a nice place there! That's where Storm got beaten up by the monster dog!'

'Oh, we were hoping for a day out somewhere. We want to try our songs out on others to see if they like them. Perhaps if we sing to the lady she will take your note more seriously?' suggested Budge.

'Yeah, we could teach you our song and you could sing it with us,' said Florry.

'Flor, that's a great idea!' said Budge.

Florry turned and smiled at his brother, 'Thanks.'

'What do you reckon then, Barkles. You going to join our band?'

'I'd love to, boys. It's just that I have work to do. Mao is going to teach me things and we are just getting going. Plus, she is going to help me with my spelling. By the way, how are you going with telling the time?'

'Oh, okay. We just look at the clock to see when we get fed. Anyway, do you want to hear our new song?' asked Florry.

'Yes, go on!' said Barkley, sitting tall so he could be as attentive as possible.

'Ready, Budge?'

'Yep!'

*We're Budge 'n Florry,*
*We're Fudge 'n Blorry,*
*Don't be in a hurry,*
*Cause at the end of the clock,*
*Is a very nice tick-tock,*
*Tick-tock.*

*We're Florry 'n Budge,*
*It's tucker time for us,*
*We're happy to eat 'n sleep,*
*For our keep.*

*Lynne is painting,*
*'n we're waiting,*
*For the end of the clock to go*
*Tick-tock,*
*Tick-tock.*

*It's tucker time!*

Barkley giggled his head off. To him this was so funny, one of the best songs he'd ever heard. He knew exactly what it was like to have a growling stomach that had to wait till he was fed at the 'appropriate hour'.

'Boys, that is really very good! You've made my day! Tell you what, if you want to sing your songs to others, let's put on a show. We'll get everyone together and you can show us your singing. What if we do it at Matilda's place? She has a swimming pool she's been making pictures in. I told her you two would like to join in the fun as well. She would enjoy playing with someone else,' suggested Barkley. 'We could go over to her place now and see what she's doing,' continued the detective, in the happy belief that this case was almost over.

Budge and Florry followed Barkley out the front, down to the corner, over the road, then turned left till they came to Matilda's place and marched up the driveway and out the back to the swimming pool.

'Matilda!' called Barkley, 'Matilda!'

'Hello, Barkley,' she said.

'Matilda, this is Budge and Florry. You would have met them in my office when we first read the picture book. They have taken to singing songs and want to put on a display. I mentioned you are creating paintings in the swimming pool. They too like to paint, don't you boys?' Heads nodded as they gazed around.

'They would like to experience painting. I have suggested that we get everyone together and they can all have a go at making pictures in the pool and singing songs. Perhaps Zenya could do a meditation, Titch could do a magic trick and Storm could, well, Storm could just be Storm. What do you say?' asked Barkley, his nose twitching over his excellent idea.

'Yes, hello, Budge and Florry. I remember you. I think this is a great idea. When shall we do it? Rain is coming, so we will have to plan it after then. I will need the leaves to be dry as the rain will make them wet and then they won't float on the water properly,' said Matilda.

'Great! Shall we say two paw's sleep after the rain?'

'Okay, great. Budge, Florry, would you like to come and play leaves with me now?' asked Matilda.

'Yeah, okay,' said Florry, with Budge nodding.

'Okay, enjoy yourselves, you two. It really is a lot of fun making pictures in the pool, and Florry, don't leave any deposits,' said Barkley quietly to his friend. 'I will go and tell everyone to prepare.'

'What about your friend? Are you going to invite her too?' asked Matilda, moving over to a pile of freshly raked leaves.

'Oh yes. I suppose I am. She did say she wanted to meet everyone, so this will be a good opportunity to introduce her. Good idea, Matilda,' said Barkley, excited that things were moving in a positive direction. 'You never know, I may have this enormous case wrapped up by then!'

Barkley wandered off, thinking of the evidence he had so far.

*Lynne was doing the artwork for Athena, so presumably Athena was the one who had given Lynne all the lovely words, or had she? Perhaps Lynne got the lovely words herself and all the magnificent paintings were Lynne's idea and she was giving it all over to Athena to produce into bedding?*

*Who wrote the little notes that were handed out to the local cats? Mao? She wrote that message to meet me under the lemon tree. I must ask Mao to show me how to hold a thing that writes. That would make my work a lot easier than scratching out letters and glueing them down, especially as my spelling is not very good.*

Every cat knew a paw's sleep meant a nighttime sleep. It always started with a front paw, then the other front paw, then the back paws in turn. Barkley watched Matilda show the boys how to throw leaves into the pool so they floated over the surface, then wait and see if they made a pretty picture, then he left to tell everyone of the upcoming show. First was a stop at Titch's place as he would need the most amount of time to get his magic act ready. When Barkley asked him if he wanted to be introduced as Joinanything, Titch nearly clobbered him. 'It's Jonathan! Not Join-anything! Jonathan! Learn to spell, Barkles, or I'll scratch the alphabet onto your ears!'

Barkley said okay and made a hasty retreat, saying to Titch if he did not behave he would get his fleas to give him a good going over, to which Titch replied he did not have any fleas because of the ghastly stuff he gets on his back every now and then.

Nervous ears made their way to Storm's place for some solace and perhaps a bit of support if he could get it. Storm was pleased with the idea and thought he would like to give a talk on what it is like to be as big as he is. He did laugh when Barkley reiterated what Titch said and suggested he introduce him as Magician Jonathan, formerly known as The Flea-Bound Grump Titch, just to stir things up a bit. Barkley did not want the alphabet scratched onto his ears or anywhere else on him. When Storm heard what Barkley and Mao were doing in the morning, he was surprised and nervous for them both; he did not wish a trip to George's place on anyone.

Zenya said she would love to teach everyone about sitting with the inner spark and asked if she could bring Puffy as proof that it works on dogs too. Barkley said best not, he needed everyone concentrating and having a good time, plus what would happen if Puffy jumped into the pool?

He would inform Mao of the concert being arranged when he saw her tomorrow. The only feline left was Miss Fi-Fi and her five kittens; Barkley did not think she would be able to come but decided to tell her about it anyway just as soon as Mr and Mrs Longford were not home so he could let himself in and talk to her properly without being chased away. Barkley wondered if he might take advantage of their absence and bring everyone over to see her and the kittens if she were up for it. Perhaps she could give a talk on what it is like to have children, an opportunity taken from everyone else when they were too young to know what was going on.

The next morning after breakfast, Barkley got the note he had made and took it to the lemon tree and waited for Mao. When she arrived, Barkley handed her the note saying he had paid particular attention to the letters, making sure he had got them all correct. Mao opened the piece of paper and read:

'Stob pressing Sed in boll's clothes.'

Mao gazed at Barkley, sighed, and put the note down on the ground.

'Come on, let's go,' she said.

'What about the note?' asked an anxious detective.

'My dear Barkley.'

*Ugh! Not again* thought a small Burmese with twitching whiskers. 'Please tell me I have not got it all wrong!' he pleaded.

'Well, let's just say it neebs a dit of lork,' said Mao with a giggle. 'We will try another tactic.'

Barkley grabbed the piece of paper and put it in his mouth. He was undeterred. As far as he was concerned, he had gone to a lot of trouble and he was going to deliver it. Normally he dropped notes for a week till they understood what he meant, so why not now? He wanted his efforts to be acknowledged.

Up the road they went, then turned left. Coast clear, they ran across the road. At the monster's driveway, Barkley suddenly became too anxious and frightened to go on. Mao took her disciple to the place adjacent, where they climbed the same tree Storm and Barkley had taken refuge in.

'There's Blackberry in his cage. Do you see the monster?' asked Barkley.

'He's probably gone for a walk,' said Mao, who then took a deep breath and miaowed her loudest again and again. Nothing happened.

'Blackberry! Where is George?' yelled Barkley to the munching rabbit.

Blackberry looked up through the wires of his cage and pointed his ears towards the door. From where they were, they could not see the verandah or who was at the back entrance.

'We want to drop a note to the lady,' yelled Barkley to the rabbit who was deeply engrossed in chewing parsley.

Blackberry turned his body and motioned towards the front; his mouth was too full to utter a word. Mao instructed Barkley to remain in the tree. Out she ventured to the front door with the note in her mouth. She could hear footsteps so figured someone was home and dropped the note on the mat, let out two great big miaows and banged the door. Footsteps were coming her way, so she made a hasty retreat back to Barkley.

They heard the lady open the door and say, 'Go on!' Out came George, sniffing and running around the front yard. Even though he knew he was safe, Barkley's nerves were ready to exit the tree and run home as fast as he could, but Mao grabbed him and said, 'No, Barkley! I know you're frightened, but you were going to run across the road without checking. Don't do that again!' admonished Mao. 'You must always put yourself in a position of safety first, before crossing a road. I know it's difficult when you're frightened, but there is always a fence, tree, under a parked car or into someone's garden for safety. Then, when you are calm and all is well, you can cross the road. I am not telling you off; I'm just reminding you what you already know. I, too, had to be reminded a lot in the early days of my training at Little Ming. Now it is second nature to me.'

Barkley was petrified and not thinking straight. He could not deal with knowing George was in his vicinity. All he knew was Mao had dropped the note and ran back to him, so he panicked; not what a detective of his standing should be doing. From the safety of the tree, they sensed George had returned inside as they heard the door shut. Barkley thought they would go home now, but Mao said to wait, for what he was not sure. His heart still pounding in his chest, he was extremely grateful to Mao for saving him from what could have been a nasty accident had he run across the road without thinking. Mao sat quietly in the tree and watched Blackberry, then saw the lady come and take him inside. Barkley sat facing the other way as looking into the yard made him stiff with fear.

'Have you calmed down now?' asked Mao.

'I will be calm when I get home,' said Barkley.

'Come on then,' said Mao. Jumping down out of the tree, she made her way to the curb before checking left, right, left – no cars – then quickly running across the road with her student in tow. 'Okay, you can breathe now.'

Just as Matilda had predicted, it started to rain. Instead of going back the way they had come, they went down the laneway that took them near Storm's place.

'Barkley, I'll leave you here if you want to stop and chat with Storm,' said Mao.

'Thank you. His presence calms me down and I am able to think clearly again,' replied Barkley, looking worn out. 'Tell me, why have you been sitting on Blackberry's cage? Hasn't the lady or George chased you away?'

'No, I only sit there when it is safe. I look out for Sebastian and send him loving whiskers. He told me he is tired of being dressed, so I said I would help him. Next time, we will make a note together and leave it on top of Blackberry's cage,' said Mao, bidding Barkley farewell.

Barkley sighed – not another trip to George's place! Still, if Blackberry came to him and asked for his assistance he would not be able to say no. A detective must fulfil the requirements of his clients – packet of sardines or not.

Barkley was not sure if he wanted to go to Storm's place or go home and sleep. He had forgotten to tell Mao about the concert at Matilda's. It was all too much for him to think about, so he decided he would go home. From the corner of Storm's street he could jump over a couple of fences and be in his own backyard down gumnut alley. Would there be anyone home to let him in though? Sleeping outside in the cold and rain was not peaceful in any cat's mind.

Fortunately, the back door was open. Barkley snuck in, had a drink and a few biscuits, then warmed his body on top of the heating duct under the couch. When everyone had left for the day and the place cooled down from the heating going off, he dug himself under the covers on Corey's bed and stayed there till his family came home and the house was buzzing with warmth and activity again.

# Chapter Twenty

The rain came and lasted for what seemed like an eternity to Barkley. He could not even go outside for a visit under the shrubs as everything was too wet. He figured if he was not venturing out, no one else was either, but he was also bored with being inside all the time. The first night after dinner, the children were teasing each other by flicking rolled-up pieces of paper while watching television. These small, lightweight toys became Barkley's amusement as he tossed them here and there, just like he had done with the leaves at Matilda's place. The children thought he was playing soccer, so said between the couch and the footstool was a goal.

The rain continued and everyone brought wet shoes inside. Sarah and Beth brought in wet everything, including soaked netball tunics and towels from their Saturday morning game. Corey's swimming things always came back soaked, although Jean wondered what he did to his towel to get it wringing wet. After catching up with all the household chores, the washing machine and drier went into overdrive.

When the house was quiet, Barkley would play soccer with his paper toys, and if Tom had left his socks lying about in the lounge room, Barkley would turn them into a mouse that needed chasing and chewing. He also pondered which magic trick Titch was going to do, not that he knew any himself. Matilda would have no opportunity to play with the dried leaves that were now wet, but he was sure Budge and Florry would be making up songs to entertain themselves with, something like 'At the end of the clock is a very nice tick-tock – it's tucker time!'

Zenya would be staying nice and warm, cuddled up next to Puffy. Would Storm be inside having the children tug at his tail and pull his fur, or would he be with Mrs Andrews in the peace and quiet? What would Mao be doing? He could not even imagine. What does a cat with Mao's knowledge do on rainy days?

The other thing he pondered was something he had not realised at the time – none of the cats Lynne had painted were wearing collars. Perhaps this was to show that they were available to everyone in some sort of way – or was this something to do with the collars that went missing? Zenya, Miss Fi-Fi, Budge and Florry appeared to be the only ones who had lost their collars – several in Miss Fi-Fi's case.

Surely it was not Lynne who was taking them? She did know where Miss Fi-Fi lived, but why would she take the collars from her own cats? Plus, there was the collar he found under the house that Miss Fi-Fi said was not hers, so whose was it? Mao's? Did she even wear a collar? Barkley could not say he had ever noticed. He was always gazing into her big blue eyes that seemed to take him to another place – one of calm, beauty and acceptance. Who had taken the collars and why? It's not like they were just lost and found somewhere – they had actually disappeared.

Barkley wondered if Lynne had taken off their collars to wash them, add a trinket or something, and had simply forgotten to put them back on, as he was sure they wore a collar the next time he saw them. It was hard to remember what he had seen, as most of this case had focussed on finding Mao. He also realised that his cravings for dried sardines had disappeared, although were he to be given a packet now he would devour one or two with enthusiasm.

Eventually, the rain drizzled out. Although the sky was still gray, Barkley was off outside as soon as someone was up to let him out so he could get some fresh air and visit his fellow felines. First, he checked in with Matilda to see how the leaves were holding up in the rain. Matilda was upset, for they had all been raked up and put into the bin. Her joy with throwing leaves into the swimming pool was gone. Now she only had what leaves the trees had dropped that day, not enough to put on a display and have other cats over for a pool party. Barkley said in a few days there will be another bunch of leaves available, so not to worry. She felt better about that but had so been looking forward to teaching everyone her game. He asked if

Budge and Florry enjoyed their time with her and she said yes, they had a blast and spent a lot of time giggling and singing.

The next closest feline to visit was Miss Fi-Fi. Barkley stopped outside and knew the lady was there, so kept going around the corner to Titch's place.

'How's it going, Titch? I mean Jon-ay-than,' he asked, noting his correct pronunciation. 'How's your magic trick going?'

Titch looked up from his slumber; he was bright-eyed and looked happy.

'Morning, Barkles! I've been practicing my magic just like my dad taught me! Do you want to see?' asked the new magician.

Barkley was astonished by Titch's cheerfulness. What had happened to him? He looked different. His face had changed — it was slender and more round at the bottom, less square and puffed up.

'Titch, you look marvellous! You really do look great! I would love to see your magic trick, but I want to be surprised and excited along with everyone else at the time,' said Barkley.

'By the way, I have had my name officially changed. Mao came and told my family that I am Jonathan from now on,' he explained.

'Really? That's wonderful! I will introduce you as Jonathan on the day. Tell me, what did she do to get your family to change your name?' wondered Barkley, curious as ever to know her secrets.

'She left a note at the back door.'

'Really? She has taken to doing the same as me? Did she leave a bone as well?'

'No, she just got some twigs, leaves and pebbles from the garden and spelled it out.'

'Goodness me! Why didn't I think of that? Mao really is very clever, isn't she?'

'Yes, she is. I couldn't wait any longer, so she did it for me. I, too, should have thought of doing it myself but... well...'

'Well Jon —a-thong. Sorry, Jon-a-than, that is amazing! She made herself understood just like that?'

'Well, it took a few goes before they cottoned on to what I wanted, so now I am called Johnny for short instead of Titchy, which is better for me. And you'll never guess what else has changed, D I Barkles! I have stopped scratching!' said Jonathan with a smile. He really was so pleased with himself.

'What? You mean changing your name has stopped you from scratching?' asked Barkley, wide-eyed. 'I can't believe my ears and eyes, the changes I am seeing.'

'Well, that and they've stopped putting that horrible stuff on my back to keep the fleas away. It doesn't mean any fleas are coming back. I am on this other stuff instead which is much nicer and not so stressful.'

Tetchy Titch had left and an exuberant, happy Jonathan had replaced him. Barkley felt he was talking to a new cat he had never met before. He bid Jonathan farewell and made his way to Storm's place. He needed to sit and analyse what Mao had done, because he realised he was feeling indignant.

'Aren't I the one who writes the notes and gets people to understand what my client wants? Aren't I the communicator around here? Blast! I shall write my own note to his family and tell them he is now called Jon… Jonathong,' he said to himself, trying to imagine the letters neatly spelled out on the page.

There was no solace to be had at Storm's place. Barkley heard a commotion as he was approaching the front door – whilst playing, one of the twins had stood on Storm's back leg. Storm whimpered, then Barkley watched the front door fly open and his giant friend bundled into the car. Carla yelled at the twins and told them to go outside and play. Storm saw Barkley sitting on the front verandah and simply called, 'Barkley, help me!' then the car drove off.

Barkley was upset that his mate had been hurt again. 'What is going on? Matilda is upset; Titch has changed for the good. Here I am grumbling about Mao writing a note that I could have done myself and Storm has been taken away in the car!' exclaimed Barkley, hoping his best mate would be alright and come home soon.

Not knowing what to do next, he ran down to Mao's place. Barkley wanted someone to talk to, someone who understood. He did not even see the lady with the pram and dog walk past the swings when he cut through the playground. At Mao's place he could hear the family moving about inside. He checked Mao's sleeping and eating room next to the back door. She was not there, so he went up into the treehouse and whiskered to her from there. Eventually, she emerged from inside. Barkley watched her walk across the garden, scratch about in the dirt and leave a couple of deposits, then return to the porch, where she sat and cleaned herself.

'Mao!' yelled Barkley, but she did not look up. Barkley called to her again and jumped down out of the tree. As he landed on the ground, his knowledgeable friend slipped through the sliding door and returned to the warmth inside the house. Barkley sighed and made his way back home. Passing through the playground he was met with three young teenagers who wanted to stop and pat him. Deciding it was not a good idea, he ran past, bolting up the street as fast as he could go. He did not like being so far from home. Going to Mao's place was new territory for him, new smells.

Arriving home, he had a drink of water then thought he would pay a visit to Budge and Florry. Granted, they were not into having deep conversations, but at least he could connect with someone today. He still had not told Mao of the concert they had planned at Matilda's place two sleeps after the rain had stopped.

'Budge! Florry!'

'What do you want, Barkles?' asked a sleepy Budge, sticking his head through the cat flap.

'I thought I'd come and say hello, see how you are,' responded Barkley.

'We're sleeping. Talk to you later,' said Budge, retreating back inside.

'But Budge, I wanted to ask you—'

'Later, Barkles. Too tired to talk.'

'Hmpf! Okay!' said Barkley and realised he was going to do the same – go home and sleep.

*I've been sleeping for days now; how can everyone be so tired? There is fresh air out here, games to play, investigating to be done, and not one whiskering to be had with anyone!*

Nothing for it but to go home. He got there just in time before the house was locked up for the day. Barkley was bored though. What to do? He wondered if Corey still had his alphabet and learning to read books so he could practice his spelling. Barkley trotted into the young man's bedroom and had a look at the books on the shelf at the back of his bed. He found one of Corey's favourite books from when he was little, *A Worm Passed By*, but there were no books on the alphabet. Barkley pulled the book down and a few other books fell with it. He sat on Corey's pillow turning the pages of the story of a worm.

> *A worm passed through an apple and out the other side,*
> *but inside the apple he was not prepared to hide.*
> *Onwards he went through a cabbage and found it a good*
> *place to store his luggage.*
> *Upon a pear he did stare, wondering if a munch would*
> *disturb his lunch.*
> *There was a strawberry, ever so juicy, which gave him*
> *hiccups and he said, "Excuse me."*
> *Eventually the worm was so big, under a branch he hid, and a*
> *warm bed was spun so tight, the size was just right.*
> *Then on a cool dawn a moth was born, and to the fruits*
> *below he greeted them with a simple, "Hello."*

Barkley turned the pages back to the beginning and read again, tracing the letters with his paw. Slowly, he began to realise the b and p faced forward – the b has a back and the p has a tail, just like Mao had shown him. The d faces backward because Regie is a dunderhead, according to Barkley, and the q is hardly ever seen. Sleep overcame the detective and he curled up next to a picture of a worm, not waking till Corey came into his room to put his school things away and saw Barkley on his bed with his books.

'Mum! Come and look at this!' Corey shouted. 'Mum!'

'What is it?'

'Barkley was asleep on my bed with my worm book,' he said, astonished.

'Well? You should learn to put things away, shouldn't you.'

'Mum, I haven't touched the book. Barkley must have pulled it down from the shelf along with these other ones – and he's been reading the book! See, the book is open. Perhaps it's the pictures he likes,' suggested the young man to his mother, who had already left his room, just like Barkley had.

Sarah stuck her head into her brother's room, 'What's going on?'

'Oh, nothing. I came home and Barkley was asleep on my bed with my favourite reader open next to him. He must've pulled it down from the shelf as I haven't touched it.'

'See, Mum! I told you he could read but you wouldn't believe me! He can write too!' said Sarah to her mum, who was busy preparing dinner.

'Well, as I said before, if he can really do that we'll stick him on the telly and make our fortune! If he can sing as well you can teach him to tap dance and then we really will be rich!'

'Zarzar, what's this about Barkley knowing how to read and write?' asked Corey.

'Oh, when Dad and I were in the shed we found stuff we'd been looking for for ages, along with all this shredded paper with letters stuck down onto the butchers' paper that Beth and I had used to make our star maps with, only the words didn't make much sense. They were all badly spelled and there were dog bones there as well. One had dad's tie wrapped around it. Barkley and dad had a fight over it. That's how he got those scratches on his hand,' explained Sarah.

Corey stared at her, then at Barkley, who sat in the hallway looking innocent and waiting to be fed but said nothing, as it was all too impossible to believe. No matter how much Sarah spoke up about it, no one was going to believe her.

# Chapter Twenty-One

**The Night of Paw One**

Barkley wondered if Storm was alright.

*And how will I tell Mao about the concert? Will there be enough leaves at Matilda's place to decorate the swimming pool? When will I have to go to George's place again?*

*Thank Felidae George is not invited to the concert. Hello everyone – this is George who has come to eat all of us! Ugh! No thanks!*

The house creaked into silence, then Barkley heard Corey talking in his sleep. 'Go on, Will! You can do it! You won!' Will was Corey's best friend. They did most things together and were even on the same swimming team.

Barkley had a drink and left a much-needed deposit in his tray. Suddenly, he heard a bang at the back door.

'Barkley? Barkley!'

'Storm, is that you?'

'Yes. I've come to tell you I'm okay. My back leg is sore, the same leg that got injured by George. I've got to take it easy for a while. Also, we are moving out.'

'What? When?'

'I don't know. We're moving to a bigger place.'

'Will you go with them or stay with Mrs Andrews?'

'I will go with them. Staying with Mrs Andrews has huge benefits, but I feel the need to be by their side.'

'Storm, I will really miss you! You have been such a good friend to me. Your strength is so powerful in ways – you have no idea.'

'Oh, I think I've got a pretty good idea how my strength works, thank you. I'm going to Mrs Andrews' place for a few days to rest. I thought I'd tell you, so you know where I am.'

'Okay. Thanks for stopping by and letting me know. I really appreciate it.'

'It will be okay, Barkley. Come and visit me at Mrs Andrews' place if you need to.'

'Hmmm, I doubt she will have me there, but thanks anyway. I am so sad you're leaving.'

'Moving was a thought my lady had today coming back from the doctor, but I sense change is on the way. She discussed it with Greg tonight after the children were in bed.'

'Well, Storm, I will bid you goodnight, and oh, will you still be able to make the concert at Matilda's place?'

'I should do, hopefully my leg will be better by then. I might have to come along the road instead of over fences.'

'I'll get Titch, I mean Joinathong… Joina… Jon-thingamy to walk with you if you like. You'll never guess – since he's changed his name he is a new cat!'

Storm laughed and they bid each other goodnight. Barkley did not know what he was going to do without Storm by his side. His presence was so reassuring and calm, plus his deep voice made everyone feel so relaxed; it was sort of melodious in a way. Then there were his big green eyes, like the colour of the ocean. Barkley knew that although Storm's lady was thinking of moving, he would have time to write her a note and tell her not to leave – surely there must be another way. Barkley was always amused that people did not know that felines can hear their thinking. Dogs can hear too, but Barkley was sure cats were better; that was his biased opinion because the only dog he actually knew was Regie next door – his toy of torment when he was frustrated or needed a bone to attach to one of his notes.

Eventually, morning came and the house stirred. Barkley begged to go out. He had not slept well all night with thoughts of moving in with Storm crossing his mind.

*If I move in with Storm, we can remain buddies. I can resume my detective service from his place and he can be my right paw. I could say to everyone, 'Pay up or I'll send Storm over!' He's so big I could get everyone to do what I say. Yes, I think it would work quite well. Mao can take over my services here. She already knows how to spell, better than I can. Yes, I think it would work quite well. I will move in with Storm! I'll miss my family here, but they will be alright. I'll have a new family.*

Barkley's mind was made up – he was going to leave home. His office was no longer available and Storm was getting a bigger house, so there should be plenty of space for Barkley too.

*Yes, after I have had something to eat I will go and tell Storm I am moving in with him.*

Barkley felt better now that he had thought about his options and was clear what was best.

After breakfast, Barkley made his way to Mrs Andrews' place to tell Storm the good news. He was just about to go down the street towards Storm's second home when he thought it would probably be best if he introduced himself to Storm's family.

*After all, I am going to be living there.*

Heading to the next road over to his best friend's place, he was met by two boisterous boys jostling to get into the car and Carla hurrying out to drive them to school. Barkley made his way to the back door and sat and listened to Greg say goodbye to Nick before turning his attention to his daughters.

'Now, where did Mummy put your socks? Do you think she put them in here? Perhaps she put them in here? Okay, here they are. Sam, have you found your shoes? Okay, that's great sweetie. Do you need help putting them on? Right, come on Evelina, into your pusher you go. Sam, here's your coat, honey. I'll help you with your shoes. Okay, off we go. Oops, better lock the back door! Oh, there's that cat again.'

'What cat, Daddy?' asked Sam.

'Albie's friend who came to visit him. It was most odd. He ran into the lounge room, Albie looked at him, then they both ran out and down the road. Do you remember?'

Sam shook her head.

'Well, he's back again. I wonder if he's alright? Come to think of it, I haven't seen Albie this morning, have you?'

Again, Sam shook her head, no.

'Hey, puss cat! Come on, come and say hello. Come on…' said Greg, coaxing the cat to come closer. Once more, Barkley decided he would wait till the opportune moment. 'Come on, let's go,' Greg said to Sam and locked the door.

Out the front door went Sam, followed by Evelina in her pushchair, then her dad. Barkley had run around to the front to watch them leave.

'Look, Daddy! There he is again!' said Sam, pointing to a cat sitting in the garden.

'Goodness me! You're right, Sam. Unless he has a twin, it looks to be the same cat. I wonder what he wants? You okay there, puss? You looking for Albie? I've not seen him today, he must be inside hiding somewhere,' said Greg, closing the front door and walking Sam to kindergarten and Evelina to day-care.

Barkley returned to Storm's backyard to have a good sniff around. There was a tree for him to climb, plenty of area for deposits, plants, shrubs and the small shed where Storm showed Barkley what a buttonhole is. Barkley tried the door to see if he could get inside. Nothing for it but to curl up and have a sleep, so he found a comfy place on one of the chairs out the back for a snooze.

*I'll go and tell Storm my news when I'm sure this is what I want.*

The detective was so fast asleep he did not hear the radio go on, breakfast dishes being washed, the washing machine going or the buzz of the vacuum cleaner. It was not till Carla came out to sweep up the dead leaves that Barkley woke with a fright and suddenly realised where he was.

'It's okay. I won't hurt you. Come on, come and say hello. Come on, puss. You want to see Albie again? I think he's gone off to his second home, not sure when he'll be back,' said Carla in a gentle voice, holding out her hand to the small Burmese cat with big yellow-green eyes.

'I am considering moving in here to be with Storm... Albie. Can you tell me what the tucker is like? And will I be well fed? Also, will I have to sleep in the laundry?'

Barkley sat waiting for a reply from the slender lady with short brown curly hair. He noticed she had brown eyes and seemed to always be smiling. What he did like most was that she dressed in practical clothes and had flat shoes, just like Mrs Andrews. Plus, Carla had an earthy look about her; one that looked comfortable digging in the garden, cuddling children and being creative with perhaps sewing, cooking or building a sculpture of sorts. Barkley tried to imagine lying in front of the fire with Carla rubbing his belly. He could smell her perfume and thought the light, delicate fragrance suited her.

Carla approached slowly, holding out her hand for Barkley to smell so he knew he was safe, then scratched his head and patted him. Barkley purred. Carla giggled. He liked the look of her and being scratched behind his ears subdued him into loud purrs and drooling, so much he hardly noticed Carla reading his nametag.

'That's enough patting now, Barkley Button Nose. I have to sweep the leaves up,' she laughed.

Barkley looked at her, 'Don't stop. What are you stopping for?' and smooched for more attention. Carla giggled again and Barkley thought Mao would really like her. Mao giggled a lot, so surely they would get on really well. 'I must introduce you to Mao, she is just like you,' he said through purrs. Then he wondered if Mao should move in too, or perhaps go and live with his family, seeing as he might be leaving them, but then who would take over Mao's current position in her family?

'What can I do to persuade you to stay?' asked Barkley, looking like he was pleading for more attention. 'If I had paper, I would write you a note and bring you one of Regie's bones. Please don't move out, otherwise I will have to leave my home and come and stay with you. Although, what if Storm came and lived with me? That way he could still spend time with Mrs Andrews and he would not be run over or stepped on and you can get another cat. Storm did say he would not leave you, but maybe I can change his mind. Ugh! If only I had an office! Wait a whisker! I could get Mao to teach me how to write with twigs and stones! Then I can leave you a note. It will be more difficult – maybe it will help me with my spelling! Yes! That's it!'

Carla kept sweeping and saw Barkley run across the deck and out the front. Barkley knew the way to Mao's from his place but not from Storm's, which meant he had to go home first and head to Mao's from there.

'Mao? Mao, are you there?' he asked. 'Mao,' Barkley called as he entered the warm room and saw her fast asleep on her bed.

The warmth was nice but it came with the drone of the clothes dryer going around and around. Barkley did not want to wake her, so he sat down quietly and waited. The tumble dryer continued its gentle whirl and Barkley felt his eyes becoming heavier and heavier.

Ahhh, such a warm room!

*It was a sunny day and all was well for the detective. He strolled along the footpath like a king in charge of his kingdom with his giant friend at his side.*

*'What could possibly go wrong now?' he thought. 'I have as many sardines as I like, Mrs Andrews feeds Storm very well; in fact, I wish she would feed me! The butterflies are out, the sun is shining. Ahhh! All is good.'*

*'Okay, here's the house here. I will knock at the door and introduce myself. You give her the letter, and in case anything should go wrong, let her have it,' said Barkley with his chest out, full of pride because he had finally mastered the alphabet and knew his spelling was impeccable.*

*Bang on the door, bang on the door.*

*'MIAOW! MIAOW! MIAOW!'*

*'Uh-humm! Good day to you, Madam, I am Detective Inspector Barkley Button Nose,' said Barkley with his sword in his paw and his oversized boots on. He had deliberately left his hat at home so he could see where he was going. 'This is my associate, Storm. It is in your best interest to do as he says as we don't want any goodnights with a Band-Aid now, do we? Please pay attention! We have received word from duss that you are not feeding him droderly. He informs me that he does not like what you give him to eat. I suggest you change his piet. There will be conse... conse-denses if you do not combly. Storm, give her the note while I give her my dusiness carp.'*

*Barkley watched his mate hand over what he thought was a butterfly. Where did he get that from? The lady stood there purring. Where had Barkley heard that purr before?*

*'I understand you. You want me to take the lovely words to....to... Ugh! Finally, someone who speaks Felidae!'*

*The lady bent down and licked his head. Suddenly, music was playing. He felt like dancing, swaying in the warm sunshine that went clang every so often. 'Ahh, sweet lady of the purrs, here to cheer, I see Storm has given you the conse-denses in butterflies and...Stand back, I will take care of this – for I am Barkley in Buttons for Noses,' he said, sniffing the worm in the strawberry. 'I tell you worm, that is the letter b. I know this because the b goes this way, the d goes that way and the p is like this. Just ask Mao, she will tell you,' explained Barkley, drawing the letters in the air with the tip of his tail.*

*The purring was getting louder and louder. 'Yes! Purr, lovely purrs...'*

'Oh! Mao! There you are! I was having such a funny dream,' said Barkley, waking suddenly. 'I dreamt I finally understood all the letters in the alphabet.'

'Hello, Barkley, glad you had a good sleep. Glad you have learnt the alphabet.'

'I have come to see you,' Barkley yawned, 'to see you about...' he yawned again.

'Yes?'

'...Titch, Jonathingamy.'

'You mean Jonathan?'

'Yes. He said you can write by making letters with stones and twigs and things. As I don't have an office anymore, could you teach me to do the same? You see, Storm's family are moving away and I want to tell them to stay. Storm is going to go with them and not move in permanently with Mrs Andrews. He could come and live with me if he wants, at least he would not be stood on and have a sore leg. I have decided if they do leave, I will go with them. Would you be willing to take over my business here? Oh, and before I forget, in two sleeps we are having a concert at Matilda's place. Will you present something to the group?'

'Goodness me, a lot has been going on, hasn't it? So, Storm's family are moving out? Okay, come on then, I will teach you how to write,' said Mao in her usual sweet voice.

Into the garden they went to collect leaves, stones, twigs and anything else that would be good; then they sat down and Mao started to put it together to make words.


`Storm is my best mate`

'Now you try,' Mao encouraged Barkley.

Barkley picked up dried grass clippings he had found on the path and formed them into the letter s, used twigs to make the y, and on he went. Barkley looked at the configuration and thought yes, they both look the same. He was proud to call Storm his friend, his best friend, his companion of strength who helped him be brave and remain calm.

'Now what letter is this?' asked Mao.

'b,' said Barkley.

'Why is it the letter b?' asked Mao.

'Because it says best.'

'What about if I pick up the stem of the b and put it here below, now what does it say?'

Barkley looked at the word, 'It says pest.'

'Correct. So, the letter b has the stem going up to the top and the letter p has the stem pointing down to the bottom. Now can you write "do not leave, puss is my friend"?' asked the Master of Academic Observances.

Barkley moved the garden waste around till he thought he had it right. Mao looked at Barkley, whose tongue was sticking out while he concentrated on his spelling. Then he sat back and looked at Mao to say, 'I've finished'.

Mao read 'po not leave, buss is my frienp'.

'So, tell me Barkley, when you see the letters, what do you see? For example, when you look at the letter b what do you see, because you can read quite well.'

'Well, when I read, I see colours. Sometimes the words jump up off the page and float away but that is mainly if I like the word. If I am not fussed by the word, it stays on the page.'

'Can you write letters with your paw?' asked Mao, pointing to the ground.

Wide-eyed, Barkley had never thought about writing letters in the dirt with his paw but thought he would give it a go.

'Can you write "the pond at the back of my place is deep",' asked Mao, moving out of the way so her student had space to write.

Barkley stood up, thought about it, balanced on three legs and with his paw, wrote in the dirt so he could see the letters. This was great fun! Suddenly he felt alive, spelling out words. Finished, he stood aside for Mao to read what he had written.



'Barkley! Well done! I am so proud of you!' said Mao, smooching her new student. 'You got it all right! It is amazing how you know how to write the letters with your paws, but cutting letters from print is slightly difficult. I asked you to write this out because it contains the letters you have difficulty with. So, how do you know the letters are correct?'

'I know they are correct because when the children were learning how to read and write they traced the letters with their finger and sometimes they would take my paw and do the same. That was how I learnt how to read, because I sat with each child when it was their turn. I did quite enjoy learning the letters with them,' reminisced the detective, now a student under the Master of Academic Observances.

'Do you know there aren't many felines who can do what you can?' said Barkley's teacher.

'Really? Surely there are! I bet Storm can!' said Barkley, puffing out his chest to look tall and strong like his mate.

'Well, we will see. For now, you need to write to his family and tell them not to leave. Can you do that with these twigs and things? You know you could tear the letters out of the papers like you have been doing, but trace them with your paw beforehand, that way you will know if it is correct,' suggested Mao.

'I suppose I could, but I tend to get stressed as I am forever in a hurry to get it done quickly and drop it off. That's probably why I make so many errors and forget which letter is which,' explained Barkley, getting the twigs, stones and other things he could find to make the words. 'Storm is not his family name. They call him Albie, only I don't know how to spell that.'

'Just write puss instead. They will know what you mean.'

Barkley wrote in the soil first.

Next, he made the same letters with the bits from the garden.

'What happens when I get there and I can't remember how to spell anything? I'll be writing at their back door where there isn't any dirt for me to practice first and copy from,' said Barkley.

'Would you like me to come with you?'

'Oh, yes please! Thank you, Mao, that would be wonderful! You are going to come to our concert, aren't you?'

'Yes, I am.'

Barkley smiled. He felt so much better and was slowly realising that he could spell after all.

'Mao...'

'Yes.'

'All those little pieces of paper that you delivered to us, you said they came from higher up. What did you mean?'

'I will explain at the concert,' said Mao, looking authoritative.

Barkley did not respond, but said he was going to Storm's place now if Mao wanted to come too and informed her that Storm was recuperating at Mrs Andrews' place from another sore leg. Barkley was normally frightened being this far from home and going along the road made him feel vulnerable; he preferred to go over the back fence, although that too had its problems if there were any dogs about. When he saw Jonathan's street, Barkley knew to turn left then right, left, left again and there is Storm's place.

Barkley marched out the back to the cleanly swept deck. Beyond it was a garden with lots of trees and weeds that needed to be pulled, leaves to be raked, dead rose heads removed and things cut back, basically a general tidy up that was probably not going to be done till spring.

Thirsty now, Barkley wished he could have a nice cool drink. He searched for a water bowl out the back but could not find one till he went to the opposite side of the house. There was a large bowl with water and thankfully, no dead bugs. Mao also had a drink. Barkley had forgotten to ask Mao if she needed to eat before they took off on their assignment.

Mao's student commenced gathering what he could from the backyard, which was not a lot; out the front he was more successful. Barkley told Mao he did not want any help but just to watch and supervise, then at the end he would ask her for guidance. Mao agreed that was a good idea and sat back and watched leaves, twigs and small branches that had blown down, empty snail shells and some long grass that Barkley had managed to chew off appear just beyond the back door. Barkley sat, thought about what he wanted to say and put the garden paraphernalia together.

Puss is my best friend please do not move away

'All I need is a bone to let them know I mean what I say,' said Mao's student, looking to his teacher for confirmation.

Mao gazed upon Barkley with such pride. She knew he could do it; she just had to find a simple way to teach Barkley to approach it from a different angle. Mao was so proud she hugged Barkley, 'Well done!'

# Chapter Twenty-Two

**The Night of Paw Two**

'Barkley, dinner!' Sarah called till he appeared from under the couch. 'There you are! Barkley, I know what you've been up to! Carla told me all about it and showed me a video of you writing, "Puss is my best friend please do not move away." Is Albie your best friend, is he, Barkley? Huh? You don't want them to move away because you will miss your best friend?'

'Who's got a best friend?' asked Beth, entering the kitchen area.

'Barkley has. You know the big ginger cat we saw? That's Nick's cat, Albie. His mum saw Barkley in her backyard yesterday,' explained Sarah, leaving out the rest of the information that Carla had shown her a video of Barkley making her a message.

'Oh, that's nice that he has a play friend,' said Beth, stroking their family pet while he gobbled down his dinner.

'Maybe not for much longer. Nick's family are thinking of moving out.'

'Really? I read this article on animals that become depressed when they lose their friend. I hope that doesn't happen to Barkley. Hey, maybe we should get another cat to keep him company?'

'I already asked mum if we could have one of Mrs Longford's kittens and she said no.'

'Oh, pity. Perhaps we can wear her down with a bit of pestering?' said Beth with a twinkle in her eye.

'Maybe. You start pestering and I'll back you up!' said Sarah, getting some potatoes out and peeling them in preparation for dinner.

'Okay. How much homework do you have tonight?' asked Beth in a pleading voice.

'Heaps! I have two essays to write – history and English comprehension, plus my maths teacher has given us a load of trigonometry to do.'

'Do you have time to help me with my algebra?'

'Yeah, okay, but you're emptying the dishwasher!'

'Ugh! Oh, okay! Thanks,' said Beth, smiling at her sister. Beth knew algebra but needed to build her confidence.

Beth chopped up onions and garlic while Sarah finished peeling the potatoes and carrots and sliced some tomatoes. They had no idea what was for dinner, only that it helped immensely if they assisted in getting things ready instead of sitting on the couch watching the telly; besides, with the amount of homework they both had there would be little time for any relaxing tonight.

Barkley gulped down his dinner. He was too busy concentrating on tomorrow's concert and who was going first, to reply to what Sarah had said to him. He thought it would be best if Matilda did her activity first, it was after all her garden and it would get everyone laughing and in the mood. Belly now full, he sat down in the lounge room, had a bath and thought about what he was going to present. Why he decided to be a detective seemed like the obvious choice, but what about learning how to write? Barkley felt he had a new freedom now he knew he could write with his paw.

*Perhaps if I go to Lynne's place and get some paint and paper I can write notes that way and have my own sign off, like Paws United. Budge and Florry would love to play with some paint and make pictures! Maybe we could sell them? One packet of sardines per painting!*

Barkley imagined them sitting on the footpath with their art and people coming to buy their paintings.

Slowly, everything became quiet. Barkley listened to the creaks of the night as the house settled and the gentle snoring of its occupants commenced. Tomorrow was the day of the concert. He imagined Budge and Florry singing their songs, and everyone else proving to Mao that they had learnt the words written about them in the book. He saw himself say that he finally knows how many letters there are in the alphabet, how to spell and that yes, he is swimming forth with greatness to touch the void of the unknown particle that already exists, where Mao will explain everything to him and he will no longer hear, 'All in good time.'

Barkley wished on all his whiskers that the day would be great and memorable for everyone, then yawned and fell asleep.

# Chapter Twenty-Three

**Concert Day**

Barkley woke with a start. Corey, who normally slept soundly, was wriggling around too much and the Captain of Cute Noses could not sleep on a bed that jiggled. Wanting somewhere warm and cosy to snuggle up on so he was well rested and prepared for the big event, he wandered into Sarah's bedroom and curled up on her dressing gown that was draped over an armchair. In the morning, he felt Sarah gently pick him up, remove her gown and place him back down on the chair. She gave him a pat and whispered to continue with his lovely dreams, then went to get ready for school. The heating commenced and the house began to stir.

'Mum, have you seen my socks?' yelled Sarah.

'Try the laundry. It's all clean, just not put away yet,' came the response.

Sarah skipped out of her bedroom singing the latest song on the radio, then came back to sit on her bed to put her socks and shoes on.

'Come on Barkley, breakfast!' said Sarah, picking him up. While she cuddled him all the way to his eating area she whispered in his ear, 'I am so proud of you Barkley! You are a very smart and special cat.'

'Miaow,' said Barkley and purred into her ear, 'open up my office so I can resume my business.'

She gently put him down and gave him something to eat. 'Go on, munch up! Here, I'll open the back door for you so you can go for a wee. Brrr! It's cold!' she said, then dashed into the kitchen to make tea, toast and get some cereal.

Beth and Corey also came into the kitchen.

Yawning, Beth said, 'I dreamt last night that I was this humungous being and I had to get over this chasm, because if I didn't, I would never get something or other, whatever it was I wanted. I can't remember that bit now, but I stood at the edge and below was this sort of dark, black gooey stuff. If I fell into it, I would have been swallowed up and turned into this horrible gunk. I had to jump over, only I was fearful of falling and being swallowed by the sticky goo. I kept on hearing this voice say, "You can do it, it's easy." I stood there looking at the distance I had to leap over and kept saying to myself, "This is real," but this voice kept laughing and saying, "No, it isn't." I had a feeling I was going to die if I didn't jump and a dread that I would fall into the chasm. Eventually, after what seemed like an eternity, I leapt over and it was easy and I was free. It was weird. What do you think that means?'

'You know what I dreamt last night?' chimed Jean, getting her coffee ready. 'I dreamt that all my children came home from school with straight As because they paid attention in class and did their homework.'

'Excuse me, but I did all my homework last night, then I went to bed and straight to sleep! The dream was so vivid. It sure felt like it was real at the time,' said Beth.

'Perhaps it means you are taking a leap into the unknown and that there is nothing to worry about,' suggested Sarah.

'Yeah, maybe. The unknown of what though?'

'Maybe it's the unknown of being your true self,' said Corey.

Everyone looked at him. For a boy so young, he sometimes came out with some profound wisdom.

Barkley, who had been eating his breakfast, stopped and stuck his head into the kitchen and stared at Corey. He too was astonished with what he had heard, because suddenly, everything seemed to fall into place. All the clues, the notes, the book, Mrs Andrews, Lynne and the lady with the big hair – it all just made sense now.

Barkley was pleased with himself that he had managed to figure it all out and did not have to rely on the Master of Academic Observances to explain it to him. He went back to eating his breakfast, then dashed outside to make a couple of deposits and charged back in to sit by the heating for a bit. *It's going to be a busy day,* he thought, while giving himself a bath. He also had to keep an ear and eye out when his family were leaving for the day so he was not shut inside. 'Can't run a concert at Matilda's place from the window here,' he said to himself.

Today, Jean was driving Corey to school. As soon as he heard, 'Corey, you ready? Have you brushed your teeth?' he knew it was time to leave for Matilda's place.

*Thank Felidae the rain has finished.*

Into the brisk morning air he went.

*Am I too early?*

At Matilda's back door, he sat and whiskered to her that he was there. The swimming pool was nice and clean and there was a fresh pile of raked leaves under the tree.

*Isn't that nice of Matilda's family to prepare the arena for us.*

'Come on Budge, we might be late,' said Florry as he came around the corner of Matilda's yard.

'Hello boys,' greeted Barkley to the brothers. He was glad to see them.

'Oh, hello, Barkley,' said Florry.

'Morning Barkles! What have you been doing?' asked Budge with a twinkle in his eye.

'Not much, a bit of this and that. Oh, Mao has taught me how to write with twigs, leaves and things. It's great fun!' said the student of Academic Observances.

'That's great, isn't it Flor?' said Budge, looking at Florry like he did not understand a word Barkley had just said. Florry nodded in agreement.

'Matilda is still inside,' explained Barkley.

'Okay. Hey Flor, do you want to play with the leaves?' asked Budge, ready for excitement.

'We're all going to play with the leaves once everyone is here,' explained Barkley to the brothers, who sat down so they were ready to pounce into fun and laughter when the time came.

Just then a gust of wind whizzed through the yard, picked up some leaves, danced them through the air and allowed them to settle in a new place. The two brothers and Barkley watched the fallen leaves be flicked across the garden. The wind died down as suddenly as it had come, but there was a loud breathing noise and it was coming their way.

Barkley sat wide-eyed as Zenya and Puffy arrived. Budge and Florry turned and looked at Barkley, wondering if this was George and why had he been invited?

'Hello. I hope you don't mind, I brought Puffy with me. He'll just sit here and listen. Is that okay?' asked Zenya.

'When everyone is here we will put it to the vote,' said Barkley, not knowing what else to say.

He was not keen on having Puffy present, breathing so heavily all day when the felines were supposed to be giggling and having fun. Zenya told Puffy to go and sit by the table and chairs next to the closed off frivolity area. To a cat, getting over the fence surrounding the pool was nothing, just jump up onto the pot plant, then up onto the wall and down – easy. There was no way Puffy was going to get in, perhaps that would be best? Maybe Puffy could keep an eye out for any people, like Lucy and Roger.

Zenya had done a balancing act to get into the yard. Everyone else just squeezed through the gap between the gates and the house but she had to bring a large, overweight dog with her. Being an Abyssinian, she was skilled in the art of opening doors and such. At home, she had learnt how to open any door to let herself in and out and had even managed to open the kitchen cupboards. Once when she was little, her family opened the drawer to get a saucepan and there she was, snuggled up in it. To let Puffy and her in, she had jumped up onto the top of the gate, saw the wire that was connected to the latch and pulled up. All she had to do was tell Puffy to push the gate and they were in.

Out the corner of his eye, Barkley spotted Matilda jump out of the window, onto the rubbish bin and down into the yard.

'Hello everyone,' she said, pleased to have visitors. Sometimes Matilda was tired of being on her own all day, longing for someone to talk to and play with. She was so happy that Barkley had suggested putting on a concert at her place. 'Just think! It will be the talk for sleeps to come and everyone will want to come over and see where it all took place!' she had said to Barkley.

'Who's that? Shall I shoo him away?' Matilda asked, staring at the large dog who was sleeping under the outdoor table.

'That's Puffy! He came with Zenya,' said Barkley, wishing he did not have to introduce the large dog to anyone, no matter how friendly he was, that is, if you could call Puffy friendly. He certainly did not bite or bark, in fact, he could not have cared less about all the cats sitting there; sleeping had a greater priority.

New visitors arrived.

'Doesn't it bother you being so big?' asked Jonathan, formerly known as Titch the Fearless, of his new friend Storm. 'Once, when I was little, I dreamt of being big, not as big as you mind, but big enough to climb the fence and go exploring. I so wanted to have a look in everyone else's garden and see what was what, especially those chickens over the way. I had never heard such clucking before. I wanted to go and see for myself. When I was big enough I got out the front and made my way around to those funny birds. I found it hilarious to watch them cluck their way through eating. One of them left runny poo and I happened to step in it! And golly, do they fight! You think I'm difficult to get on with, you should watch those chickens! They seem to have this order of who gets what when and if you take what isn't yours, you get chased out. There were feathers flying that day! Once I spent the night there. It was a good sleep too, very warm sleeping next to a chicken. I think in the morning they laid extra eggs because I had purred them to sleep the night before. I couldn't wait to get out of their enclosure though, whiskers, did it smell! How many dinners do you get a day? What about breakfast? What do you eat?'

Barkley smiled at Storm, who looked at him as if to say, 'You couldn't get him to talk nicely at all before, now that he's changed his name, you can't get him to shut up!'

'Welcome, come in,' said the Detective of Ceremonies.

Budge looked at Florry and Florry looked at Budge as if to say, 'Look at that cheerful chap! What a transformation!'

'He must've gotten rid of all his fleas!' said Budge.

'Yeah, and changed his diet and all,' said Florry, looking back at Titch, astonished with his chatter.

Storm was still limping but not as bad as last time. Fortunately for him, Puffy had left the gate open so Jonathan and he just had to walk through and not jump over anything. Getting into the pool area did mean jumping over the fence, so Zenya called Puffy to come and put his paws up onto the railing.

'There you go, Storm. All you need to do is walk up Puffy's back and you'll be on the fence, then you can jump down, if that doesn't hurt too much,' she said.

'Huh? You do realise I am almost as tall as him?' said Storm, amazed that he would even consider standing on Puffy.

'Oh, that's okay. He won't mind. He's used to me climbing on his back.'

'Yes, but that's you. I'm four times as heavy.'

'It won't matter. You don't mind, do you Puffy? See, he doesn't mind. Up you go!'

Storm looked at Puffy, who stood there on his hind legs, front paws on the railings, wagging his tail and puffing madly with his tongue hanging out. Zenya got out of the way to give Storm some space. The giant cat stood on Puffy's back, then carefully stepped onto the railing and jumped down. There was a slight whimper with pain, but otherwise he was good. Puffy never moved a muscle. He appeared to not even know Storm was standing on him.

'That is some dog if he will let you do that,' said Storm.

'Oh, he'll let me do anything, won't you Puffy?' said Zenya, walking up Puffy's back like she was accustomed to jumping off and doing summersaults, then like Storm, stood on the railing and jumped down. Puffy wagged his tail again and returned to sleeping under the table.

'How many whiskers till Mao gets here, Barkles?' asked Budge.

'I don't know. Hopefully she'll be here soon,' he replied.

'And what about Miss Fi-Fi?' asked Matilda.

'That I do not know. She said she was coming but I am not sure when,' said the detective turned organiser of entertainment. 'It will depend on whether her kittens can be left on their own for a bit.'

Barkley was getting nervous. He wanted everyone to arrive on time so the performance could commence without any distractions. He heard a car come up the drive, a door slide open, footsteps at the front door, a thump, then the footsteps retreated, the door slid shut and the car left. He looked at Matilda, wondering what was going on – she should know the sounds of her own place.

'It's just a delivery man for Lucy; it happens all the time,' explained Matilda.

Barkley sighed with relief. The last thing he wanted was for their fun and games to come to a halt before they even got started.

'Hey Barkley! Is that Mao in the tree there?' asked Budge, nodding to a branch hanging over Barkley's head.

Barkley looked up. There she was, sitting quietly, watching everyone chat and sniff around the yard.

'Mao! I didn't see you arrive! Care to come down and join us?' asked Barkley, wishing that the day would go to plan.

'I'm okay up here, thanks. I've got a good position to watch all the proceedings,' she explained.

'Right, the proceedings! Best get on with it then,' he thought and called everyone to attention.

'Hello everyone, welcome. I don't think we all know each other. I will introduce you in order of appearance. These are brothers, Budge and Florry. Boys, stand up so everyone can see you. Budge and Florry are going to sing some songs for us today. Then we will do some leaf art at the swimming pool with Matilda. Next, we have Storm, who probably needs no introduction. I think he is well known around here for his size alone. Storm is going to give a talk on what it's like to be that big (everyone cheered with glee). Next, we have Jonathan, who some of you may have known as Titch. Jonathan is following in his father's footsteps and doing some magic. Zenya is going to take us on a meditation. Miss Fi-Fi, if she can get away, is going to talk about being a mother, and for those of you who have not officially met, this is Mao,' he said, pointing to the overhanging branch, just to find that she had disappeared. 'Where has she gone now?' he sighed in frustration.

'Hello. I am Mao, Master of Academic Observances,' said Mao, emerging from under the hedge that lined one side of the pool area.

Barkley heard a myriad of miaows say, 'Hey! I know that voice! I've heard that voice before! We've heard that voice before, haven't we Flor? Where do I know that voice from? I remember, your voice was in the dream I had the other night! You were telling me not to do something, what was it?'

'Okay, calm down everyone! Calm down! Let's have some peace,' yelled Barkley, trying to control the situation. He was becoming more tense as the moments went on.

Suddenly, the place became quiet as everyone nodded and responded with a timid 'Hello.' Then no one said anything; they just sat and stared. Barkley, who was still under the tree, watched in amazement as everyone looked on in awe, as if Mao was some great cat from Kitty Cavern. Then Budge piped up, 'Come on Mao, tell us where we know you from.'

The sweetest voice they had ever heard said, 'Perhaps you would know this better,' and started to purr loudly.

'Yeah, that's it! That's what we've heard, isn't it, Flor?' said Budge, nudging his brother. 'Yeah, you more than me,' Florry responded.

'Hey! Have you been coming to visit us while we're sleeping?' asked Budge.

Mao kept purring and nodded her head.

'It was you! You came and said we should sing!' said Florry.

'I remember waking in the night once, thinking I had heard someone tell me to go outside and make paintings with the leaves. I did see you out the front once jumping around the pots,' said Matilda. 'Yet how do we know you when we have never met you? What happened to giving a whisker? If we all know your voice, then you have come to see us while we were sleeping, yet you could have come and introduced yourself when we are awake like any normal cat. What is wrong with you?'

'Puffy said he had seen another feline around and I didn't believe him, but now I think you must have come to visit when we were fast asleep on the bed out the back. Puffy said he had a dream that he was playing and running around with another dog. I had this amazing dream that I was playing with another feline. We were jumping and running through grass and everything smelt so sweet,' said Zenya.

'Mao, why couldn't you just come and say hello by giving a whisker like anyone else would?' asked Matilda again, realising her patience was becoming short. Matilda was a straightforward feline and did not like being mucked around, just tell it how it is. When she first moved in with Lucy and Roger there was a lot of dithering going on with them both, but she soon sorted them out. Even though it took time, she now has them in a good place where they are decisive and do exactly as they say they are going to do. Her dinner is served on time and she had recently got Lucy to place the rubbish bin just so and leave the window open so she can come and go as she likes; not too many cats in the neighbourhood would know the trick to getting inside.

'You have been very elusive and hard to catch,' said Storm, remembering the times he gave chase. 'As Matilda said, what happened to coming and giving a whisker?'

Barkley came and joined the group. He wanted to hear what Mao was going to say and to see if he had finally understood it all, because each occasion he managed to pose a question the response was, 'All in good time.' Perhaps now was not a good time, but he wanted Mao to explain – she had, after all, been at the core of this mystery. He also wondered if this case was finally coming to an end.

*It has been the most cryptic case I've ever had. I've eaten all the sardines, lost my office and Regie's bones for bribing. Pretty soon, I'll probably leave my family and go live elsewhere if I want to continue with my services – or give it all to Mao (she seems better at it than me).*

Astonished, Barkley noticed that he was no longer jealous of Mao's abilities. He suddenly felt free and knew he was ready to let go of everything he thought he stood for. He watched Mao standing proud in front of everyone.

Mao looked at Storm with a twinkle in her eye and said, 'You are very good at chasing. It took all of my agility to lose you on both occasions.' Turning to everyone assembled, she continued, 'It is a pleasure to finally meet you all. I didn't say anything because it would defeat the purpose. I am one of four felines in my family. When I was young, we got to play all day, run around outside in the grass, go exploring, sniff flowers, sleep as much as we liked. It was tremendous fun...'

'Pretty much the same as most felines,' said Matilda, remembering her own playfulness.

'What have you been doing in our home?' asked Budge, wondering if he could have been attacked while he slept, or worse, had his food stolen.

Mao purred her lovely, sweet purr and walked over to Barkley so she now sat to his right.

'Budge, Florry, aren't you commencing the concert with a song?' asked Mao.

'I think I know what you've been doing,' Barkley piped up.

Mao turned and looked at her student.

'Really? What is knowing? Knowing is to not err at the sight of magnificence but to understand the Way is best.'

'WHAT? What are you on about? Speak normally so we can understand!' said Matilda, losing her patience. She, like everyone, wanted answers. If she was not going to get them she would just shoo Mao away and get on with having fun. Matilda, for all her loveliness, never put up with nonsense.

Mao looked her straight in the eyes and said, 'Mastering academic observances is about seeing what is there and what is not there. Creativity is the expression of you found in the space between. Let me ask you, if I had come and given a whisker, showed my paws, would you have sat and spoken with me or sent me away? Would you have taken to singing, meditation, frivolity and having fun if I had suggested it, or would you have just brushed it aside? I do not come to cause any malice, but now that we are all together, let me ask you, what do you know of the words written about you in the picture book?'

'Not much, but we've been singing and dancing ever since, haven't we, Flor?' said Budge, interrupting Mao's stare towards Matilda. Florry nodded.

'Yes, and I have been playing outside with the leaves and watching them float across the water. I thought I was doing this because I watched you tossing leaves out the front that day,' said Matilda.

'And Puffy and I have been meditating more. It's really very nice.'

'Excellent!' said Barkley, attempting to keep things moving so no claws were extended. 'What say we get on with our concert before Matilda's family come back.'

Everyone agreed to continue showing their talents rather than destroying the event with misunderstandings displayed as anger.

# Chapter Twenty-Four

'Budge, Florry. We'd love to hear your songs,' said Barkley, stepping aside to create space.

Budge and Florry moved to the front of the group, turned to face everyone, then got into position with Florry on the left, Budge on the right.

> *If you are ever in need of a chat,*
> *Just come and see us cats.*
> *He's called Budge,*
> *And I'm called Florry,*
> *Together we make Fudge and Blorry!*
>
> *We are cats,*
> *Mischief is where it's at.*
> *Bundles of joy,*
> *But no, not a toy.*
>
> *We're into cuddles 'n purring,*
> *Playing 'n sleeping.*
> *Creating laughter,*
> *Cos it is a pleasure to know ya.*
> *We're cats,*
> *Come and see us for a chat.*

A slow melodic song was next, but the twinkles in their eyes and small cheeky grins gave the punchline away.

> *A gentle paw*
> *Was all that was needed,*
> *To touch your heart at the core*

*And float away all that heeded,*
*To allow you to dance*
*And give one more chance,*
*For you to focus*
*AND GET UP AND FEED US!*

The brothers giggled so much they lost their balance and toppled over. Everyone joined in the laughter. They all knew what it was like to be sitting there staring at their family, miaowing for something to eat. How many times did, 'I'm hungry,' fall onto deaf ears when they were staring at those funny zombie-making things?

'I have a song,' said Zenya.

Everyone looked at her and said, 'Go on.'

*Do not underestimate the power of us cats,*
*One little purr and you will love us all the more,*
*One little glance and our love will last and last,*
*Do not underestimate the power of us cats.*

Zenya looked shy, but she did not need to wonder as they all cheered her on with purrs and smooches. Storm showed his appreciation by raising a paw in respect.

'Miss Fi-Fi!' said Storm enthusiastically.

Barkley whizzed around to see the French feline making her way down off the fence and into the concert area. He was so happy to see her! He wanted to run over and give her the biggest smooch he could find, but thought he should remain composed while he was managing the day's activities.

'Hello everyone,' said Miss Fi-Fi, looking at Barkley and Storm in particular.

'Hello,' they chorused back.

'We were just singing a few of our songs,' said Florry.

'Yes, I could hear you from out there,' she responded. 'I cannot stay for long; my little ones will be wanting me soon.'

'Seeing as you cannot stay for long, what would you like to do while you are here?' asked Barkley, ready to change the protocol.

'I have been hearing such lovely stories of how much fun it is to throw the leaves into the water to make a pretty picture. Could I do that?'

'Of course! There is a pile of leaves over there. You can throw those in and see what happens,' said Matilda, pointing to Roger's neat pile of raked leaves.

'Ohh, thank you,' she said, making her way over to pick out some of the best leaves she could find to bring to the pool. Storm decided he would assist and brought some extra leaves. Delicately, she placed each leaf into the water and waited for them to float away, only nothing happened. A couple of them got stuck to her claws, so she flicked and flicked till they fell into the water.

'Monsieur Storm?' she asked, looking at him, 'I don't understand why it isn't working.'

'You need the wind to carry them over the water,' he explained, then sat down with his back to the pool, put his tail in and gave it a swish. Being so big, he was the only one whose tail was long enough to reach the water. Miss Fi-Fi watched the leaves bob up and down as they moved, ever so slightly, away from the edge.

'Miss Fi-Fi?'

'Hmmm?'

'What's it like being a mother?' asked Zenya.

'Yeah, tell us what it's like,' said Matilda, keen to know.

Everyone stopped and eagerly awaited Miss Fi-Fi's response.

'Well, it is like nothing you have experienced before. You have these little bundles that smell so nice and are helpless without you. You must feed them, and they are hungry all the time. Their little feet squish against your belly, and that is very soothing. They are so little, and at first, they cannot see or hear anything so you have to help them, but it really is such a lovely experience to have something so tiny and dependent on you. I let them know all is well with my purring and licking them clean. I must get back to them soon. They will be cold and hungry again and I will give them their bath.'

'Yes, but how do you know what to do? Did your Mamma teach you?' quizzed Matilda.

'Oh, when you lick them clean and make the purring, it is passed on to your little ones, so if they ever get the same chance, they too will know and so will their children. That is how it comes naturally. There is something inside you that just comes out because it was all given to you when you were little. Besides, there is always the Great King Cat in the sky who knows everything and passes it on to us.'

'How are they now, Miss Fi-Fi?' asked Storm, who knew he was too big to invite himself in through the cat flap.

'They are wonderful. They have opened their eyes and are getting used to focussing on things. They can hear more and are just beginning to purr. I can tell you, listening to them make the little purring is so warming to my heart.'

'Can I come and visit you and see the kittens?' asked Matilda.

'Yes, of course. Yes, you are most welcome. I have to go now.'

'Miss Fi-Fi? Before you go,' said Storm, pointing to her leaves that had gently floated across the water.

'Oohhh! Look at that! How pretty! I think I can see a giraffe.'

'Yes, I can see it too,' said Storm.

Everyone moved to look at Miss Fi-Fi's giraffe. Budge and Florry were not really interested in what it was like to have children; all they wanted was to sing their next song. When Miss Fi-Fi was speaking, Budge looked at Florry like, 'What is it to us? We'll never have the opportunity, so why wonder?' Florry nodded.

'Barkles? Could we sing one more song?' asked Budge.

'Okay.'

Budge and Florry started to hum the tune and sway in time. Everyone cheered because they knew the song but had not heard it since they themselves were kittens. This was always known as the 'Chum Song', the song cats and dogs sing when they become best mates.

*Oh, great Pal,*
*It is good to see you well.*
*Friendship is the greatest gift,*
*It gives me such a lift.*
*It doesn't matter what you do,*
*We will always be friends,*
*Through and through.*

*Oh, dear Friend,*
*Every time you smile,*
*I am transported to a place,*
*I had forgotten for a while.*

*Mate, chum,*
*I'm glad we have become,*
*The friends we were meant to be,*
*Because with you I am the best of me.*

*Warmth, hugs and laughter,*
*This is what we are after.*
*Boundless memories,*
*Of you and me, yes please!*

*Oh, dear Pal,*
*It is good to see you so well.*
*Mateship the greatest gift,*
*It gives such a lift.*

Everyone smiled and laughed. It felt good to come together and sing something they had not heard in many years, plus to their amazement, they remembered all the words.

Barkley gazed at his friends and realised no one was trying to pick a fight, not even the new Jonathan. He had quietened down a lot since he had gotten rid of his old name. Sometimes in summer, reminisced Barkley, he would hear felines fighting at night and wondered if that was Titch pushing his muscles onto innocent felines who perhaps just wanted to get past. For all the years of comments about Titch being the biggest grump ever, his new demeanour will change the gossip to how nice and chatty he is.

There was talk once that someone walked their dog past his place and Titch got up and had a go at the dog. Apparently, it was an enormous dog – Barkley wondered if it was George. 'I mean, Felidaes to him. If he can take on George and win, then I will definitely give up my love of sardines!' he had said when he heard the story. Plus, everyone knew when they wanted the use of Barkley's detective service they were not to pick fights. How could they pick a fight with the greatest detective around these parts and still expect him to solve their case? 'Besides, I don't want my cute button nose to be clawed, otherwise I might have to change my name to Barkley of Scratched Noses,' was another reason the detective gave to anyone who knocked at his door.

Barkley sighed.

*Where am I going to get a new office from?*

'Well, goodbye everyone! Enjoy your concert. I liked the song you sang. Will you teach it to me?' asked Miss Fi-Fi of the brothers.

'Don't you have a similar song in your language?' asked Budge.

'Yes, it is called "Oh Mon Ami, Quand Tu Souris".'

'Goodbye Miss Fi-Fi!' they chorused.

'Thank you for coming!' said Zenya as she watched the French feline jump over the swimming pool fence and make her way towards the gate.

'Everyone, get some leaves and take them to the pool!' instructed the Master of Ceremonies as he too got up, put a bunch of leaves into his mouth, sat next to the edge of the pool and threw them in, one by one, then waited for the surprise to form. They were all excited to be throwing their leaves in and watching the pretty pictures form in the slight breeze that had arrived. Some of Miss Fi-Fi's giraffe got mixed up with Zenya's leaves and made what she thought was a giant bear, just like the one that sat on Lucy and Roger's bed. Lucy loved the teddy bear she put on the bed each morning after she had made it look clean and tidy; Roger could not see the point of it.

Barkley did not think his looked like anything till Zenya threw her leaves in. Together, they thought it looked like a tree – one that was ready to climb and have fun in. Barkley almost fell in when he threw his last leaf in. Fortunately, Zenya managed to pull him back before he toppled over headfirst into the cold water. He was so glad he was not going to spend the afternoon chilled to the bone and having to lick himself clean, let alone work out how to get out of the freezing water with leaves stuck to him. He would have ruined everyone's pictures and fun.

Storm thought his leaves looked like a bird and Matilda thought hers looked like a massive leaf. Jonathan threw his leaves in from every corner of the pool; he was so excited to be playing games. Now that his name had changed, he felt so free. He ran around and did as he pleased, threw a leaf in after each lap around the pool, then jumped over the fence, ran up the tree and gazed out at everyone's designs. 'Ahhh, no more Titch the Fearless. Now I can be Jonathan, a gift from Dad, a magician just like him,' he yelled.

Storm looked up at the boisterous Jonathan playing in the tree, jumping down into the garden pot, then leaping over the fence, back into the pool area, picking up leaves and doing it all again. Storm glanced at Barkley as if to say, 'There is no comparison between what was before and is now.' Barkley took it to mean it was time to move on to the next event.

'Okay everyone, Storm is going to give us a talk now on what it is like to be big,' said Barkley, bringing everyone back together.

They all quietened down while each found a spot and waited for the giant to speak.

'Hello everyone. Let me see, where do I begin?'

'Start with Harley,' Barkley suggested.

'Oh yes, well, my brother Harley is bigger than I am.'

Everyone gasped in amazement.

'Believe it or not, I am the smallest in my family.'

'No!' they chorused.

'When we were kittens, we used to play and run around. Harley would run up the walls, holding onto the wallpaper as tightly as he could with his claws. I tried it once, but I fell off. I was pretty good at climbing the curtains though. Then we got our nails cut and half the fun went. Because we were so big and had huge appetites, I was given to my current family and Harley stayed where he was. Being this big means I can jump fences with ease, but I am not as light on my feet as you, Miss Mao. For all the times I chased you, I could never catch you! Harley was always braver than I. When dinner was being prepared, he would stand on his hind legs, put his paws on the benchtop and snitch a few morsels for us, till he got a smack on his paws. We could smell what they were cooking and we didn't want to go without tasting a bit of an excellent, well-cooked meal.

Sometimes a bit would fall off the children's fork onto the floor and Harley and I would gobble it up. This was huge fun for us, but not so when the parents found the children were feeding us.'

'Yes, but where did you get all those muscles from?' asked Matilda.

'I don't know. We are all like that, including my parents. There are seven of us in the family.'

Wide eyes looked at Storm. None of them could believe there could be that many large cats.

'I remember my dad being very strong and he had big feet. When we were kittens, he used to lie on his back, put his paws in the air and balance us on his feet. Sometimes we faced Dad and he would smile and flick his ears. Other times, we were the other way around and watched his tail flick from side to side. We would wave our feet in the air trying to get to what we thought was the biggest toy ever. It was great fun and we giggled and giggled. After playing, we always had delicious sleeps, all curled up together. Then Harley and I moved in with a family. We both grew too big to keep together, so I was given to my current family. I hear news of Harley every so often because his family is related to Greg.'

'And how is Harley?' asked Zenya.

'He's good. When he knows they are coming over, he smooches against Bob's legs to leave his scent, then I pick it up when Bob gets here.' Storm laughed, 'Bob is always amazed why I am smooching him and sitting on his lap when he visits. I'm only leaving messages for Harley,' he giggled.

'I would so love to see you both together. Just so I know I have seen two giants,' commented Zenya.

'Yeah,' agreed Barkley. He was a bit starry-eyed listening to Storm speak. Those deep, melodious tones in his voice made him relax so much he had forgotten what he was supposed to be doing.

'Shall we continue?' asked Mao, proposing that the next act commence.

'Yes! Yes! Let's continue,' said Barkley, waking up to the prompt. 'Who is next? Titch — I mean Jonathan, I think you are next.'

'Okay, thank you everyone,' said Jonathan. Making his way over to the corner of the area where the hedge met the boundary fence, he bobbed down behind a shrub. Everyone waited, listening to rustling sounds. Goodness knows what he was doing back there! Suddenly, up he popped with a small leaf in each ear and smiled his best smile.

'There was once an owl who did nothing but scowl.' His left ear wiggled.
    'Woot! Woot!' said the scowl.
    'But his friend smiled the biggest of smiles.' His right ear wiggled.
    'I am sure my dinner will feel much better, if the last thing it remembers is a smile so tender.'
    'Hoot! Hoot!' said the smile.
    'Your Woot Woot is too loud!' His right ear continued to wiggle.
    'Your Hoot Hoot is too soft!' His left ear wiggled.
    Jonathan pulled his ears back and his eyes became as big as an owl's.
    Then his ears stood up and said, 'WHOOT! WHOOT!'

Suddenly, he bobbed back down behind the hedge. 'WHOOT! WHOOT!' they heard, then silence for a breath.

    'WHOOT! WHOOT! WHOOT!'

Everyone turned around – there was Jonathan behind them.
    'How did you get there so quickly?' asked Zenya.
    'Yeah, you were there and now you are here. How did you do that?' asked Budge and Florry.
    Jonathan did not respond but simply leapt over Storm and landed back near where he had started, jumped over the shrub again and out came a ping pong ball, then another and another. Before any rolled into the swimming pool, Jonathan was catching them. He threw them here and there, tossed them in the air, caught two under his paws and the third with his tail, then rolled one out along the paving, got another one, and with precision paws, rolled a second ball so that it hit the first one and did the same with the third ball. Everyone was laughing and having a good time.
    '*What a transformation a change of name can make,*' Barkley thought.

No more flea-ridden scratching Titch − here was laughing Jonathan, having a good time entertaining everyone. Jonathan did not stop there. He ran around the swimming pool again, but not only that, he cut across each corner and leapt over the edges, making his body longer on each leap. Towards the last lap he jumped so hard everyone thought he was going to fall in, but he kept going and finally came to a stop just before Storm. Turning to face everyone, he took a bow. Everyone miaowed in appreciation and Zenya smooched him for being so brave to jump so high. Matilda wondered if she could do the same but did not want to fall in the water as she did not know how to get out.

'Jon-a-fin, that was wonderful, wasn't it everyone? Now I think it's your turn, Zenya,' said Barkley, allowing the purebred to take over.

# Chapter Twenty-Five

Zenya stood, looked at Puffy, who was fast asleep under the outdoor setting, and said in a calm voice, 'Please make yourselves comfortable and close your eyes. For the next few moments, I'd like you to focus on your fur and how warm and how clean it is.'

Zenya paused for a moment.

'Now listen to the sounds you can hear.'

They sat listening to the birds chirping, leaves rustling, Jonathan's fast breathing that was beginning to quieten, a car going past, Puffy's snoring, people walking a dog out the front, a raking sound, a rubbish bin being wheeled along and the lid opening, and became aware of the smell of fresh wee. Bang! A car door shutting. Bang! Then voices – someone talking on one of those things they talk into, a mother yelling at a child, a pram and footsteps coming from across the road. The whirling noise of a refrigerator, computer, insects buzzing. A few trees away was a possum sleeping, chickens clucking, and then two ducks flew over going quack, quack.

'Do any of the noises change? Do they become deeper, higher, stop or fade away?' she asked.

Storm could hear a ball bouncing in the far-off distance, then he sensed his lady talking to someone about the value of their house and repairs that needed to be done. This was not an audible thing. Even though he was far from home, he could smell her perfume and knew her vibrations had changed.

Jonathan's breathing had quietened. Puffy's breathing was louder because he had just woken up. He sat watching Zenya show meditation, just like she had done with him on many an occasion. He knew what was coming next so stretched his body, rolled over onto his back and rubbed it on the paving, then sat up and watched everyone do the same.

'Now sense your family's energy. How does it feel? What has changed?'

Purring started. First the leaping Jonathan, then Budge, Florry and even Mao. Hearing the sweet tones of Mao's purring, Barkley began to relax and forget he was in charge of proceedings for the day.

*What shall I do? Go with Storm to his new place or stay where I am with no office? Will I get an office at Storm's place? Would they mind if I ran my business from there? Dilemma. Dilemma.*

Then he remembered, 'At the ultimate outcome to all dilemmas, I will still be… Still be… At the ultimate outcome to all dilemmas, I will still be cared for!'

Barkley opened his eyes and glanced at Mao, who was looking at him.

*Perhaps I should move in with Mao? We would make a formidable team. I can do the detectiving, while she questions my clients and makes sure I am paid properly.*

Then he remembered he had not had a craving for a salty dried fish for ages. Barkley was purring now, everyone was. He vaguely heard Zenya say something about listening to our purring and how did that feel? It felt good, as always.

Barkley's mind continued to drift. He was glad dogs did not purr as well.

*Could you imagine Regie purring? He would be salivating over his bone so much he wouldn't be able to chew properly. Come to think of it, I haven't seen Regie for ages either. Perhaps he has moved on? What luck if he has! Pity I won't be needing any of his bones anymore as I have now learnt how to write better. I wonder if Mrs Longford has learnt the alphabet yet? The children learnt when they were young. I wonder why she took so long to learn how to spell? Maybe they didn't have the alphabet when she was little? Poor thing! Fancy having no alphabet! That is probably why she couldn't understand the note I wrote; she didn't have an alphabet. Maybe my note prompted her to learn? You know, one of those 'will get around to it people' and never does. Now she finally is and it all could be down to me! Gosh!*

Barkley purred loudly, sitting up and puffing out his chest to be like Storm. Then he opened his eyes and noticed everyone starring at him.

'Okay, thank you, Zenya, for the lovely meditation. I was purring so loud I didn't hear you finish,' said Barkley, trying not to yawn.

'You were purring and started mumbling about moving in with Storm or Mao. You going to leave your family and go and live elsewhere? Why?' asked Budge.

'Yeah, why?' asked Florry.

'I have asked Barkley to come and join me so I can teach him the ways of Little Ming as I was taught. It is entirely up to him if he wants to come,' said Mao, addressing the group.

'Yeah, but what about your office and writing letters? And why wouldn't you be getting bones from that Regie anymore?' quizzed Matilda.

'Because my office is gone. As you know, after the hole in the roof was fixed, Sarah and Beth cleaned it all up. Then Tom locked the door and there's no way in,' explained Barkley.

'Plus, Storm's family is thinking of moving to a bigger place and I am torn what to do. I don't know if I should stay where I am and give up my detective business, go with Storm and live with him or go with Mao and learn the ways, although I think I am beginning to understand what it all means.'

'Dear me, Barkley. I had no idea you had lost everything. It must be very stressful for you,' said Zenya.

'It has not been nice, but I do know from the note Miss Fi-Fi got that I will still be loved and cared for, it just depends on who that will be.'

'You can come live with us, if you like,' said Budge. 'Lynne's got plenty of paper. She might give you a bit of space to write and even help with your letters.'

Florry gave his brother a nudge, 'We can't invite him. Lynne's going away, remember?'

'Oh yeah. Sorry Barx, Lynne is going away for a few days. Her mum is coming to feed us. Here, Flor, I hope we get good tucker and none of that ghastly tasting stuff you get at Lilly's,' said Budge, making yuk faces.

'Lynne is going away? Do you know where?' asked Barkley, putting his detective hat on again.

'She's going to – Budge, where is she going again?' asked Florry.

'I don't know. She's going to some place with her friend, Daphne. They're going to sit and look at the view, is what she said,' responded Budge.

'Yeah, that's right. A change of seen… scenery,' added Florry. 'We can ask her when she gets back if you can come stay.'

'Thanks Budge, Florry. That would be very nice of you. Okay everyone, that just leaves Mao and myself,' said Barkley, still pondering his options.

'Why don't you go next?' suggested Mao in her sweet, melodious voice.

'Yes, why not. Okay. Um, well, being a detective is not all that great. I mean, sometimes it is, especially when you win the case, but it's a lot of hard work. Sometimes you're outside in the cold in unfamiliar territory all night long and the possums and bats make a lot of noise, not to mention the cicadas in summer.'

Everyone nodded in agreement.

'And when an owl comes past – that's quite scary. You can hear a mouse in the bushes and it's very tempting to go get it, but you're not there to hunt, you're there to collect clues, catch the culprit if you can. It's hard to focus on what you're there for when you know the delight of a snack is just there, but then there's a whoosh and out of nowhere an owl comes down, grabs the mouse and flies off silently into the night. Once, when I was sitting near the pond watching the fish in the moonlight, a cockroach came across the rocks just near me. An owl swept down, his wings glanced against my ear, and before I could look up to see what that was, he was gone. I was mighty glad he didn't think I was going to be his next meal!'

'Then there are the times you need to let off steam and run around like a mad thing, zooming here and there, but you might give the game away when you are supposed to be incognito. I have never not solved a case, although I must say, Mao, this one has been the longest and hardest I have ever tackled!'

'Most of my cases are about getting your breakfast and dinner sorted into something that you like or teaching the dog that bit you a lesson – it's amazing what a scratch on the nose can do! Once, I had a parrot come and ask for my help. She hated them saying "Good boy" to her, but all in all, I enjoy being a detective. It is very satisfying, and nice to know that a good deed has been done and won. There was another time when I first started, I was leaving calling cards around the place when this very large dog that looked like he would eat me up in one gulp came to see me, like you Ti… Jonathan. He wanted his name changed to something more masculine. He did not like being called Cookies when he had broad shoulders and a jaw the size of my head,' said Barkley, with his eyes popping out in fear.

'What did he want to be called?' asked Matilda.

'He thought Walter was more akin to his demeanour and I thought he was right. He looked like a brute but was really very gentle and distinguished.'

'How do you spell Walter?' asked Matilda.

Barkley ignored her question as he did not want to admit it had taken him six attempts to get Walter written correctly, as on his first three spellings he had left the 'l' out. He remembered Walter's family thinking he wanted more water, so they put several bowls out for him to drink. Great in summer, but being forced to drink water was not Walter's idea of fun. 'Here Cookie, have a drink. Have a drink, Cookie.' He would look at them forlornly and say, 'My name is Walter!' Then Barkley remembered how he got the 'i' and 'l' mixed up and his family thought he wanted to be a waiter, so they taught him to fetch those things they stare into, pull the duvet up to make the bed and take the empty cereal box to the recycling bin. He didn't mind the training, he just did not want to be called Cookie all the time – Walter was better.

'Well, anyway, I will have to decide what I am going to do next. Clearly, I cannot continue my services with my family now that my office has gone. If I give it up, what else shall I do? I am already established and have got the knack of it now. Well, time to decide later. Mao, I believe the whisker is all yours now,' said Barkley, trying not to look sad at having to give up his enterprise.

The elusive cat that everyone was curious about looked at all her new companions and simply asked, 'Have none of you figured it out yet?'

'If you give us cryptic clues, I will box your ears and send you home!' yelled Matilda, whose temper was ready to flare.

'I think what Mao is trying to say, if you will permit me,' said Barkley, with Mao nodding in response, 'is that we all have special talents, gifts to bring to our family, and that these talents assist the people we look after. If all these talents come together there is an endless amount of fun to be had.'

'Yes, fun for you and the mastering of observances for the people you look after,' said Mao, continuing with her speech. 'With the exception of Sebastian and Miss Fi-Fi, you have all heard the words written about you in the picture book.' All heads nodded in response.

'Hang on a minute, how do you know we've all heard the words?' Matilda interrupted.

Mao started to respond but Barkley answered again, wondering why on such an auspicious day the words in the book were not meant for George but for the kitten.

'She was listening from the hole in the roof.'

'Did you know she was there at the time?' asked Matilda, looking at Barkley.

The detective shook his head and Mao continued.

'Thank you everyone for coming to display your talents. I have enjoyed it immensely, have you?'

'Wait, aren't you going to explain everything to us?' Matilda asked, expecting explanations to be flying through the air like bees after they had visited a myriad of flowers.

'I don't need to. You have all understood very well. I came to show you all that you are capable of doing all of these things and more. Today, you have proven that to everyone.'

'I will never be a mother though,' said Matilda.

'No, but you do have the ability to be a leader and care for your new family,' replied Mao.

'I thought you were going to tell us about Little Ming and what you learnt there,' said Florry.

'Yeah, where is this Little Ming place, anyway?' asked Budge.

Again, Barkley interjected, 'Little Ming is a treehouse in Mao's backyard.'

Florry looked at his brother as if to say, 'She's got her own house up a tree? She is the luckiest cat that ever there was!'

Everyone just sat there, saying nothing. They could not believe their ears and wanted more information. Surely Little Ming was more magical than that and there were many wonderous things to learn.

'Mao, what does Little Ming mean?' asked Barkley, realising he had not figured that bit out yet.

'Ming means bright.'

'So, the house where you live is Big Ming and the treehouse is Little Ming?' quizzed Barkley.

'Great Ming,' said Mao, realising Barkley had solved the case.

'Hey Budge, does that mean Mao learnt all that stuff in a treehouse?' asked Florry.

'I suppose. I don't know. Does make you wonder if it's some kind of magical place,' said Budge.

'Yeah. Perhaps we should go visit?' suggested Florry, looking at his brother like this was a good idea.

Budge knew Florry was up for the adventure, why else would he go and visit Lilly so much when her tucker was ghastly and made him feel sick? He was curious and thought a visit to some magical place just might be in order.

'Well, I think that has brought our concert to an end. Thank you everyone for coming,' said Barkley, making his way to the fence. They all followed him except Storm, who pushed his way through the hedge and came out and around to get to the gate.

'I'll walk home with you,' said Jonathan to his new buddy Storm. Storm said nothing and simply made his way through the gate, bidding Barkley farewell.

Before he left, Barkley called out, 'Storm! Do you mind if I come and live with you?'

Storm stopped, thought about it for a second and said, 'If you can put up with the racket, being stepped on, the youngest pulling your fur and are prepared to watch them all grow up as well, then I don't see why not. It might give me a bit of peace. You'll have to get your own bowl though – I'm not sharing my tucker with anyone!'

Barkley smiled to his beloved friend, who left with a twinkle in his eye and Jonathan by his shoulder, chatting to him about the day's proceedings like they had known each other since their paws first touched.

'Come on, Puffy, let's go home now,' said Zenya and watched the big dog get up and make his way to the gate.

Reaching the top of the driveway, Budge turned to his brother and asked, 'What have we learnt, Flor?'

'I think we have learnt that magic really does happen.'

'Do you think while Lynne is away, she would mind if we painted some pictures?'

'I think we would be looking for a new home, if we did that,' said Florry.

That left Mao to chat with Barkley, as Matilda had already gone inside, or so they thought.

'You have solved the case, Barkley. Well done!' said Mao, smooching him.

'Thanks, but have I really? Like – Mystically Acquired Occurrences – Magnanimous Affection Overdone – what does all that mean? Why does every page have words with MAO?'

'MAO stands for all those things, and it also stands for cat in Chinese.'

'You mean your real name means cat? What happened to Master of Academic Observances?' asked Barkley in astonishment.

'Mao also means Master of Academic Observances. Remember all the words in the book? They were all about academic observances, weren't they. It just so happens they all had pictures of cats.'

'Except for George. Why was he the only dog in the series?' asked Barkley, still astonished that Mao's real name meant cat.

'At the time I gave Blackberry the message, I had no idea such a massive dog resided there. He must've been out for a walk. The note was originally meant for the kitten, who unfortunately is too young to comprehend, but I thought with a bit of persuasion from Blackberry, Sebastian would understand and tell the mother to get her daughter to stop dressing him up in doll's clothes and dragging him around. Sebastian doesn't need to learn gentle loyalty; it's the daughter that does. Still, George has mended his ways now and no longer chases the laundry around the clothesline, so all in all, it has been a great success.'

'It is a long way for you to go that far, are you not scared?'

'Not usually. Sometimes I have to pay extra attention when crossing the road, but otherwise I know I'm safe,' said Mao.

'What if you are chased by a dog?'

'Do you know any dogs that can climb trees? Do you know any dogs that have not whimpered after a scratch on the nose? I may not be as big as Storm, but I can defend myself when I need to, and as you know, I am very agile.'

'Are all the messages in the picture book for people?'

'Yes, of course.'

'Budge and Florry said the pictures were being made into bedding.'

'Yes, that's right. Athena's creativity has finally gotten out and this is the result.'

'Yes, but where did she get the idea to paint the portraits and have the lovely words next to us?'

Mao said nothing but just looked at Barkley as if to say, 'From me.'

'So Athena is your lady and you gave her all those wonderful words?'

'Yes and no. I simply pointed her in the right direction once she had received my idea for the design.'

'How did you know she was going to pick up your idea? Oh, don't tell me, you were sitting on her lap purring and told her what to do, then purred in her ear when she was asleep.'

Laughing, Mao said, 'Of course, Barkley! What else do cats do?'

Barkley knew she was right. He thought of Regie, who had to be trained and told what to do, whereas Barkley just did as he pleased and miaowed till someone got him what he wanted. George too needed to be trained into good behaviour, but there was no way he was going to put his paws up for that!

'So, Barkley, what do you think about coming to live with me? We could be great you know. Storm's place is further to get to so you might not be able to see him so much, but he is moving away anyway,' said Mao.

'Tell you what, why don't you move in with Budge and Florry. You can watch Lynne do her paintings and I'll move in with Storm?' suggested Barkley as they walked to the gate and made their way out. Matilda, who'd been listening to their conversation, put her paws up on the gate and gave it a shove till it shut, then went to leave a deposit in the garden, jumped up onto the rubbish bin and went inside for a bite to eat and a sleep; it had been an eventful morning. She knew what Roger would say when he came home and saw all those leaves in the swimming pool.

Barkley and Mao bid each other goodbye and made their way to their respective homes; Barkley, diagonally across the road and up the street a bit; Mao, way down the road, through the playground, then back to Great Ming.

# Chapter Twenty-Six

**B**arkley was hungry, cold and tired. He wished he had a window open to let himself in like Matilda did.

*Perhaps I could get someone to create for me the same set up Matilda has? Then I wouldn't have to sit in the cold waiting to be let in as I would already be snuggled into someone's bed!*

Barkley scouted around the house in the hope someone was home or a window or door was perchance open.

*The garage? My office? I could sleep under the house. Brrr! Too cold under there!*

He thought of going to Budge and Florry's place for a sleep.

*They have a cat door and Lynne knows me, so I wouldn't be trespassing too much. Would the brothers let me in? Would they mind if I let myself in? Would they mind sharing their food with me?*

Even though he wanted a good sleep in a nice warm bed, Barkley, the greatest detective known in the area, sat and pondered the concert.

*The picture book is right. All is well for he who has gratitude. Some might say that a treehouse is a castle in the air and to a child it is, yet some might be disappointed with said castle because it does not fit with their heart's desire, but what does the heart know when it is not in its kingdom?*

*The heart can only speculate what it would be like, hence the ideal falls into sorrow and sadness because living is done through made up stuff that stops one from seeing and feeling with truth. If I accept myself, I trust myself, and therefore I am grateful for all that I am.*

*Budge and Florry, having grown up around painting, would know that a brush filled with paint that touches paper is letting the expression of the moment explore possibilities and as Mao said, the*

'Excuse me, are you Detective Inspector Barkley Button Nose?'

'Yes, I am. To whom do I have the pleasure of this whisker?'

'I am Lilly. I have come to ask you to stop another feline called—'

'Florry, yes, I know him. Have you come to tell me he is stealing your food?'

'Yes, and to also ask if you can get my family to give me something different. Florry and the birds eat most of my food, leaving hardly anything for me. My family think I like it, so they keep buying more. I'm tired of eating the same meal, plus Florry is usually sick or he leaves stinky, runny deposits in my garden or at next door's place. I am being blamed for it all and I've had enough.'

'I'm sure you have. Florry is a friend of mine; I will let him know. He tells me you are his girlfriend,' said Barkley, looking at the small white cat with blue eyes who he could tell was normally shy and quiet, but now was determined enough to come all this way to seek his assistance.

'At first, I thought he was cute. He talks a bit, then just lounges about.'

'Does he let himself in through the cat flap?'

'No, my meals are placed out the back for me. Florry usually comes over in the morning, leaving me hungry all day, then I am fed the same food again at night.'

'Wouldn't you prefer to be fed inside?'

'Yes, I would, but my family are out all day, so they feed me out the back.'

'Do you have a warm bed to sleep on?' asked Barkley, wondering if it was just right for a cosy nap.

'I have a small basket.'

'If you would like to show me where you live, I can get started on your case straight away,' said the detective, knowing the case would be easily solved.

'That would be lovely; however, I cannot pay you with sardines, but I did leave a few biscuits at your door.'

'That's okay. If I finish early, perhaps we could doze in your basket?'

'It's not big enough for two. I will show you the way. Perhaps you could show me where Florry lives so I can go and eat his tucker, see how he likes it,' said Lilly as she went along gumnut alley, past Barkley's old office, jumped over the fence, went around the fishpond, down the street, past Mrs Andrews' place and up her own driveway to the backyard.

'This is where I eat and sleep,' said the white cat.

Barkley looked at the food that was there, sniffed it and walked away, realising it was no wonder she struggled to eat it and Florry was sick afterwards.

'What do you do when it's raining?' asked Barkley, noticing her area was not under cover and she had no protection.

'If it's raining really hard, I go and sit under the house next door. It's not comfortable there but I am dry.'

'Plus, your tucker gets all wet – what do they do then?' asked Barkley with a yuk look on his face.

'The birds have usually eaten it all by then.'

Barkley got to work straight away and asked Lilly to help him get twigs, stones, leaves, empty snail shells and whatever else she could find. When he thought he had enough, he started to write the note to her family.


Change puss food


Then he wrote another on the other side of the door.


Change puss food or I bite and scratch


'There you go, that should do it,' said Barkley, looking at her like 'I need a sleep!'

'Thank you. What does it say?' she asked.

Barkley read to her what it said and told her he would need to come back for the next few days and do it again and could Lilly manage to collect some things for him to make letters with. Lilly looked at him wide-eyed and laughed.

'You can't say that! My family will be very angry.'

'It will be alright, Lilly. Come and tell me if they don't change it for you,' yawned Barkley, really wanting to curl up and have a good sleep as exhaustion had finally gotten to him.

'Okay, well thank you, Mr Barkley Button Nose,' said Lilly, expecting him to leave.

Barkley took his cue, bid her farewell and left. He was so tired as he walked back along the street.

*I don't care. I'm going to Mrs Andrews' place for a kip.*

Barkley went up her drive and snuck out the back, hoping she would not be home.

*I'll just curl up in these bushes, have a good nap and then go home.*

Barkley slept like he had not slept in ages. He woke and sighed with relief that the case was finally closed – no more headaches! Yet why did he feel that there were still questions that needed to be answered, like who stole the collars?

*I have a new case, must go and have a word with Florry. Hopefully someone will be home, I'm starving!*

Barkley slipped back into sleep. When he woke again, he felt refreshed. It was almost dark. He saw the lights were on at Mrs Andrews' place but went straight home without attempting to say hello, disappointed that his presence would agitate her.

*Just as well Storm doesn't live with Mrs Andrews all the time! I would have no opportunity to move in with him. Then again, if he did live with her all the time, she wouldn't be moving to a bigger home! I wonder if Storm would reconsider staying with his family and move in permanently with Mrs Andrews?*

Barkley yawned, then got up and went home to a warm house, good food and long sleeps on top of the heating.

*Tomorrow, I will go see Florry.*

As the family got ready for bed, Barkley pondered where he would rather be – here with his family with no office, with his best buddy Storm or with Mao.

'Decisions, decisions! But at least I will still be loved, heard and accepted.'